Alexandra Büchler left her native Prague in 1978 for Greece, Australia and the UK. She now lives in Glasgow. She has translated prose, poetry and plays from Czech, Greek and English. Her recent work includes the translation of David Malouf's *An Imaginary Life* and of contemporary Australian and Scottish short stories.

This Side of Reality

Modern Czech Writing

Edited by Alexandra Büchler

This book was published with assistance from the
Arts Council of England

Library of Congress Catalog Card Number: 95–71063

A catalogue record for this book is available
from the British Library on request

For permissions see page 229

First published in 1996 by Serpent's Tail,
4 Blackstock Mews, London N4, and
180 Varick Street, 10th floor, New York, NY 10014

Phototypeset in 10pt Times by Intype, London
Printed in Great Britain by Cox & Wyman Ltd, of
Reading, Berkshire

Contents

*This book is dedicated
to the memory of
Ladislav Fuks (1921–94)*

Introduction

For most of the post-war period, Czech literature existed in a peculiar state of fragmentation and dividedness, subjected to censorship, ruptured by exile, and deprived of the influence of a valid critical and theoretical practice. It was particularly during the time of 'consolidation and normalization' following the Soviet invasion in 1968 that some of the best Czech authors were forced into exile, both internal and external, that crucial cultural forums were disbanded, vehicles for publication and critical dialogue banned, and major works erased from official history. The unofficial, shadow literature continued to be written and published in underground conditions of clandestine meetings, samizdat editions and exile presses. A number of dissident writers, some of whom have in the meantime gained international recognition, were forced to leave the country and stripped of their citizenship. Those who stayed were subjected to police harassment and persecution, or at least relegated to a twilight zone where their work, while not directly banned, was not available in bookshops and libraries.

What these writers had in common was not only their implicit or explicit rejection of formal and ideological dogmatism, but also a genuine concern for the continuity and integrity of national culture and for essential human values crushed in an atmosphere of fear, apathy and general complicity. Drawing on a legacy of irony and humour and on the tradition of the absurd and the surreal, they often abandoned the conventions of literary realism in favour of collage, fragmented and episodic narrative through which they examined the continuously distorted image of the past and present, explored the ever-shifting line between imagination and reality, and tested the communicative capacities of language corrupted by the hegemony of ideology.

Yet the attention paid to the dissident writer by the police state also reflected the traditionally privileged status of the written word, its immense power and influence in a culture in which writers, the 'engineers of human souls', were seen as the ultimate moral arbiters of their society. The centrality of the writer and of storytelling as a way of mediating between society and its representations, between reality and fiction, is evident in most of the texts presented in this anthology as is the preoccupation with the very process of writing and with literary constructs and conventions. These questions, however, are approached not from the perspective of a heightened literary self-consciousness but from the position of concern with moral values to which the issues of artistic integrity and responsibility are intrinsic.

Many of the stories told here share a sense of confined experience and a desire to cross boundaries in a quest for meaning denied to the reality from which they arise. From Fuks's moving story of a Jewish boy dreaming about leaving the occupied Czechoslovakia to see the world, to Murrer's Kafkaesque tale of self-repeating history, or Kratochvil's bizarre proposal to relocate a whole city to the Amazonian rainforest, 'away from all roads, ideas and bad intentions', much of the writing speaks of journeys, real and imaginary, of experiential claustrophobia, of breaking out of reality's prison.

Finally, this anthology traces some of the history of the past decades. While Ivan Klíma's story sums up the situation of the dissident writer in 1970s Czechoslovakia, and Michal Viewegh's editorial asides reflect the more liberal but still uneasy atmosphere of the 1980s, the last two texts take us into the new, post-1989 era. In an intensely personal account that seemingly ignores the momentous events of the times, Ludvík Vaculík focuses on the most essential of private and civic responsibilities, the education of a child. But it is Jáchym Topol's narrative that opens the floodgates to the nightmarish new reality governed by the twin superpowers of today, the media and the mafia. Literature is knocked off its high ground by market forces and censored by business priorities, the books for which authors and readers once risked their freedom are remaindered by street vendors, while the very word 'freedom' has been hijacked by the jargon of economics. Ironically, this story resonates with the same concerns underlying the writing of Topol's predecessors and older colleagues, bearing witness to a new, deeper corruption of values from which there is no escape, for there are no more walls to fall.

Alexandra Büchler

Ladislav Fuks

Kchony Sees the World

I

Sadness is yellow and six-pointed like a Star of David. It was a great sadness. At the end of February, when it was freezing cold, my Papa said: 'Why don't you invite Kchony over to our place sometime?'

I invited him the next day as soon as I walked into the classroom. To avoid delay, I told him to come that same afternoon even though Papa's brother Vojta, that is, my uncle, was supposed to be coming.

'But don't be disappointed,' I said. 'I know what you like. But I haven't got as many pictures of the world as you have. All I have is one book with a few stupid photos.'

'That's OK,' Kchony squeaked, 'I'll come anyway. But I'll have to bundle up, you know, because it's February now and it's freezing outside, and I can't afford to catch a cold. Know what I mean?'

'You won't catch a cold at our place,' I said. 'At our place we use only central heating. None of that coal-stove stuff! It's like an oven at our place.'

Kchony nodded approvingly. It looked as if he had something more to say but all he could manage was a sigh. The bell rang and we ran to take our seats. The dreaded class was about to begin.

As soon as he had finished taking rollcall, the geography teacher began to test the students on everything they had learnt since the start of the school year. Each one got three questions and then a grade of F: Mínek, Carda, Bronowski; Turkey, Arabia, Egypt.

'Here we are at the end of February and you know less and

less every day,' the teacher growled. 'What's going on? Are your memories rolling up on you?'

All of us were scared except Krappner, who was the teacher's pet, and we tried to work out what it meant for someone's memory to roll up. But Kchony was more scared than anyone. The teacher picked on him most of all, even more than on Arnstein and Katz, who sat in front of him. So Kchony would sit on his bench by the stove, praying secretly to God in Heaven that the teacher wouldn't call on him—that's what his neighbour told me. Whenever the geography teacher did call him up to the blackboard, everyone in the classroom breathed a sigh of relief and secretly thanked God in Heaven, knowing they were safe for the rest of class.

At last the teacher called Kchony up to the front of the class, saying, 'Here we are at the end of February, your memories are rolling up on you, and I have yet to test you on Palestine.'

He asked what the population of Palestine was. 'Fifteen,' Kchony answered timidly. 'Million.'

The teacher asked Kchony if he counted himself among them and then went on to the next question: what kind of government did they have there? There was a long silence before Kchony was able to speak, and then 'A monarchy,' he blurted out.

'A monarchy, a monarchy,' the teacher nodded, 'is that right? My, but we are confused. The Arabs would have your head for that! This is no Council of the Elders of Zion here, do you understand?' He went on, 'What grows there?'

'Barley, dates, oranges,' Kchony stuttered.

'And what else?'

'Lemons,' Kchony whispered.

'And?'

That was all Kchony knew. He turned to his classmates, desperate for help, but no one dared give him a hint. In this class the punishments for helping were severe.

The geography teacher smiled good-naturedly and offered to help. 'Recall, if you will,' he said, 'that fine parable from the New Testament.'

Kchony was on the verge of tears and probably near fainting as well. Krappner and some of the other boys broke into laughter. Next time round the teacher would go easy on them; this was one of those moments when he enjoyed a laugh.

'If you can't remember the parable,' the teacher said, even more cheerfully than before, 'then pray to the Virgin Mary, the Christians' faithful servant.'

Two big tears rolled down Kchony's cheeks and he leant his right hand against the blackboard for support. 'The parable about Christ, Our Lord,' he gasped.

The geography teacher slammed his fist down on the desk and shouted that it was the parable of the withered fig tree and that the fig tree was Kchony, and go ask his father, he ought to know, he preaches. Then the teacher gave Kchony an F and wrote in his grades-book: David Kohn does not know that figs grow in Palestine. He confuses geography with religion.

After school I met Kchony in the hallway and reminded him to come over. Today at four.

'Course I'll come,' he said, 'but it's important for me to bundle up. I didn't finish telling you.' His voice dropped to a whisper. 'You don't know *why* it is I have to bundle up.'

'So you won't catch a cold,' I said.

'But *why* I can't catch a cold,' he said excitedly, 'you don't know *that*. And it's not 'cause I'm sensitive. Give me your word of honour and I'll let you in on it. But not even Arnstein and Katz are allowed to know.'

'Word of honour,' I said, and offered him my hand. But Kchony only let out a sigh, looked round the hallway and said he'd tell me that afternoon when he came over to our place.

No sooner had we finished lunch than someone rang at the front door. Růženka, our maid, shouted that it must be the young master and jumped up so fast to answer it that she practically knocked over her chair. What a nitwit. It was only two o'clock.

It was Papa's brother Vojta, that is, my uncle.

He didn't spend much time with us. He and Papa rushed

straight into the study and closed the door. I sneaked into the bathroom and heard my uncle saying in a hushed voice that this should never have happened. I think it had something to do with a ban on the newspaper he works at, or maybe it was something about the Sudetenland again, like last autumn, but it didn't have anything to do with Papa. My Papa is head of the Police Commission and he's been investigating suicides since the events in the Sudetenland; don't ask me why.

When they came out of the study, my uncle said he was in a hurry, quickly said his goodbyes and left. No sooner had he walked out the door than Papa instructed Růženka to light the stove in his study.

That's strange, I thought, today of all days. Kchony's coming over and we're going to use the stove for heating. Doesn't matter, though. Kchony won't be going into the study, anyway. Maybe the chimney sweep came and recommended that we light the stove every once in a while. Could be that, I reassured myself.

I fiddled around the apartment testing the warmth from the central heating, but I couldn't figure it out. The door to Papa's study was locked, which meant I wasn't allowed to go in, not even if there was a fire. Růženka was in the kitchen, pouring petrol from one bottle into another, but it was no use trying to talk to her. She'll probably set the apartment on fire, I thought. What a pain. I wish it was four already.

Finally four o'clock came and Kchony appeared, looking like a little bear in his warm, furry coat. He started taking off his shoes in the hall as Růženka handed him some sandals, but just then Papa walked in: 'It's dry outside. Don't bother,' he said. Dry, and here we are at the end of February.

While Papa talked to Kchony, the little furry bear hung on the wall among the coats, and through the open door of Papa's study I could see papers everywhere—on the desk, on the chairs, on the carpet. I couldn't believe my eyes and I pulled Růženka aside to ask her about it. Her eyes bulged as she told me that Papa had been burning papers in the stove.

I quickly led Kchony back to my room and offered him a seat. He sat down on the couch next to some newspapers. 'You read newspapers?' he asked in awe.

'Uh-uh,' I grinned, 'all I read's the sports page.'

'I don't read newspapers.' He shook his head. 'My Papa won't let me. My Mama reads them and you should see what it did to her. She's ill. Like everyone who reads the papers. That's why I'm not allowed to.'

'Not even the sports page?'

'Not even that,' said Kchony, 'word of honour.'

'Let me show you my toys,' I said, and I pulled out my electric train, my building set, my car, various types of cats and mice, and my bead game. Not the tin soldiers, though, because they were all battered and one of them was missing his head.

'I don't play with them any more,' I said. 'I've had them since I was little. I just run my train every once in a while. But that's not actually a toy.'

'No, it's not.' Kchony nodded in agreement. 'What do you say we give it a run? Does it work?'

So we set up the tracks, the railway station, the bridge and the tunnel, and I put the train on the tracks—the locomotive, the passenger carriages and the freight cars, that's all I have—and turned on the power. The train started up. Through the station, over the bridge, through the tunnel, and over again, round and round, dashing along, clackety-clack, smelling of paint, and it was a wonder it didn't fly off the tracks as it took the turns. Kchony loved it.

'If that's an express—it is, right?—then it's an international train,' he said. 'I know, I go to the railway station and watch. I've got some toys too, but not an international express train.'

Just then he caught sight of the battered soldiers in my wardrobe.

'Soldiers!' he shouted. 'I see soldiers in there! Let's stop the train and put the soldiers in it.'

'Oh, all right,' I sighed. 'I do that too, but only in the freight car. They don't fit in the one for passengers. I found them in the street one day.'

Kchony stopped the train and put the soldiers in. 'They're great, especially this headless one,' he said, his head bobbing with enthusiasm. 'How'd it happen?'

'That's the commander,' I explained. 'He lost his head in a

battle when he was on the front line. But he's OK otherwise, so who cares?'

'So who cares?' he agreed. 'He's OK. Toy soldiers always are. I could play with them for ever. Just like with the train—hey, have you still got the head?' Kchony asked. 'We could glue it back on.'

'No such luck,' I said. 'Růženka swept it out from under the couch along with the dust and threw it away.'

'Then I guess we really are out of luck.' He nodded sadly, and then, using his finger to make sure the soldiers were firmly in place, he asked, 'Is this switch here the one that turns it on?'

I nodded. Kchony flipped the switch and the train started up. Through the station, over the bridge and through the tunnel, round and round, dashing along, clackety-clack, through the turns; it's a wonder it didn't fly off the tracks.

Kchony watched for a while, then lay down flat on the ground and put his chin right up next to the tracks.

'It's beautiful,' he sighed. 'This train runs just like a real one. Does it ever get derailed?'

'Sure,' I said. 'The cars tip over and the soldiers fall out and die. Some of them could even get their heads knocked off.'

'And then what?'

'Then there'd be a funeral.'

Kchony grumbled and, his eyes still fixed on the train, said, 'Let's not have any funerals. Then I'd feel bad for the soldiers. Look how they shake. If only I could climb in there with them. I love riding in trains. Paris, Africa, doesn't matter where to. That's why I go to the railway station so much. But I've never been anywhere,' he said enigmatically from his position by the tracks. 'The furthest I've ever been is a castle called Karlštejn near Prague.'

That brought us to the pictures of the world, my little book that really didn't have much in it at all. I pulled it from the bookshelf and laid it on the table. Kchony sat down in a chair and put his hands in his lap. I could tell he was burning with eagerness.

'You're going to be disappointed,' I reminded him. 'It's a

stupid book. There's nothing in it. I don't even know where we got it from.'

One of the pictures showed a domed cathedral with columns lining the square in front of it and an obelisk in the middle of the square.

'That's Rome, St Peter's Cathedral,' he called out. 'Gosh, would I like to go there. What else is there?'

'There's this,' I said and turned to the picture on the next page. It showed a piece of sea and, on the shore, the dome of a church with four pointed towers.

'Constantinople,' he cheered, 'another church! A mosque! I want to go there too. Next?'

The third picture showed only the shadow of a sad stone wall with people in black skirts and hats facing it. I didn't want to show it to him. But he pushed my hand away and took a good long look.

'What is it, what is it?' he asked. 'I don't know anything about that place.'

'That's Palestine,' I whispered, 'Jerusalem, the Wailing Wall.'

We sat in silence for a while, until Kchony lifted his head and said he wanted to go and see that too, and he looked over at the newspapers lying on the couch.

Just then my Mama called us to the kitchen table.

As we ate our snack, Papa asked Kchony how he liked school and how his father and mother were.

'I like school,' he said, 'and my Papa's well. But he doesn't preach much any more because his vocal cords hurt and he's afraid it hasn't done any good anyway. He's thin, too, and his hair's grey and he gets dizzy, and sometimes he spends all day in bed—but my Mama, she's sick,' he blurted out, 'she talks about dying and I'm worried about her. But that comes from reading the papers. I'm not allowed to do that.'

Then my Papa said that Kchony was handsome and clever, that he liked foreign countries and would soon see the world. He said Kchony was going to do a lot of travelling and that travelling was wonderful and healthy. As my Papa was saying all that, Kchony blushed and glanced at me with a meaningful look in his eyes.

It wasn't long before the clock struck six, and Kchony said he had to run so he would reach home before it got dark and the damp cold set in. I asked if he had been cold at our place.

'No, I wasn't,' he said. 'You've got central heating, so you don't use the stove at all, and that's really important for me. Some day I'll tell you why if you give me your word of honour.'

'But you promised to tell me today,' I protested.

'And you won't tell even Arnstein and Katz?'

'Word of honour.'

'Not even Katz?' he repeated. 'Fine, then, I'll tell you.' His voice dropped to a whisper. 'But I can't do it now. It's six already and the cold mist is setting in. I'll tell you when you come over to our place.'

Kchony put on his warm, furry coat in the hall and suddenly turned back into a little bear. He said his respectful farewells and left.

I went back into my room to put away the toys, and before long Růženka appeared. She said the book lying on the table was beautiful and the young master must have enjoyed it. I said it was a pretty stupid book and there was no way the young master could have enjoyed it. Then I asked if she knew what was going on in Papa's stove.

'The stove's gone out,' she declared importantly, 'and there were two pails of ashes. I ran into Ševcová, the superintendent's wife, when I was bringing them out to the yard. Lord, how that woman's loose tooth wiggles!'

Ten days later Kchony came up to me before class and asked if I could come over to his place that day.

'It's your turn now and my Papa wants you to come. My Mama too, only she's locked in her room so you might not see her.'

I promised I'd come, even though I wasn't feeling well. The last few days I had been unusually listless. Růženka claimed that it wasn't anything serious, just springtime fatigue—which was possible, after all, since it was the middle of March.

'Oh, that's just March fatigue,' Kchony said, brushing it

aside. 'Nothing serious. Everyone gets it, even wrestlers and soldiers.'

He was about to add something, but just then the bell rang and he ran quickly to take his seat on the next-to-last bench by the stove. It was time for the dreaded class.

The geography teacher began testing us on everything we had learnt since the start of the school year, giving every boy an F after each question: Mínek, Carda, Bronowski; Turkey, Arabia, Egypt.

He said our memories were rolling up on us. 'You knew more last autumn,' he growled, and again we tried to work out what it was for a memory to roll up, and again, except for Krappner, everyone was scared. We prayed for the teacher to hurry up and call on Kchony. Kchony was more scared than anyone and was praying he wouldn't be called on.

At last the teacher called him up and gave him Palestine. Did he know what was in Jerusalem?

'The Wailing Wall,' Kchony stuttered.

'Delightful. And what else?' the teacher asked.

'A temple,' Kchony whispered.

'A temple?' the teacher said, shaking his head. 'You must be confusing it with something else. You are sorely mistaken!'

Kchony shuddered in fear and turned to the class for help. But in vain. No one dared give a hint. I shuddered to think the teacher might start on the Virgin Mary again and make Kchony cry. But this time he chose something different:

'A temple adorned with splendiferous stones and with gifts dedicated to God, and not one stone shall be left on another. Let those who are in Judea flee to the mountains, let those in the city get out, and woe to those with child!'

Then the teacher told Kchony to pray to the Virgin Mary, the faithful servant and Mother; he told him to go to the Wall if he wanted to whimper about his F, and in his grades-book the teacher wrote: David Kohn is lacking in religious education.

As the tears flowed down Kchony's cheeks, some of us started to laugh so the geography teacher would notice. Krappner laughed the loudest of all, making squealing sounds and pointing at the sobbing Kchony. And at that moment, for the first time in my life, I realized something awful, and it made me shake with terror.

After school, in the hallway, Kchony shyly reminded me that I was supposed to come over. Four o'clock that afternoon.

'I'll show you a photo album of pictures from all over the world,' he whispered. 'I haven't got an express train or any tin soldiers, but I have got that. I hope it's OK—and I'll tell you my secret too. Give your word of honour?'

I said I would and he added, 'Don't say anything to my Papa about that F or what the teacher said to me. It would only give him more to worry about. It's enough that I'm afraid. You know what of—that I'll fail.'

'But Kchony,' I whined, 'you can't fail!'

Then he ran back home in his warm, furry coat, looking just like a little bear because he was afraid he'd catch a cold. And it really was weather for catching colds that day. Damp and chilly, the middle of March.

II

When I got home at 6.30 that evening, the apartment was as quiet and empty as a locked-up church. Only then there was a crashing noise from the kitchen, so actually it wasn't quiet at all—that must have been Růženka getting supper ready. When I walked in, she was kneeling on the floor in front of the range, a bottle of petrol in one hand and a salt-shaker in the other. Uncle Vojta had been over at our place again, she said, standing up. There had been a big argument. What it was about, though, she didn't know.

'You can't hear properly through that door, that's just it,' she complained. 'It's there just for spite.'

I reminded her of the keyhole, but she dismissed the idea. 'Same thing. There's a key on the other side, and all you can see anyway's the window.'

Then she said Papa had been burning things in the stove again. Five pails of ashes. As she was bringing them out to the yard she had run into Ševcová, the superintendent's wife, and had to pop over to her place. That tooth of hers, the wiggly one, had fallen out.

'But just so there's no misunderstanding,' she added, 'it didn't really. It's all just her imagination. I must have been at her place for quite a while because by the time I got back, Papa had gone to the police station and Mama had gone into town to buy groceries.' She shook the bottle of petrol.

Then she asked if I had heard anything out on the street or during my visit to the young master's, and she put the petrol on the table and the salt-shaker on top of the range. She said she was going out of her mind and supper would be at eight, provided all went well.

There was a loud cracking sound as the heat split the salt-shaker in two. She swept the salt from the range top with a broom and threw it into the oven. Then she sat down and asked me to tell her about my visit to the young master's.

'His father was very kind to me,' I said. 'He patted me on the head twice.'

She wanted to know if he had said anything to me.

'He said I was very handsome and polite.'

Her eyes bulged in astonishment. 'That can't be. A gentle-man like him wouldn't lie,' she said, horrified.

'He also said that I was obedient and that I was doing well at school,' I went on.

'Well, I never, that is unbelievable.' She hurried over to the range to see to something and then asked if Kchony's parents had given me anything to eat.

'They gave me hot chocolate and cake. But not home-made. It came from a sweet shop.'

How could I tell that? she objected, and started clattering about with the dishes.

'How could I not when they took it out of a box?'

'They could have stuck it in there beforehand.'

'Right, sure, that's why the box had the name of the shop on it, sure.'

Suddenly she decided to accept my explanation and asked instead about the lady of the house.

'She came out of her room,' I said. 'She's sick.'

Then Růženka asked what kind of dress she had on and what she was wearing on her head, how many rooms they had and whether they had a vacuum cleaner. And then I had no choice but to tell her the last bit too—how Kchony had showed me the album of photographs from around the world.

'He showed me the places he wants to go, every single one, because he wants to go everywhere. All over the world, which is ... wait, now, how did he put it?' I stared at the bottle of petrol on the table and tried to remember. 'Oh, I know—colourful, vast and varied. He wants to travel the globe.'

'Oh sure,' said Růženka, mixing something in a pot on top of the range. 'That's very nice and all, but only if they've got the money for it. A preacher like that can't have much. Not unless he got a loan from some Jewish banker.'

I kept my mouth shut tight so as not to spill the beans. What Kchony had told me was strictly between him and me.

'You see,' Kchony had said once we were alone in his room and I had given him my word of honour, 'it's like this. Me and my family are getting out of here. We're going to get on a train and ride. Not round and round like the soldiers, though. We're going to ride straight all the way, out into the world, which is colourful, vast and varied. And not on a freight train, either. We're going to ride in a passenger carriage. I'm already getting my things together now. Right here's my notebook with all the stations and cities we're going to, and I also wrote down all the stops we're going to make. And right here I've got another notebook with all the famous buildings we're going to visit, but see, it's already full, so I have to run over to the stationer's tomorrow and buy a new one. You know what a passport is, right, and a visa? Well, we're going to get our passports and visas in half a day. My Papa said your Papa was going to help him. Do you collect stamps?'

I shook my head.

'Too bad, you should. You could peel them off the postcards I send you. We're going to take everything we have with us. We're going to have a new apartment in a new building. I hope I'll find friends there too. But I'm going to have to speak English or French, that's it. And I'm going to go to a new school, too. I hope there won't be another geography teacher like the one we have here. What do you think? Tell me there won't be.'

I said no, there wouldn't. 'There's not another geography teacher like that anywhere on earth,' I said, and Kchony nodded happily.

'Yeah, but you know what's important,' he suddenly remembered, 'is that we can't leave until Mama's done with her cure, that's the thing. You know what a cure is, right? My Mama's eager to leave—she'd like to go tomorrow—and me too, but we have to wait a week. After all, it won't kill us. But I have to be careful not to catch a cold. That's why I was asking if it was warm at your place. That's why I wear that furry coat, see? So now you know. Now you know it all. Absolutely everything. But you can't tell a soul. Not even Arnstein and Katz. And you know why?

'Well, I'll tell you,' he said with secrecy in his voice. 'Because I wouldn't be able to stand up to them. They'd say that I can't see the world because I'm as fragile as a dandelion. So you have to give me your word of honour.'

And that's why I couldn't tell even Růženka.

As I sat there in silence, she suddenly shouted out, 'Good Lord, I forgot to salt the food!' And she rushed over to the wall where the salt-shaker was hanging. Then she remembered that the salt-shaker was broken and she had thrown the salt into the oven. 'Lord,' she said distractedly, 'I thought I threw the petrol away. I'll just have to pop over to the superintendent's. Be back in a jiffy.'

An hour and a half later Růženka returned, even more agitated than she had been when I came home from Kchony's.

'There are terrible things going on,' she said, her voice trembling. 'Everything's in turmoil,' she said, 'turmoil.' I'd never heard that word from her before. 'There was a corporal over at the superintendent's, and his wife is all swollen up and she lost the knife she uses for cutting meat.'

Supper was at nine. The food was too salty and impossible

to eat. But nobody noticed. Mama was preoccupied and Papa asked me how it had been at Kchony's.

By the time I went to bed I was worn out. Must be that springtime fatigue. All I dreamt about was trains and soldiers. Růženka says it's a bad sign, like teeth falling out or a knife getting lost. Either stomach troubles or something to do with love.

III

The morning after my visit to Kchony's I was woken by the doorbell. From the hall I could hear that a policeman had come for my father and they were leaving together. I leapt to the window. Papa's car was standing in front of the building and there was another policeman at the car door. Papa got in and the car pulled away even before the door had slammed shut.

A light snow mixed with rain began to fall as I walked to school, and slush was forming in the streets. The foul weather made the day seem especially gloomy; the first hour was geography and the teacher was going to test us on everything we had learnt since the start of the school year.

But no sooner had we walked into the building than we learnt the happy news: no school! We were to take the shortest route home and come back tomorrow. I looked everywhere for Kchony but couldn't see him. Maybe he was there and I had just overlooked him, or maybe he had already run back home. The rest of us got out fast too, before the geography teacher could turn up and force us to stay for his class. But, as we soon found out, there was no need to worry.

The geography teacher was standing in front of the school building, listening to the rumbling from the neighbouring streets, looking at his watch and gazing about with a slight smile on his face.

Foreign troops were entering our country.

Armies were entering our country.

I hurried home. The streets were impossible to negotiate. Everywhere full of people, smoke and pandemonium. Full of cars, trucks and tanks. Full of petrol and rubber. Full of helmets and soldiers. And swirling down through it all were the snow and the rain, everywhere on the ground mud and muddy pools of water. Oh my God, I thought, what if Kchony caught a cold yesterday?

Růženka was at home.

'Mama went to buy groceries,' she shouted excitedly. 'We're going to starve to death! I'm cooking lunch now. It should be ready by evening.'

As she was shouting, a pot fell from her hands and smoke started to pour from the oven. Then a plate fell to the ground and shattered. Soon one plate after another was falling, until every single one of them was broken. Růženka dashed over to the window, looked out and yelled that 'they' were on the way.

She must have lost her mind.

I walked out and went to turn on my electric train.

Mama got home at noon and Papa soon after.

As Růženka carried in a bowl of something that was supposed to be lunch, Papa told us that Uncle Vojta wouldn't be coming to see us any more. He had been arrested. By the German police at nine o'clock that morning. Růženka's eyes bulged, and Papa told her to light the stove. Right away. I couldn't even eat, I was so excited. Then the telephone rang: it was police headquarters and someone hurriedly gave my father instructions. When he had finished the call, Papa looked at me for a minute and then told me to finish my lunch and go and do my homework.

IV

The next day when we got to school our first class was geography, since the geography teacher had traded with the teacher of Czech to make up for yesterday's lost lesson. He walked into the classroom with a strangely cheerful gait and a smile that lifted our spirits. Brachtl whispered to me that we weren't going to be tested today and I could feel the entire class, except for Krappner, breathe a sigh of relief.

The teacher ceremoniously stepped up to his desk and told us to look around and see who was missing. That meant we could all turn round in our seats, and the teacher called Bronowski up to the front of the class to say who it was.

Chadima and Dostál, he said. Who else? the teacher asked. Take a better look. Kohn, he said. The teacher nodded and told Bronowski he could sit down again.

Next he called Carda up and asked him if his father was still laying roads and what were the names of the towns along the Riviera where rich people spent their vacations. Then he called Mínek up and asked where in Europe there were people as poor as road-layers and where fur coats were made. Next he called Daubner up and asked where soap was manufactured.

One after the other he called them up to the board, and each one sat back down with an F.

Finally he called up Katz and Arnstein from the benches by the stove. He asked Katz if his family's pharmacy was prospering and if they stocked poisons too. He asked Arnstein if his family still had a shop selling fur coats and if their apartment was connected to the gas mains.

Then the teacher closed his grades-book and asked with a smile if we knew the parable of the lost sheep. That was Kohn, he said. Kohn had gone astray. At least now, said the teacher, there was one black sheep fewer among us.

The geography teacher then stepped to the window and declared, 'The temple has been thrown down. Not one stone has been left on another. Those who were in Judea should have fled to the mountains. Those in the city should have got out. At this moment Kohn is in the bosom of Abraham the progenitor.'

Laughter sounded from the middle row. It was Krappner.

Then the teacher told Bronowski that his father would find Kohn in the morgue when he performed the autopsy, for the morgue is Abraham's bosom.

'After all, your father *is* a professor of pathological anatomy.' The teacher smiled and raised his eyes without moving his head.

Then he told me that my father ought to know better than

anyone how they had found Kohn in the apartment with his tongue hanging out on the table. 'After all, your father *is* the head of the secret service in this damned monarchy.'

Then he said that yesterday Kchony's sick mother had gone insane and poisoned everyone in their apartment with gas.

Then he stepped away from the window, closed his gradesbook with a smile, and went back to testing us on everything we had learnt since the start of the school year.

I walked home frozen with horror.

I blurted out the news.

Papa didn't take his eyes off his letter-opener.

I stammered through the story of how the teacher had said at least there would be one black sheep fewer among us.

Papa went on listening and looking at his letter-opener.

I breathlessly told him what the teacher had said to Bronowski, and then finally out came what he'd said to me.

Papa said nothing, just tucked away his letter-opener, asked the teacher's name and walked out of the room.

Later that afternoon, when I awoke from my feverish sleep, I staggered groggily into the kitchen and learnt from Růženka that they had found poor Kchony in the bedroom lying next to his father, Dr Ephraim Kohn, a rabbi from a synagogue in Jerusalem; his mother had turned on the gas without them knowing it. Lying open on the table was an album full of photos, as if Kchony had been pointing to it, plus a pencil and a notebook with its pages still blank.

And that was how Kchony saw the world.

I never did reveal the secret of Kchony's journey, not until now, that is. But I'm sure if Kchony were alive today he would have freed me from my word of honour. 'Sadness,' he would have said, 'is yellow and six-pointed like a Star of David.'

But no, that's not right. He would say, 'I've seen the world now, so go ahead and tell my secret. Now it's all right even if Arnstein and Katz know.'

(*Translated by Alex Zucker.*)

Věra Linhartová

The Road to the Mountains

The institution was housed in the buildings of a former convent, situated above the town and a good distance away from it. Twice a week a bus would stop at the gates to discharge the new patients, accompanied by their nurses—there were not many of them, as a rule, and they never returned to the town—or else a few sad relations, who, having done their duty, would go back an hour later, reassured or even further saddened, but nearly always in silence. If there was something wrong with the bus, especially in winter, or if the road was icy and too dangerous for traffic, the institution might be cut off from direct contact with the town for a week or even longer.

It was separated from its surroundings by a high, smooth wall, over which no one could get in or out, as it lacked any handholds or footholds; only a single gate in it opened on to the road, which ended at that point. Here the buildings turned their blind walls to the gate; there were only the doors to the domestic offices, through which the things that were needed for the running of the institution were passed inside. It was only to this first forecourt, a paved and enclosed area, that outsiders would come to hand over to the nurses whatever they had brought from the town; they never entered the premises of the institution itself. The monastic customs continued to be observed here almost unchanged, mainly because they suited the institution's purpose, and also because the people who drove up were the same ones who had been coming here over the years; they accepted the change that had taken place but they saw no reason why they should change their own established practices. As a rule they put down their deliveries and left again without talking to anyone.

The life of the institution proper revolved around the inner courtyard, just as it had at the time it was a convent; it was an arrangement dictated by the building itself—the small doors of all living quarters gave on to a colonnaded cloister which surrounded the rectangular courtyard, and the only access to them was from there. Another facility which retained its former use was a parlour, projecting towards the forecourt— the one place where the patients could meet their friends from outside. This was a room divided into two by an iron grille, and although the small door in it was kept open it was rare for patients to walk through to their relations or the other way round. Because no one wished to be the first to cross over, everybody remained in the section intended for them, talking to each other through the grille, the openings in which were not all that numerous. There, too, between the parlour and the patients' rooms, was the flat of the head physician; this had direct access to the outside, to the fore- court and gate, as well as to the inner courtyard; the nurses, male and female, had their rooms in the domestic quarters and annexes by which the convent, originally not very large, had been extended over the years.

A strange aspect of the post of head physician was that there was no one here for him to treat; the only patients sent here were those who had already been pronounced incurable and beyond treatment elsewhere. Nevertheless, the doctor played an indispensable part. For one thing, the patients' relations would have demanded it; though aware of the doc- tors' helplessness in the case of their sick ones, they would not have entrusted them to an institution without medical supervision. And for another, the presence of a man in a white coat was reassuring to the patients themselves; they came and talked to him about their illnesses, as they were accustomed to doing from all the hospitals they had passed through. If there were no physician here they would know they were not expected to walk away again. As it was, they came here as though to a transit station, much like all the others they had been to before; they could not have borne the thought that their condition was permanent, and although they all suspected just that, the uncertainty that was left to them was their only hope.

The doctor's strange position among his patients, not as a leader and healer but as an observer, a counsellor, and almost one of them, together with the relatively great distance from the town, the poor roads and irregular communications, all resulted, once the institution was established, in there being no interest in that post, even though the work was evidently not demanding, its prestige fairly high, and the pay adequate. The man who eventually got the appointment had been aware of its peculiarities even before he began; he knew that he would be far from the bustle of the town and locked into an isolated building, doing a job which could never lead to any discoveries, and that, therefore, he was ending his scientific career. However, not only did he not mind, but perhaps it was just this that made him apply for the post.

While the patients may not have been sure whether they would remain in the institution permanently, Jan Kraus was entirely sure of it, both for himself and for his patients. He would not be able to leave this place after a few years, because all those who had started out at the same time he had would by then be too far ahead and somewhere else, and because in any other post he would have to start again at the very beginning. The work he was doing here led to no results; he was not curing the sick, he was observing the incurable, and he was trying to make them reconciled to their condition. Every word of his, every attempt, if it was not to peter out uselessly, had to be absorbed by the patient and penetrate deep into him, and even so the result was really in the attempt itself, for it produced no visible consequences. This kind of work was quite different from work in other hospitals—where each attempt had to be followed by a change for the better in the patient's condition—and, after all the time he had spent here, he would have found it difficult to do any other kind of work. But this aspect of his stay, too, suited rather than disturbed him.

However, he did not have a lot of experience behind

him. This was his second post since he had qualified, and he used to be afraid that, although this kind of work attracted him and fully satisfied him, he might not be up to it, and the patients might not have as much confidence in him as would be necessary for their own good. But his concept of work in the institution, as he had thought it through beforehand, was beginning to enter into everything he did; this attitude, which contented itself with itself and did not expect results, was not the right one for dealing with people, and so he soon realized he had no choice but to accept the post or else to stop thinking about it amid the conditions of normal hospital work. He decided to accept it and, giving up his former flat in the town, moved into the institution with everything he possessed; the major part of his belongings was books.

Along with the rest of the keys handed to him when he assumed his post, he received the key to the library. Apart from him no one ever entered it, because the nurses had set up their own library of new books, which they ordered from the town, and no one was interested in the old volumes which had lain untouched since they were acquired by the institution. The library contained several thousand books and was accommodated in a large room specially built for it. Although it consisted of just one room, it was, from the outside, the most massive and eye-catching part of the building. It was not, however, visible from the gate: it projected from the rear elevation and with its height kept part of the inner courtyard in the shade. Inside, tall windows alternated with dark bookcases filled with books. In order to remain undisturbed he would lock the door behind him, and if a nurse told someone who was looking for him, 'The doctor is in the library,' this meant that he was inaccessible. But often he did not even read. There were too many volumes which he knew he would never read, so he would rather not even touch them in order not to disturb the neat alignment of their spines; and if, after all, he took one down, he only browsed through it, read the page where he happened to have opened it, and returned it to its former place. Because the books he had brought with him were so ridiculously few, he would rather return to them in the hope that he might understand them in a way that would enable him to do without all those other unread volumes—because those were so numerous he would not know where to start. Most often he just stood for hours over stacks of old maps or engravings, or over the globe which, when he touched it, revolved slowly, with a grinding sound from its rusted axis.

In the course of the day there were a number of fixed points he had to observe. If it was reception day, at a certain time he had to be in his surgery, where the new patients would be waiting for him to examine them and make the final decision on whether they would stay at the institution. They were so used to a strict daily routine from other hospitals that it was necessary, initially, to maintain it for them. They got up, had their meals and went to bed at prescribed times, and this continued until it occurred to them to change their schedule to suit themselves. He also had to observe a timetable with regard to the mail, official business and indispensable management matters, because these depended not only on him but also on officials, shop staff and people providing transport, for all of whom regular contact is one of the main prerequisites of communication. As for the rest of the time, between these set tasks, he dealt with it as he pleased. He would change night into day and sleep during daytime; he would quite irregularly visit the patients who had themselves adopted a similar pattern; they could send for him or come to see him. But none of this was governed by caprice; he was guided by what he considered necessary so he could think, work or rest.

All patients had to be brought to the same conclusion, but each one of them had to be brought there by Doctor Kraus in a different way. This depended, on the one hand, on how long the patient had been in the institution, and, on the other, on how his disease was progressing and how firm a hold it had taken on him even before his arrival. Having thus created two sets of pairs of conditions, which intersected with one another, the doctor was able, according to his distance from the two, to assign to each patient his own place in this imagined set of co-ordinates, at least approximately, and then to move it like a chessman on a board. But he did not like the idea of a two-dimensional plane; more often he located things beside each other or on top of each other, like pieces of something in space, but he used even this scheme reluctantly and only in order to get where he wanted to get, after which he might again abandon any such notion. This was the easier as he was not on his own and aloof from them, able to survey them with a single glance, but right among them and therefore able to arrange them around him and within him.

Many rooms at the institution were still empty. The patients had single rooms, so that most of the time they were on their own. They were, of course, free to go out and sit in the courtyard, which was laid out like a garden, with trees and little paths, along which stood metal garden chairs which anyone could place in the sun or in the shade, just as they pleased. At any time during the day, therefore, one might see several patients in long overcoats sitting on the chairs, strolling along the paths, or just standing in one spot gazing in front of themselves; no one ever disturbed anyone else, and if ever they got into conversation they first had to be convinced that they would not be bothering the other person; besides, the conversations initiated here were more like prolonged silences broken now and again by a word. Or else they could walk in the open colonnade that ran around the courtyard, where they were protected from the changeability of the weather. They were also allowed to walk out into the extensive wooded park that surrounded the buildings and was bounded by the smooth wall. More often than not, however, the patients stayed in their rooms and saw one another rarely; indeed some did not know each other, and only the doctor and the nurses knew about all of them and could, especially the nurses, act as go-betweens for them. They did not carry messages because no one sent any messages, but the patients used to speak to them of their ideas or dreams, and the nurses would pass these on, in a changed form, sometimes because they were at a loss what to talk about, and sometimes because they believed that one patient or another might like a particular dream because he had such dreams himself. Doctor Kraus was aware of this and never prohibited it, and they therefore believed that they were doing the right thing and went on telling the patients about themselves.

But even the vacant rooms already had their occupants, of whom Doctor Kraus was aware and whom he had been expecting sooner or later for some time, sometimes for years. The doctors in the town would notify him of cases of sickness and send him their diagnoses, so that, unless the sick persons had meanwhile been taken to some other medical institution, he was able to follow the entire history of their sickness until finally, when all other options had failed, the patient would be brought to him and he would meet the person whom until then he had only read about in the medical files. However, not all the signalled cases actually got to him—in some of them the doctors were wrong, others would through their own efforts return to normal life, and in the case of yet others, when it was certain that they were incurably sick, their families might refuse to send them to the institution and look after them at home instead. But all these people already belonged to the institution, and unless they succeeded in overcoming their disease, or unless they were kept back by their families, they would sooner or later arrive as though at a place they already knew, where everything was a matter of course to them, and where there was nothing to surprise them.

(*Translated by Ewald Osers.*)

Arnošt Lustig

The River where the Milky Way Flows

T he light from the Milky Way flowed through the room. Everything was in its place—a little table and a vase of pale pink gladioli, two rather old wardrobes, armchairs with oak armrests and a wide double bed. A red-headed woman with a smooth complexion and a tired, listless face sat on the edge of the bed. She was completely naked.

The doctor had been standing over her for a long while. He turned to the boy.

'Open the door all the way,' he said.

'Is that better?' the boy asked hesitantly, as if he were ashamed. In the doctor's voice he caught the echo of an unknown adult world.

'I've seen worse cases,' the doctor answered.

The boy carefully opened the door between the room and the hall and returned to the doctor. He took his place at the foot of the bed again, slightly to the side so he would not be in the way. The woman hadn't noticed anything. She had big white breasts, a little droopy but still firm; her nipples, rough pink circles, were like raisins in a cake. Several reddish hairs grew in the middle of the white skin between her spreading breasts. Flesh covered her hips in folds, leaving red creases as if she had worn something too tight.

'It's probably going better now,' the doctor said to the woman, as both a question and an assurance.

'I don't know,' the woman said.

The doctor's hairy nostrils twitched, and he sighed aloud. He obviously had asthma. From the movement of the woman's eyelashes, he judged again that she was better. He wished to look as though he understood his work before the woman and the boy and himself; he wanted them to feel they had done well to call him, even though he didn't belong to their health centre.

'I thought right away that it would be better,' he repeated.

The woman tried to nod. She sensed in herself some dead world which was now slowly coming alive, like a star flying through a freezing infinity and appearing again in the range of its original course, marked by an inexplicable touch.

She probably felt as if she was drowning and somebody was saving her against her will. Instead of a deep pool somewhere there was the room, the bed she was sitting on, the light above her head, and she was choking on the air as a drowning person chokes on water, but at the same time she was engulfed in her own thick-headedness and in what was stupefying her with apathy. The door and the window let in a draught, the air was fresher from time to time and the woman's thighs became covered with goose-flesh. But if she was cold herself, you couldn't tell. Her eyes held a bleakness like the desolation of ice deserts, or abysses, the void between the stars and the most distant universe, and the reflections of gas, fire and ice. The skin of her naked body could be a temperature gauge for the boy and the doctor to read. She didn't say a word: they had to work out for themselves how she was.

'Do you want to go to sleep?' the doctor asked the woman.

Obviously, he wouldn't get an answer. She looked indifferent again.

'Do you have the feeling that you're completely stiff?' the doctor wanted to know.

Then he inquired, 'When you open your eyes, can you see everything at the end of the room . . .?'

Obviously, what he was really trying to do was to keep her from remaining indifferent to his questions and from falling into apathy. Now and then he gave the impression that he imagined himself in the woman's position and that he himself was trying to answer his own questions.

'I won't annoy you any more,' the doctor added. 'It will soon disappear. Everything will be OK.'

For a moment she looked as if a struggle or an interest in something was being revived, but the doctor saw that she was not interested in herself or in him or in the boy.

The boy's curiosity continued, mixed with pity, but he realized that it was only curiosity, just the simple desire to see her up close. He felt there should be the presence of a double mystery. The boy noticed that the woman, her eyes lowered, looked somewhere far away; she was all agog and pursed her lips, but either she didn't want to look there, or couldn't, or else she acted as though she wanted to achieve what they had prevented her from doing. Her face still wore a slight grimace. She opened her mouth like a fish gasping for air. She probably wanted to throw up but didn't have anything to throw up, nor enough force; she constantly gave empty coughs. She had marble-white skin and a strong body; when the boy stared at her sideways, he saw that her legs were a little short.

'Sleep, that's the best thing to do,' the doctor remarked again.

'Here's a pillow,' the boy added.

'You can lean against it, if you want.'

In the doctor's voice could be heard an effort to introduce both calm and quiet; it carried an echo from the world of unknown, healed people.

The boy let go of the bedpost he had been holding. He placed a large white damask pillow behind the woman's back and stepped away again without taking his eyes off her. The woman was not paying too much attention to him in spite of her nakedness. For the boy, though, her nudity was so imprinted in his memory that even if it were covered up immediately he would never forget it. She was the first naked woman he had seen in his life.

He understood and didn't understand what it was. It was older than he was, older than the woman, than the world, the stars at night and the sun in the day. It was the mystery of the body, and beyond it the mystery of man, the world and existence. It spanned baring all and hiding it, after which there was no more of anything, because what more can a person—a woman, a man or a child—uncover beyond nakedness? The light emphasized and immortalized it, probably as pillars reinforce a bridge from underneath so it can bear even the largest strain. It was and it wasn't the fact that the nude person before him seemed more naked because she was a woman. He was embarrassed, but it wasn't only shame he felt, or mere curiosity. He had sometimes glanced at his mother when she was half-dressed, even if he had never had the chance to see her totally naked. It was a physicality that for the time being had been refused to him, concealed, and found its basis in mortification as well, bordering on shamelessness. The first thing that had struck him was that the woman on the bed did not even try to cover up her nakedness, at the very least with her hands, or fingers, or with anything. Her body was like the bedding the bed was made up with.

He was ashamed of the way he was looking because he knew that he was seeing everything, even if he was acting as if he hadn't seen a thing, and that it wasn't the main thing that drew his attention. The woman's face held an indifference to the world around her, but her body continued to signify everything a body means. Breasts and legs, the darker triangle in the crotch when she opened her thighs a bit. Even though there was an open window in the room and now the door was wide open as well, the air still wasn't fresh. But the woman's body gave off a different scent from that of the room, which to the boy was connected with her nakedness. He was gazing like someone who had never seen anything like it before, like someone who didn't know when they would get a chance to see it again. He contained the feeling of excitement in himself because he knew it wasn't appropriate.

Without letting anyone hear he repeated to himself: she is naked, she is totally naked. And also: that's how a woman looks naked.

And again his shame helped him not give himself away.

The doctor was thinking about something.

'Close the window, that's enough,' he said.

'I should pull up the blackout shades first,' the boy answered.

'OK,' the doctor said. 'I should have thought of that . . .'

'I'll turn off the light,' the boy responded.

'Or—just wait a second,' the doctor replied. 'I'll tell you when . . .'

The woman had been sitting without moving all this time. Her clothing and linen were lying in disorder on the beige stool near the bed. She did not seem to be cold. Her underwear, all white, looked quite ordinary, like most things in the apartment. Simple, narrow lace bordered the neck and hem of her nightgown. It was a little rumpled. Her body was quite short and stout. When she bent forward or sat, her breasts sagged even more and rolls of fat folded over her hips; but in the mirror her bent back with its taut skin was quite smooth. She was hugging her legs against her chest, her smooth, plump knees almost under her chin. She seemed to be resting after some kind of exhausting trip and to be thinking still that she was alone there. Her green eyes stared somewhere towards the window, past the boy and the old doctor. She had spittle in the corners of her mouth. She looked like a hunted horse or dog. She didn't have a very pretty face; it was rather round, with rabbit-like eyes that appeared motionless, even though she darted them here and there.

'It's getting cold here,' the boy suddenly said. 'Should I close it now . . .?'

'In that case, it won't do any harm,' the doctor said.

'So the blind can stay pulled down and we don't have to close the window at all . . .'

'I shut off the main pipe; everything has been aired for a long time,' the doctor said.

He looked into the corner of the room. The boy followed his glance and again he saw the gas burner on the stove. The mirror reflected the woman's plump, fat back; from behind, she looked like Buddha.

'When did you find out?' the doctor asked.

'At 5.00 p.m . . .'

The boy was obviously happy that the doctor had started to ask him questions because he could look at him and not at the woman, nor at her back in the mirror. When she sat without hugging her knees or leaning against the pillow, her back arched up like a cat's. He didn't want to look at her because she didn't have anything on, but it was difficult not to, since she was so close. Suddenly, he wasn't sure what he actually wanted or didn't want, and what else he wanted.

'Was the door locked?'

'No.'

'Can you tell me how it happened? You needn't be afraid . . .'

'First I rang the bell, but it wasn't connected, so there wouldn't be a short circuit. Somebody had turned off the electricity. Then I knocked. For a long time, nobody answered. Then I tried the knob. I wanted to break down the door. I know it's supposed to be like that, but the door was open . . .'

'Sometimes the whole house blows up . . .' the doctor said.

'I know . . .'

'That would have been a pretty spectacle . . .'

Then the doctor asked him what he had seen when he got inside, but in such a way that the woman could not hear him.

'I smelt it right away,' the boy muttered quickly. 'It hit me in the face. We have a gas stove like that at home, and we're really careful with it. I heard a hissing—when I had stopped knocking—like a radiator. I went right over to it and held my nose. It had probably been lit, and she fell asleep. Then they cut off the gas. The main pipe here is on the other side, not where it is normally . . .'

'Was there a lot here?'

'Not so much that I couldn't come in, but I got frightened . . . there was enough. Then I was afraid I'd run out of breath. It stank something awful—'

'How old are you?'

'Twelve. Almost thirteen . . .'

'Thirteen already?' The doctor was surprised, and his voice sounded with new astonishment. Suddenly he smoothed the boy's hair. He seemed to want to say something else, but he probably changed his mind and thought about the woman again.

The red-headed woman raised her green eyes and noticed, like the boy, that the doctor had begun to jot something down in his notebook. His fingers were shaking. They were quite thick, full of veins and wrinkles and brownish freckles. He wrote in jerky motions with a blue Pelikan fountain pen which was worn and tarnished. Quiet lay in the room like the green surface on a pond. They could hear him writing energetically at broken intervals even with two windows open to the street. The boy racked his brains over what the doctor could be writing for such a long time, if it were just a prescription. But probably it wasn't just a prescription.

The woman slowly moved her eyes away. She sighed aloud and started to cry. Her hips and breasts started to shake like pumpkins when she moved her knees. She did not even wipe her mouth once, and the boy would have liked to do it, but he didn't dare. To suggest it to the woman, he wiped the corners of his eyes and lips with his fingers, even though there was nothing there. The woman didn't notice him. Shivers ran up and down her spine and she was trembling all over.

Suddenly she seemed to be crying from relief.

The doctor stopped writing. He covered her shoulders with the checked blanket which had slipped off them. The blanket had been half lying on the stool near her clothes. She helped him and held it around herself now with both hands. This was the first thing she had done for herself during all that time.

The boy raised his head. He felt that something was ending. What had been uncovered was veiled again, even if only with a blanket. He was more happy than not. The whole time he had been confused and it surprised him that he didn't show it. He had known that it would end. He stored everything that he wanted to remember in his memory, perhaps even more than he wanted. He wasn't sure. The only thing that couldn't be denied was what the woman had done. He wasn't even sure how he got here. Or of everything that happened afterwards. He could tell what was going to happen next.

'No,' the doctor said, 'no, no . . .'

The woman stopped sobbing. The doctor's voice had probably made an impression on her; it had in it some kind of magic, new to him, which the doctor was now trying out.

'You'll soon be better,' he said.

He noted down something else. His writing created the feeling of a common, oft-repeated activity, and the notion of past and future consequences as well. The passing time was acquiring some sort of new sense.

'It'll be all right, don't worry . . .' he added. Only this time he took out of his doctor's bag a notebook with prescription blanks and again he spent quite a long time filling them out. He filled out three in all. He put detailed instructions on each.

'You're doing well enough now for me to examine you a little . . .' he said.

The woman agreed without a word.

He looked long and carefully into her eyes. With the tips of his firm fingers he pulled down her lower lids so that the shiny reddish-white of her eyes was barer than the boy had ever seen. He recalled vaguely the image of a blind person.

'Where have I put my stethoscope?' the doctor asked. 'My dear . . . here. . . . mmm—' His voice was full of a strained effort to soothe her.

'I'll listen to your pulse and we can count it—it's not as bad as it looked . . .'

She still had saliva on her lips, but the doctor didn't mind. Only after counting her pulse did he take out his handkerchief and wipe her lips. Slowly he began to pack the instruments he didn't need any more. They were lying on the white sheet next to the woman on the other side of the double bed. The bed had two clearly outlined places like the imprints of complete bodies. Finally, the doctor took his big chromium-plated needle.

'This will be all now. We're still going to ask the young man a question . . .' he added, to the boy. When he stopped trying to give his voice that soothing intonation, he suddenly sounded almost like an old man. The woman seemed to have calmed down, judging by her face and eyes.

'I've already told you all I know,' the boy pointed out. He was surprised by the sureness the doctor demonstrated while examining the naked woman's body. But during the examination, the boy seemed to be expecting something. Present within him was the familiar suspicion that in the naked body

of the woman there reposed a secret he hadn't yet discovered—an opportunity, and a temptation. He didn't know
what that secret was, but he knew he was closer to it than he
had ever been; he also felt the nearness of some definite
disillusionment. In his eyes in the mirror he discovered a
hunger for knowledge, mixed with lust. He rebuked himself,
full of complicated feelings, which however he excused; it was
as if there were pouring out dimly from an unknown star in a
single perceptible moment some unfamiliar fragrant yellow
and silver light. The light caught on the woman's body and on
all things, on the doctor and his instruments, in the boy's
heart and in his conscience, only greyly. It was streaming
down from an unclear countryside, where he had not been,
but without lighting, it reflected backward into those
unknown heights. The boy knew that he would pay for his
temptation with disillusion.

He sensed inside himself a question that lay ahead, and its
never-ending echo: why? Why did his first naked body of a
woman mean disillusionment? Where did that come from?
Where had it lost or regained its sense? Why wasn't it pretty,
even when it wasn't only ugly or distasteful? Or was it possible for something to be pretty and odious? He half-closed his
eyes so he could confine the thing that he was ashamed of. It
evoked a pandemonium in his soul which the silence outside
him drained away. It was the thought of how he was connected with the woman's body, with the entire circumstances
which allowed him to view her nudity. And at what price. In
his mind, he penetrated her nakedness more and more
deeply because he sensed it was only temporary and he
realized that the echo of silence which surrounded her and
overcame the room, deafening him, as if he could hear the
roll of invisible drums in warning, was not perceived by either
the doctor or the woman. It was an ancient forest that he
found himself in, but one whose terrain he knew, as well as
the way out. The nakedness of the woman flowed from the
blanket like a wild river emptying into soundlessness. Only it
descended from within and not from outside. He felt a new
flash of anxiety which startled him. He suppressed it. It was
an invisible struggle going on within him about which the

doctor didn't suspect. Only once did it occur to him that
the woman was sitting there like a small white monster,
bound by invisible cuffs. It was a vile thought and he didn't
mean it in offence, which would be even more unfair than
how he had become witness to the woman's nakedness. He
didn't know yet that there are no limits to thoughts of any
kind, be they backwards or forwards, or any that concerned
beauty or revulsion, but every such thought contained its own
relief that it was only a thought, and not the act. He was
ashamed of the pleasure which he got from the chance of
seeing the woman naked, and regarded her with sympathy
for what had happened and why it probably had and to
whom. And to everybody else it concerned. He felt how fear
and courage fused together and added to what he was seeing.
And he felt how and whereby the world took off its mask
before him.

The silence and voices from outside dissolved in him as
they did in the room. Now it seemed that the woman's skin
was shining in the places that weren't covered by the blanket.
Was it a shine that only a woman's body has? Or the body of
a child? At the same time he felt like an ant which bores its
way into the earth and comes out where it didn't expect. But
his actions hadn't been as innocent. If the curiosity which
took him to the limits of unscrupulousness was part of the
craving everyone knows about, but prefers to keep quiet in
front of other people, and which they willingly or not so
willingly satisfy, but don't speak about, then he wasn't so
innocent. He felt innocent and guilty. He overcame the
power of the secrecy which had revealed itself in front of him.
The nakedness of woman. Her body. He didn't know his skin
was so thick.

The lure of the woman's naked body caught him unawares;
regardless of what kind of state he had found her in, it had a
magnetic power which he didn't want or perhaps couldn't
resist. He perceived an inscrutable pressure that disturbed
him without affecting the woman or himself. He had wanted
to do something good for the woman, to atone for the feeling
of guilt and shamelessness. He knew the doctor looked at him
from this point of view, being one with himself and his calling,

the same way that the boy wanted to be himself. He relied on the confused circumstances as an explanation for how he had got inside the flat and found the woman. And for everything that had happened, what he had done, and how he had acted up to that point. And why he was staying in the office. He was surrounded by almost imperceptible confusion, which enabled him to remain and in its own way protected him because he didn't look as if he was a mess himself. It excused him for still being there. It did and it didn't. But wasn't most of the world yes and no, not only here and not only today but for almost as far as he could see into the past and for as far as he wanted to look ahead? He thought about it for just a split second. The naked woman on the bed in front of him embodied the mystery of the world, people, what a person signifies, a woman and a man, the past and the future, everything from which the universe was born and a person from the universe. Pain and painlessness, suffering and sympathy, or understanding. What had happened, for whatever reason, and what couldn't be undone only because he didn't want it to. For a moment it seemed to him that the naked woman stood for something that was missing, something that would make him grasp what a boy must know— and one day a man perhaps—in order for the world to be whole to him. Only he couldn't answer the question why it had to happen the way it had, in such circumstances as these. He had to be content merely that it had happened and that he was there.

He suspected what it was preparing him for, and how it was doing so. What would no longer be the same for him, or innocent again. And why he was entering the rest of his life hampered with the shame of it, even if at the same time it was with the feeling that he had been good for something, that he had been able to prove his usefulness. His manhood. The seed of maturity.

'What happened after you turned it off?' the doctor asked. He pointed to the gas burner.

'She was crying . . . only quietly, not like before . . . ,' the boy answered.

'Nothing else?'

'She was holding her neck like that,' the boy said, turning to the doctor and showing exactly how she had done it.

'Yes . . .'

'First I thought something was choking her . . .'

'Even before you entered . . .?'

'No, I would have heard it. Probably after . . .'

'You helped her take off her clothes?'

'No, I only picked them up off the floor where they fell.' The boy lowered his eyes.

'She was pale . . .?'

'She was awfully white . . . and she wanted Egon to stay downstairs, as if she was afraid somebody would come. Or as if she was expecting somebody. The woman who brought you here was the landlady. She still said it couldn't be true . . .'

The doctor remained quiet for a while. She was his third case since the end of that autumn. Looking at the woman, he felt as though his strength were ebbing, even though this was the easiest case.

'I have to report it. It can't be omitted. I've had more cases like this one, but not in this district. This isn't my district. But it isn't so bad, at least not this—'

The boy probably didn't understand him.

The woman relaxed her bent legs a little because they were falling asleep. She pulled the blanket up to her neck. The pillow covered not only her back in the mirror, but also part of her hips. Something like soapy foam appeared again in the corners of her mouth.

Suddenly, the doctor looked at the boy and asked quietly, 'Is she your mother . . .?'

'No,' the boy explained quickly. 'She's Egon Lederer's mother. He's downstairs now at the landlady's. We used to be in the same class. Sometimes somebody from our class stops by here. We aren't allowed to attend school any more . . .'

'I just heard about it . . .'

The doctor frowned. He sniffled. His nostrils were as hairy as his eyebrows. Everything he wore was dishevelled.

The woman raised her eyes again. She hugged her bluish knees still closer to her body, almost tucking them under her chin. She was holding her knees with her hands. They could see that her whole body suddenly started to shiver again.

'It's OK now,' the doctor said. 'When we can feel cold or warmth, we're already better.'

He obviously knew what he meant by that. He finally put the needle away too and rubbed his hands as though to warm himself. He suddenly looked more satisfied too.

'A person has to know whether he's cold or warm. I've been practising for a long time . . . I got my diploma almost forty years ago . . . cold or warm! Now only warm . . .! Maybe I won't report it. I'm not even from your district. We won't do anything unpleasant.'

The woman seemed to feel a moment's shame. Her green eyes flashed with a dark gleam, as if a ray of dark sun had flown over them.

'Now even the most common things are unpleasant,' the doctor said. His voice rang with another meaning he was not mentioning, and he added, 'No one would understand it . . .' as if he were satisfied with himself. His growling voice filled the whole room. Something sincere rang in it. His voice had a strength of the sort that unites people into an unknown, unnamed human brotherhood only in those moments when the strength is genuine; but also his voice sounded with the echo of the two preceding cases, and not only those, but also something from his heart.

The boy saw that the doctor was doing what he could, even though he was afraid, as the young boys from his class were afraid because not all of them would drop by to see him.

The doctor looked round the room, then at the woman and the boy. The boy turned his eyes away. Something that had existed had disappeared. Something else had taken its place. It was like thin sheets of platinum foil, incredibly transparent, which could be separated from one another in the imagination, even though these sheets of foil were lying on top of each other. The boy felt that the part of his curiosity connected with temptation was already gone.

He came out of the ancient forest. The drum rolls subsided. The wild river wound obediently between its banks. He no longer felt such guilt or remorse coming from his lack of shame. He no longer felt like a hyena creeping up to a dead body, unsure whether it was still alive. The feeling of distastefulness left him and then he alternated between regret and tolerance and sadness. He already knew that to suppress sadness and not let it show was part of being a man, just like not crying was, even if you sometimes couldn't prevent your eyes from going moist. Even his deepest anxiety and fear inside settled to where he was able to control it. He followed the woman's pulse on her wrists, as he did at her throat. He might have a fever. Maybe the woman did too, with shivers at the same time, he thought. But that's what the old doctor was here for. He had entered into some unanticipated game and now the only thing important to him was to remain within the boundaries of rules that were agreed on. It struck him that the doctor didn't have very strong muscles. He was already old and had become soft. What the doctor had probably retained was his judgement. The things he said. How he was able to orientate himself in the situation from the few words he had said to him about Egon and how they were no longer allowed to go to school. He could figure it out. He may have disliked being called into a district that wasn't his. But even if he didn't like it, he could accept it with patience and understanding.

The boy could feel what was ebbing away. His heart wasn't beating so much any more and his breathing had calmed down. His eyes lost their hungry look; they no longer shone with that same repressed eagerness as when he had turned off the gas pipe and opened the window and done everything it had occurred to him to do. It wasn't exceptional any more. He suddenly felt ashamed that he was still there. He took his hands off the foot of the bed. The landlady probably also feared the report. He thought he should turn round right away and leave. He looked at the gladioli. The flowers weren't even too faded. The white curtains were hanging on the wall. The seven-pronged menorah had been knocked over on the beige olive-wood stool. He righted it and put the missing candle in the pretty holder. He thought about the possibility of leaving. He had an unpleasant feeling even without looking at the woman, the impression that he had stolen, even though she already had the checked blanket over her.

'What's wrong with you?' the doctor asked.

'Nothing . . .'

'You don't feel sick because you breathed in so much?'

'No . . .'

'Are you sure . . .?'

'Positive . . .'

'You should go for a run . . .'

'Seriously, there's nothing wrong with me . . .'

In his mind he was back with his curiosity, which he had repressed shamefully. He was constantly too close to those half-opened crevices which he couldn't forget, and already in this moment he sensed, far ahead, that even later he would never forget her. Mentally, he was returning to the transparent rosy flesh which he had never seen before. He knew that never again would he feel greater surprise, looking at a woman's body, than he did now. He sensed that this sight, like a caressing breeze, would touch everything in the future, and already it too daunted him ahead of time. He was discovering a strange, miraculous and corrupt beauty in the fact that he had just seen his first naked woman: fleshy thighs and ginger-coloured mons Veneris, and everything else different from what he had imagined. Only, something had been explained to him.

'Will you stay here a moment longer?' asked the doctor.

'I don't know, probably not much longer,' he said, as though answering with a question rather than a real answer. 'Not even an empire as big as the German Reich can win a war against the whole world. Not even the longest war can last forever.' The woman didn't say a word in reply.

'Someone should stay here,' the doctor said. 'I don't like to leave my patients without supervision. I'll send a more experienced nurse here. I'll call our district office. I can arrange it by phone . . . It shouldn't take too long—'

'OK,' the boy said.

'You can get dressed, by the way,' the doctor said, and opened the woman's mouth again.

'So, I'll wait here,' the boy said.

'I think it would be best if you wait here. You know what to do—'

The woman started to get dressed. She let go of her knees and let her feet fall, reaching for her underwear on the foot of the bed. The boy turned round. By the sounds, he could follow the way she put aside the cotton blanket and got dressed. He heard how she buttoned her white blouse and skirt and that she sat down again, tired.

'I'll drop by the house for a moment, so they'll know where I am—' the boy said after a moment.

'I hear you,' the doctor replied.

The woman never answered him, as if he weren't there. She was ashamed, and nodded when the boy couldn't see her. She was already dressed, and she made a completely different impression, the boy thought. It would come back to him sometime, when the event was in the distant past; perhaps it would happen again, after everything had been forgotten. He tried mentally to reconstruct it.

'Go wherever you have to, but hurry up for my sake . . .' the doctor said.

When he was alone with the woman, the doctor turned off the light, pulled up the blackout curtains and closed the window. Then he turned on the light again and approached the woman, who was looking at the floor.

'It can't be done that way, my dear,' he said. 'And that way they would win without a fight. Now there's almost a year gone, and what we used to count in years we'll start to count in months and weeks. And even if it weren't so . . . we would have to grit our teeth and hold out.'

Then he remarked: 'Not like that . . .'

And finally: 'One simply has to know when he's warm or cold and what steps he should take so he can wait it out. And then, you're not the only one. Life—even if it sounds trite—is a responsibility; there are only a few moments when it seems easier—only, they would like it if we'd all do it to ourselves . . .'

The woman kept silent. She lifted the sheet and used the end of it to wipe the foam from the corners of her mouth where it had reappeared.

'You'll forget it,' the doctor added. 'You're still young. The whole world can still belong to you . . .'

'Yes,' the woman said finally.

'Now the main thing is to keep warm. I hope you understand me. I'm not reporting anything. The landlady shouldn't let her tongue wag.'

The woman suddenly started to cry again, but differently from before. The doctor inhaled loudly—short, strong, forceful breaths, as if the next moment he would gasp for air. He was looking at the gladioli, which someone had probably brought her before it happened. The woman's lips were very small. Only the ends drooped while she wept and this gave her an expression of harsh disbelief. It was as if a human being were composed of different layers and each experience would be one of those layers; however, a human being wouldn't increase according to their quantity, but, on the contrary, would decrease.

'In any case, you mustn't get angry,' the doctor said. 'Don't read the newspaper. Try it for a few weeks, and you'll see how everything will go beautifully even without the paper . . .'

The doctor's sharply hewn, hairy nostrils twitched. He looked twice at his watch. But his glance didn't reflect consciousness of the time, only constant shame and fear. He felt in a hurry. He was waiting for the boy and perhaps it occurred to him that the boy wouldn't come, and what he would have to do if he really didn't come.

'Don't cry, no one will find out about it,' the doctor said. 'It was simply a weak moment. Nowadays all of us are fighting it. It's behind us already. It won't last that long. Certainly not as long as it has lasted up to now.'

'I don't know,' she said, bewildered.

The boy showed up shortly in the doorway, and the doctor breathed a sigh of relief. Again he looked at his watch, and this time his look reflected something.

'Maybe I could make some toast,' the boy said.

It wasn't clear to whom he said it, the doctor or the woman.

'That's an excellent idea,' the doctor said. 'Only it should be plain . . . for the time being . . . or if you have a little garlic—'

'Egon went shopping somewhere,' the boy replied. 'When he comes back I'll tell him it was only carelessness. The land-lady already knows that you're not going to report it anywhere . . .'

He got a little out of breath from speaking.

'Definitely don't put anything on the toast . . . anyway, it's some artificial filthy pork product . . .' the doctor continued. And he repeated, 'That's not a bad idea . . .'

He was already wearing his coat with its broad fur collar, although it was only autumn. The coat had long since lost its original elegance. In his hands he held his doctor's bag of Italian calf's leather into which he put his medical instru-ments. As he automatically snapped it shut and let his glance wander around the apartment, he noticed the family pictures on the wall. There was a chubby boy with black hair, a woman with a red fringe and next to her a man who was going quite bald. There was also a river at night and stars. The last picture in the corner had a piece of black ribbon on it. Under it, standing on the stool with the flowers, was a small lead war urn. It looked like a sports cup or a trophy. In the frame on the wardrobe there was a photograph, a group of unknown people on some snowy hillside; they were all laugh-ing for some reason.

'You needn't even mention that I was here,' remarked the doctor pensively. 'No one actually knows about it, only the landlady, and I'll stop at her place on my way out. We won't make any trouble for each other.'

He didn't try to sound good-hearted any more. Suddenly he felt very tired. Obviously he was glad to have done it, to have arrived in time, and also to be able to leave again already. The woman looked at him questioningly.

'It's not necessary,' he said. 'No, thank you.' And then he added, 'It's not necessary to annoy them needlessly.'

As soon as he left, slowly, somehow without energy, the boy started to cut the bread. He soon knew his way around the apartment, where he had been many times already, and the woman could rest, seated, and look to see how he was doing. On the table in the kitchen stood an electric toaster. Because they hadn't turned off the current from the electric power plant yet, the shining silvery machine soon started to heat up.

'Egon will be here in a minute,' the boy said. 'I had come to see him.'

The woman nodded.

'I'm preparing toast for three people,' the boy added.

The woman nodded again. In her look was remote resignation, the germ of a smile, gratitude, shame and some new, perplexed hope. She wiped the corners of her mouth and then she looked at herself in the mirror.

(Translated by Josef Lustig with the author.)

Ewald Murrer

Swallowed by Earth

Two chains of footprints in the snow.
A jay lets out a mournful cry
over the meaning of this tour.
Were the two in conversation?
Were they walking hand in hand?
Was one prodding forth the other with his bayonet?

Ondřej Fibich

Lying in this ghastly small space was becoming unbearable. If at least I had been here alone, I would have had a hope of lasting longer with the limited supply of air. But there were five of us and the door (if one could call the small square of boards a door) was tightly shut, weighed down with a boulder and with earth piled on top. Worst of all was the burning candle which breathed for two. We knew that with the candle we were madly wasting oxygen, but no one extinguished it. We were all afraid of darkness. For in this dim light, shimmering on the low ceiling of our cell which more than anything else resembled a grave, our imaginations were enclosed and we could perceive nothing beyond the inner space. The mere idea of darkness engulfing our prison opened up for us a view of the landscape outside that we feared. We expected danger to come from there. We expected the arrival of an enemy horde who would either shoot us on the spot or drag us through the woods God knows where, but who would certainly deal with us with the utmost cruelty.

And so we remained stretched out like this for hours, without the slightest movement. Then an old man with grey hair who was lying next to the candle could no longer bear it and began to crawl frantically to the door, moving hastily, with desperation, like a drowning man struggling to the surface. He fumbled in my face with his hands and in the face of Master Velebný with his feet; he crawled over Master Otto, and then, having removed the boulder and the earth, he leapt outside. There, he collapsed on the ground and sobbed with his face in the moist spring grass.

We sensed that the moment we had been hiding from, the moment we had feared, had arrived. We could feel the enemy horde drawing close. Yet we all rushed outside. We came out of the burrow like newborns emerging from the mother's womb, and we shouted, blinded by the sun, still clinging to the umbilical cord of damp darkness under our eyelids.

And there they were, steadily approaching from the woods, with their unshaven faces and dirty uniforms and with weapons in their hands. They were here and we lay helplessly in the grass, bathed and swathed in the swaddling clothes of space. And soon they stood over us, lighting their cigarettes and stacking their weapons into neat pyramids. Then they sat down next to us and their faces were the faces of experienced nurses. They smiled at us and caressed us, gave us names and wrote registration numbers on our snow-white clothes. They did not shoot us, they did not beat us; instead they offered us cigarettes and watched as we sucked in the smoke. Soothed, we fed peacefully on this maternal milk and the fragrance of the breast was sending us to sleep.

Then they helped us up from the grass and supported us, leading us through the woods. Their strong shoulders were tender, their arms showed us the way on a road free of pitfalls and danger. And it was clear that we had not fallen into the hands of the enemy, but had been saved. We were walking with a group of friendly comrades and that was very good. We could smell the forest and it spoke to us through the kind voices of the birds. The sun was warm, like the heart of a wise, indulgent father.

The soldier supporting me had the good-natured face of a

child. I looked at him as if he were a friend I had not seen for years. He noticed my gaze and said, 'There, Michal, everything will be all right. We are going to the village and you will be looked after. There will be food and drink and a bed—a generous bed with a soft white eiderdown!' Master Velebný, Otto, the silver-haired old man and Master Polák were all talking to their rescuers and looking forward to our arrival in the village.

Everything was so good and our sense of relief so enormous that even the unexpected shooting from the woods did nothing to destroy our happy smiles. But it destroyed our benefactors. All of a sudden they lay dead at our feet, a grimace of surprise on their faces. Their murderers approached us from the woods, shouting and waving their loathsome rifles wildly in the air. The same rifles that had so abruptly ended our idyllic journey. We froze with shock. They were here, the hateful horde we had hidden from in the grave.

They arrived and stopped near us, stacked their weapons into neat pyramids. Then they dragged the dead bodies of our fellow-travellers to the side of the road where they buried them. Speechless with terror, we were grabbed by the arms and hauled forward. I expected certain death. I could already feel the hole in the back of my head, when the man who was dragging me along spoke: 'See, everything is well again, Michal. Now we are going to take you to the village. You will be fed and have a good sleep.' It was awful. Astonished, we all stared at these killers, whose faces glowed with a certain tenderness despite their unshaven and tired appearance, uncannily resembling the faces of those who had just been shot dead and buried, those who had so suddenly departed on this road.

And so we were hauled along until we approached the village. 'We had already lost all hope of finding you, Michal.' The man next to me spoke again. 'We'd been searching for you for days—but it was as if the earth had swallowed you!' The forest still spoke to us with the familiar voices of the birds. 'My name is Petr—Captain Petr Komers,' the man introduced himself. He winked at me cheerfully. 'Now, all is going to be well—you've been saved!'

Then a barrage of shots sounded from the woods. Our ears, already used to this music, registered it as a triumphal fanfare. And then these men too lay dead on the road. Captain Komers fell at my feet with an expression of amazement on his face, still clutching a flower his hand had seized in mortal spasm. He grasped at the dead, shrivelling bloom like a shipwrecked man clinging to a splinter from the vessel that only a short while ago had been his only certainty.

And, having arrived from the woods, they were here. 'You are saved! The village, sleep, food, drink! It took us a long time to find you! Where have you been? As if the earth had swallowed you! I'm Sergeant Tajtl! You are safe now!'

And then these men, too, lay dead on the road, while others ran towards us from the woods. 'You are free. We shall accompany you to the village. My name is Jarkovský.'

And Jarkovský also died on that road, followed by Sergeant Rataj, Major Klika, Corporal Harant, Captain Velický and Captain Voldan. All those who had saved us and were going to take us to the village.

We walked down the hill, leaving the woods behind. Ahead, we could see the red roofs of village houses. The sky was cobalt blue with little white clouds floating high above. The sun was still shining with fatherly kindness. We entered the village. With a smile, Colonel Briks pointed to a farmhouse. 'There. They will give you food, wash you and put you in white feather-beds—ah, what happiness is a soft white eiderdown stuffed with feathers grown to protect the weak, vulnerable goslings. What happiness is the tender, maternal embrace of a warm bed!'

With a wide gesture he invited us, dazed and mute with terror, to enter the farmhouse. Inside stood a woman in a colourful apron; next to her a small girl, all dressed up in lace, who held a basket of fresh bread. A dog chained to his kennel eyed us with sympathy: being a prisoner himself, he understood. He could read our faces and welcomed us with a knowing growl.

The woman showed us into the house across the sunny

courtyard. The colonel waved to us with a handkerchief he had pulled out of the pocket of his dirty uniform. The girl had disappeared, probably to make our white beds.

The woman opened a door. We descended into a small cellar, far too small for five people. A candle was burning there, using up air for two. The door was locked behind us. The key grated in the lock. The key screeched darkly, and then there was silence. Silence.

(Translated by Alexandra Büchler.)

Ota Filip

extract from the novel
Café Slavia

Prague in the twentieth century is the true protagonist of this novel, its history enacted against the theatrically lit backdrop of bridges, palaces and winding streets through which the narrator, Count Nicholas Belecredos, makes his daily journey to the famous Café Slavia, one of the last remaining constants in times of change and uncertainty.

Night and day, high above the Vltava work was in progress on the gigantic statue of Stalin, to become the largest statue in the world. So far St John of Nepomuk still screened Stalin's granite-hewn shoes and ankles, but each evening, as I stood leaning against the plinth of St Ludmila, I watched Stalin grow on the huge brightly lit plateau above the river. By May he was already half assembled from the enormous granite blocks, and his left shoulder was being lowered by a crane. Two workmen were standing on the smooth surface of his elbow. Stalin's shoulder with the epaulette of a generalissimo hovered on a rope above the heads of the pair of them, whose duty it was to make sure that the edges of the granite blocks were precisely aligned.

I heard the ropes whirr and the crane screech, and suddenly the block of rock dropped, no, it did not drop but slid too quickly into its proper place. The workmen threw up their hands. It was strange—they grew smaller and smaller, they went down on their knees and screamed. Then there was silence above the river. I saw Stalin's upper arm, with the shoulder settled down accurately on the elbow. A leg hung down from the crack between the two blocks; two or three streaks of blood coloured the grey granite. The crane-driver tried desperately to raise the granite shoulder again. The engine gave out a roar, the ropes strained, but the stone did not budge. Someone climbed up a ladder and tore the leg from the join between Stalin's elbow and upper arm.

The harsh light of the building site reached down as far as Charles Bridge, and as I lifted my head I saw St Ludmila's stone face smiling above me. The saints to my right and left— I think they were St Francis Seraphim and St Francis Borgia, the one framed by two angels and the other by two females— were smiling too, but evilly and maliciously. Only St John of Nepomuk seemed to be inclining his head even further to the left. A deep shadow lay on his pious face. Just then a figure appeared at my side.

'No, no! You're not standing right! You're seeing it all from the wrong perspective!' he shouted, waving his hands before my eyes. 'St John is blocking your view! I actually designed Stalin's statue to be viewed from Charles Bridge and I intended to have St John of Nepomuk removed altogether because . . .'

'Why?'

'Quite obvious. He's in the way. Besides, it's not even known if he is a genuine saint or a false one. History doesn't concern me. I am an architect. But just consider a few facts: King Wenceslas ordered John of Nepomuk to be thrown into the Vltava from this spot, and drowned. It was only some centuries later that the drowned man was rehabilitated and a statue erected to him on Charles Bridge. Now people will be viewing my Stalin from this spot here, and St John might lead them to make totally inappropriate comparisons. For instance, St John was not rehabilitated until three hundred years after his death, and then he got a modest statue. Stalin, on the other hand, was regarded almost as a saint in his lifetime, but three years after his death was labelled a criminal, and a colossal monument is now being rashly built for him. There must be something wrong here, people will say. So how am I to answer them? The comrades in the Central Committee forced me to design the statue differently from what I had intended. I wanted to place Stalin a little further back from the edge of the crumbly slate slope above the river, his implacable gaze fastened on the saints on Charles Bridge. In my concept Stalin was to triumph over the past. But, as you see, nothing came of that . . .'

'Why are you telling me all this?'

'I've been watching you for a few days. You see, the comrades don't understand perspective. As I've said, I was forced to move the statue closer to the scarp of crumbly slate above the Vltava. This gave rise to problems. The hillside had to be consolidated by injections of concrete, and now Stalin is facing straight down Pařížská, our Paris Street. What d'you think? Shouldn't the street be renamed, say, Moscow Street or Kremlin Street or Greater Siberia Street, seeing that Stalin is facing east? Anyway, Stalin now looks down Paris Street to the Old Town Square, because that's what the fools on the Central Committee wanted, and that philistine in the *Literary News*—can't think of his name now but never mind—do you know what he wrote? Stalin looking towards the monument of John Huss in the Old Town Square would symbolize the direct link between the Hussite tradition and Communism. When I pointed out that Stalin couldn't see the Reformer because the Huss monument doesn't stand directly on the Stalin–Paris Street axis, they actually considered the possibility of moving the Huss monument, so the two could look each other in the eye. Besides,' the architect sighed, 'the statue of Charles IV, the father of our nation and the fatherland, has its back towards Stalin, so it will probably have to be turned round in the Square of the Knights of the Cross. You know what Prague people are like: they immediately make jokes. I'm a bit unsure about the saints on this bridge. The most important ones are turned away from Stalin, like, for instance, our St John of Nepomuk, and those who have to bear Stalin's stony gaze from the side have for centuries had their faces turned heavenwards or else stare at the pavement. That's my problem, and it worries me. And that's why I come here every day to find a solution.'

The man was silent for a while.

'As yet there isn't much to be seen of Stalin,' he continued more softly, 'but just you wait till they put his head on! Can you see his left leg? It's slightly forward, as if he'd just arrived in Prague and stopped short in surprise at the city's beauty and nobility.'

'Yes, but if Stalin had really just arrived in Prague he would have stopped on the eastern bank of the river,' I observed matter-of-factly, because I could not have cared less where Stalin stood, or where he had come from, or when the devil would take him.

'One might also explain it differently,' the architect went on, a little irritated. 'Stalin, on the march against the rotten and decadent West, is leaving Prague. He stops for a moment high above the Vltava, for one last glance at the city.'

'If he takes another step forward, he'll fall into the river,' I said.

'You think so?'

'I've never yet seen a statue take a step,' I replied in a conciliatory tone. 'But in fact I've only just noticed that Stalin is standing too close to the edge of the Vltava scarp. The weight of the granite is quite terrific, and if the slope were ever to slip, then . . .'

'I've had everything reinforced. After all, I'm an architect!' he interrupted me with an almost despairing cry.

'It was just a thought.' I tried to lighten my voice.

'Be quiet, be quiet,' the architect hissed at me. 'Another word and I'll have you arrested! I'll report you!'

Then he vanished in the dark at the double.

The following day the right shoulder was put in place, then the collar; the neck was made up of two blocks. Finally came the great moment: in the course of an evening and a night shift Stalin's head was put on, complete with a cap.

Three weeks later I discovered that Stalin was moving.

When I leant my head against the north-western edge of St Ludmila's plinth, in such a way that the edge of the sandstone touched the middle of my occiput, I saw that Stalin's nose touched the extreme left-hand star in the five-star halo over the head of St John of Nepomuk. The following day the star covered the entire nose, and a month later Stalin was leaning forward to such an extent that the tip of his nose was threatening the second star above St John's head. Moreover, so it seemed to me, the granite colossus was performing a very peculiar movement—he had raised himself slightly, and the whole platform on which he and his entourage stood was tilting towards the river.

One evening I was standing on Charles Bridge once more, waiting for the moment when Stalin would topple over into the river. His nose meanwhile had reached the third star above St John's head.

I inhaled deeply the cool, sweet damp which rose from the river and supposed that I would have to stay on the bridge until dawn. Towards ten o'clock the architect came reeling from the direction of the Old City bridge tower. Three or four steps from me he stopped and slurred: 'Oi, you still here? What's there to goggle at, then? All you see is a Stalin that's not quite come off. Admittedly,' he raised his right forefinger, 'there exists a bigger one, but mine is the most beautiful.'

The man flung his arms open and seemed a little unsteady in his knees. 'Stalin towers above the avenue of saints on this bridge. With his colossal dimensions he crushes the past. No matter where you stand in Prague, you can still see him. On the one side the castle, symbol of a glorious past, and on the other the majestic Stalin, our present and future.'

He dropped his arms and scrutinized me with sad eyes.

'Impressive, isn't he?' he asked in a croak. 'I wanted him in bronze, but do you know what the comrades said? Bronze is a material in short supply and has to be imported from capitalist countries. Granite, on the other hand, is abundant in Bohemia. I told them straight away: He'll be too heavy in stone, and the hillside above the river is crumbly slate. The comrades wouldn't believe me, and now we have this mess!'

The man breathed into my face: 'You know it already. Stalin's toppling over!'

'For a year it has seemed as if Stalin . . .'

'Shut up!' he yelled at me. 'You've seen nothing, understand? And even if you've seen something you've still seen nothing, because you've seen a state secret. I'll have you locked up till you rot!'

'That's not going to help. He'll topple over just the same.'

'The devil take him!' the man howled, and he made a movement as if to embrace me. 'Know what I'll do?' he then asked me softly.

'No. And I don't care.'

'I'll fling myself into the river and be drowned because I can't swim. Stalin demands his sacrifices!' he exclaimed plaintively.

The architect walked backwards towards the statue of St John.

'And you're not going to stop me!' He raised his fist menacingly.

'I wouldn't dream of stopping you.'

'But you'll be a witness!' The unhappy architect climbed up on the parapet. 'You'll be able to describe how I met my end. Promise me!'

'Yes, I promise you.'

'You've put my mind at rest. When the fire brigade fishes me out of the river, say it was an accident or something like that. I wouldn't want to spare the comrades the expense of a state funeral. But you're my witness for the future. One day, when this stupid period is over, you'll have to tell them that it was no accident, but suicide from despair. So you're not going to stop me?'

'I've told you.'

'You think I can't summon up the courage to do it?'

'You've got the courage all right,' I heard myself saying loud and clear. 'Go on, jump! Your witness is waiting.'

'That would just suit you, wouldn't it?' the man on the parapet suddenly yelled at me. 'Driving an honest Communist, an artist who rendered outstanding services to socialist realism, to suicide! No, I'm not going to give you that satisfaction.'

He climbed carefully down from the parapet, approached me, and hissed at me: 'Get away from here. I don't want to see you on the bridge again. And be glad I'm not having you arrested. Who are you, anyway?'

I took a deep breath and answered in a mild and melodious voice, 'I could be your father.'

'What?' The man stood open-mouthed.

'Calm yourself, my son,' I said gently and kissed the architect on his left cheek.

I began to pray.

I stood leaning the back of my head against the edge of the plinth of St Ludmila on Charles Bridge. The tip of Stalin's nose was touching the fourth star above the head of St John of Nepomuk.

'Holy Ludmila,' I addressed my revered saint, because this was no false saint. 'In 921 you were strangled. From a political point of view your kinswoman Drahomíra had no alternative: quite simply, you stood in her way. Ah well, if a statue were erected to everyone in Prague who in the name of God or for some other convincing reason was strangled, drowned, hanged, beheaded or burnt at the stake, the city would be too small to accommodate all those unjustly put to death. Yes, dear Ludmila, they subsequently canonized you and your murderess gave birth to Wenceslas, another saint. That's how this bloodthirsty history was regulated. The murderers and their victims became legends and now live peacefully side by side in a permanently falsified history. You, dear Ludmila, had taken up the cause of the blind, which means also those who, blinded by heathen phantasms, refused to see the glory of God. And how did they repay you? When the murderers came to kill you, you fell on your knees and asked them to cut off your head with a sword, so that much blood should flow, because your blood, as you called out to the heavens, would find favour in the eyes of God and He would adorn your head with a crown. And what do you know, they only throttled you in the end.'

I was silent in the Café Slavia.

Everything there was to be said between myself and Mr Alois, the waiter, had long been said, and so we just gazed at each other. He always stood patiently behind me, and when he began to breathe deeply, or when he actually opened his mouth, I would raise my right hand and silence him. I knew only too well that he would try again to repeat that ancient history about Rudi and Sarah, which touched both of us so painfully, and relate it in ever-gloomier tones. In a reproachful voice he had already recounted to me all the probable, as well as fabricated, variations of that story. Sometimes I would be the villain, and other times Rudi and Sarah would have brought their fate upon themselves. Only the end of his countless episodes about Rudi and Sarah were always the same—Mr Alois would admit to his only love, to Sarah and to his adopted son, and would curse a world which had allowed Sarah to be shot dead outside a hut in the Siberian winter and Rudi's ashes to be scattered on an icy road somewhere in Bohemia.

I had an uneasy suspicion that he wanted to shuffle on to me the responsibility for Sarah's and Rudi's deaths and that he was tormenting me to get me finally to break my silence and resignedly to admit my guilt: Yes, Mr Alois, I too am a sinner. If I had not met Sarah we would both have an easy conscience today. Especially me, Mr Alois, because you are innocent.

But I did not say a word. Only once had I flown at Mr Alois: 'Be quiet! Let be the question of guilt or innocence. No history, not even ours, tolerates final judgements. It only deals out blows.'

The masks which I then put on were applied too heavily. They were not only to change me according to atmospheric disturbances and my states of mind, but also to protect me. Grease-paint and a beard were my armour. On my aimless daily roamings through the city I eventually had only three points of orientation—the statue of St Ludmila, the shadow of Charles IV and the Café Slavia.

The following night a Turkish moon rose. The Vltava resembled a silver snake which had settled down for the night under the numerous arches of the bridges.

Just then came the earthquake.

Stalin began to rock on his pedestal; it seemed to me that he was about to take a step forward. His reflection on the silver surface trembled. Charles Bridge shook; there was a danger of the towers of Prague keeling over eastwards, but they maintained their vertical position. The firm foundations of my former palace rose slightly, the walls groaned, plaster fell from the ceiling, two window-panes flew from their frames and shattered into countless glistening splinters.

Stalin turned on his axis; slowly, as if he had tripped, he fell forward on the slope by the river.

Belatedly, the detonation thundered across Prague to every point of the compass. A grey cloud of dust veiled Stalin's figure up to his neck. For a split second the cloud shone in all the colours of the rainbow. His head still towered from that strange light, but suddenly, with a lightning-like movement, it dropped forward, as if some terrible force had broken the generalissimo's neck.

Stones struck the dully shimmering river, others drummed down on the roofs or fell on the pavement. A lot of fragments whistled past my window. A little later the echo of the explosion came back into the city. It fell from all sides into the river valley, and above the dust-cloud which hung like a grey bell over the spot where less than a second before Stalin had stood above the Vltava, it came together again. A gust of wind blew the cloud away. With lightning speed it reached my window, and with all its strength flung dust and a sweetish stench into my face.

Then silence fell again.

(Translated by Ewald Osers.)

Bohumil Hrabal

Palaverers

I

Some old men on a bench in front of the cement factory were shouting at one another, grabbing one another by the lapels and screaming into one another's ears.

It was drizzling cement dust, and all the houses and gardens were coated with finely ground limestone.

I walked out into the dusty field.

A little man was mowing grass with a sickle under a lone pear tree.

'Excuse me. Who are those old men over by the gate, the ones yelling and screaming at each other?'

'By the main gate? Those are our pensioners,' said the man, still mowing.

'Nice way to grow old,' I said.

'Isn't it, though,' said the man. 'I can't wait to join them. Only a few years now.'

'Hope you make it!'

'Oh, don't worry about me. This part of the country is good for the health. Average age here is seventy,' said the man, without a break in his skilful one-handed mowing. Cement dust poured out of the grass like smoke from a fire just doused with water.

'But can you tell me what the old men are arguing about? What makes them scream all the time?'

'They like to watch the cement factory at work. They think they can do better. Anyway, the more they shout the thirstier they are at night. They've worked all their lives, you know. They grew up with that factory. They couldn't live without it.'

'But why don't they go and pick mushrooms or just pack

up and move up near the border? They'd each get a little house and a plot of land in the woods.' I wiped my nose with the back of my hand. It left a slimy black line.

'Well, let me tell you,' said the man, stopping his mowing, 'one of the oldsters by the name of Mareček moved out into the woods beyond Klatovy. Two weeks later he came back in an ambulance. The fresh air'd given him asthma. Two days later he was his old self again. The one closest to the gate, the one yelling the loudest—that's Mareček. Believe you me, our air here is as strong as plum brandy, as thick as pea soup.'

'I don't like pea soup,' I said, stepping under the pear tree.

A team of horses galloping past on the dusty road kicked up a cement screen so thick that it completely hid the cart they were drawing. The driver kept up a cheerful song inside the dust cloud. Suddenly the gelding on the right gave the reins a jerk, tore some of the smaller branches off the pear tree and shook down a good hundred pounds of cement dust. I groped my way out of the cloud, my arms stretched out in front of me.

I'd started off in a dark suit; I was now wearing a grey one.

'Can you tell me where Jirka Burgán lives?' I asked.

The man had gone back to his mowing, balancing his weight with his free hand as before. All at once his sickle hit a molehill and he dashed into the field.

'Wasps!' he shouted, brandishing the sickle above his head.

I ran to catch up with him. 'Excuse me, but can you tell me where Jirka Burgán lives?'

'I'm Jirka's father,' he called back, still on the run, lashing out at the aggressive insects with his sickle.

'Pleased to meet you. I'm a friend of Jirka's,' I said by way of introduction.

'He'll be happy to know you're here. He's been expecting you,' Mr Burgán shouted, and put on a burst of speed.

But in the midst of waving the sickle and lashing out at the wasps, what did he do but drive the point of the sickle into his own unlucky skull. He didn't slow down, though, and was always slightly ahead of me, the sickle sticking out of his head like a feather in a cap.

We stopped at the gate to his house. Not even his nostrils

showed the sign of a tremor. Blood trickled down his dust-laden hair and around both ears, coming together in a rapid stream below his chin.

'Let me pull it out for you,' I said.

'There's no rush. Our boy may want to do a picture of me like this. Here comes my wife.'

A heavy-set woman had passed through the gate, her sleeves rolled up and her hands greasy. She might have just finished gutting a goose. One of her eyelids hung down below the other, and her lower lip sagged.

'I've been keeping an eye out for you,' she said, kneading my hand. 'Welcome, welcome.'

Then rosy-cheeked Jirka came running up. He shook my hand with one hand and motioned towards the countryside with the other. 'Beautiful, isn't it? Have I been lying or haven't I? The colours! The landscape! The fresh air!'

'Lovely, lovely, but look at your father,' I said.

'What's wrong?' asked Jirka.

'What's wrong? Why, this!' I answered, wiggling the sickle that stuck out of Mr Burgán's head like a gigantic beak.

'Ouch!' said Mr Burgán.

'Oh, that,' said my friend with a wave of the hand. 'I thought something serious had happened. Look, Mother! Father must have been after those wasps again. Naughty, naughty!' Then turning to me he laughed and said, 'We always have such fun. Once when somebody'd been stealing our rabbits, Father decided to teach him a lesson, so he laid down some boards over the manure pit in such a way that if the man even set foot on them at night he'd fall straight in. The rabbit hutch is right next to the pit, you see. Well, wouldn't you know: Father forgot all about it and fell in the next morning himself.'

'It's not all that deep,' said Mr Burgán.

'How deep is it?' asked Jirka, leaning over to his father for the answer.

'Oh, up to here,' said Mr Burgán, holding his hand up to his throat.

'You see!' Jirka roared. 'Then there was the time he decided to play sanitary engineer and poured a bucket of carbide into the cesspit. But he forgot all about it and emp-tied his pipe into it a few minutes later. I just happened to be leaving the house, and what did I see? A cannon shot of an explosion, a quarter of a ton of flying faeces, and Father, twenty feet off the ground, somersaulting his way through it all! He was lucky though: the manure broke his fall.'

'Ho ho ho ho ho ho.' Mrs Burgánová laughed so hard her belly shook.

'That's not true. I wasn't anything like twenty feet above that manure,' said Mr Burgán, beaming. The blood around his ears had dried into an enamel gleam.

'How high was it then?' asked Jirka, leaning over again for the response.

'Oh, fifteen, say. And there couldn't have been more than a fifth of a ton of faecal matter,' said Mr Burgán. 'Our son is always exaggerating,' he added. 'It's the artist in him.'

'That'll do it every time,' I said. 'Now please don't get me wrong, Mr Burgán, but that sickle in your head—it makes me nervous.'

'Oh, it's nothing,' said Mrs Burgánová and, taking hold of the handle, she wiggled it loose and yanked it out of the wound.

'Mightn't Mr Burgán get blood poisoning?' I asked, con-cerned.

'No. We treat everything here with fresh air,' answered Mrs Burgánová and, making a loving fist, punched her husband in the forehead. 'It's always a good idea to give Father a punch between the horns first thing in the morning. Why? Because he's a naughty boy.' She took her husband by the hair, drag-ged him into the yard and, shoving his blood-stained head under the pump with one hand, started pumping with the other.

'Father's got a lot of energy in him,' said Jirka. 'This year during the holidays he spent some time fixing the drainpipe, walking up and down the edge of the roof laughing, with never a thought about safety straps or the like, and Mother standing watch so that if he tripped she could run for the ambulance. On the fourteenth day he finally strapped himself down—and off he fell. There he was, hanging by one leg, with me passing him things to drink through the window and Mother spreading out all our quilts on the cement walk. And what do you think happened when I cut him down? He fell head first on to the cement, just next to the quilts!'

'Ho ho ho ho ho.' That was Mrs Burgánová again. 'Right on to the cement. But by nightfall he was down at the pub again,' she added, pumping away.

'Father rides a motorcycle, too,' said Jirka in a loud voice so his father could hear. 'Our friends who drive tell us, "No offence meant, but the way your father follows the traffic laws you'll be bringing him home in a basket one of these days!" Ha ha ha! Well, one day Father didn't come home, so we took a basket and went out looking for him. And all of a sudden down the road at a bend lined with thorn bushes we hear this bleating noise. So we go over to investigate, and what do we see, Mother?'

'Ho ho ho ho ho.' Mrs Burgánová still had her husband's head under the pump.

'Father and his motorcycle wedged into the thorns!' said Jirka, almost choking with laughter. 'Instead of taking the bend, he'd driven straight into the bushes. So anyway, there he was, perched on the motorcycle, hunched over the handle-bars, held in place for two whole hours by thorns and nettles and thistles.'

'I had one thorn up my nose and one under my eyelid, and I was dying for a sneeze!' Mr Burgán yelled over, raising his head. But Mrs Burgánová grabbed him by the hair and shoved his head back under the pump.

'How did you get him out?' I asked with a shudder.

'I brought over the sheep shears, then the garden shears,' said Jirka, 'and performed what's known as a Preisler incision. I had him out of there within the hour.'

Mr Burgán lifted his head to add something, but slammed the back of his neck against the pump's iron spout in the process.

Suddenly there was a flash over a nearby hill and an explosion from the same direction.

'Ten o'clock,' said Jirka.

'The rascals,' his mother said tenderly and looked up at the hill, where a small white cloud was forming above a clearing. A number of soldiers had appeared from among the dust-laden pine trees on the hill, and one of them came out into the clearing. On a flag signal he released the pin of his hand grenade, hurled it into another clearing and dived for cover. Another explosion followed and another milky cloud. The force of the blast reached deep into the valley, shaking cement dust from countless hazel shrubs and sunflowers.

'The rascals,' said Mrs Burgánová gently. She pulled her husband away from the pump by his hair, then parted it near the wound and examined it with great care. 'It'll dry up just fine in the fresh air,' she said, and politely motioned to me to enter the house.

II

The kitchen was hung with dozens of dust-laden pictures. Moving a chair from canvas to canvas, Mrs Burgánová huffed and puffed her way up to each and dusted it off with a wet rag. Bright, dazzling colours suddenly lit up the room.

Every five minutes explosions from the training camp shook the house and rattled the cups and saucers on the dresser. With every hand grenade the brass bed would roll a little further out of place on its casters. Each time, Mrs Burgánová looked in the direction of the explosion; each time she said tenderly, 'The rascals . . .'

Meanwhile Mr Burgán was showing me the pictures, using his sickle as a pointer.

'Now when our son painted this *Sunset Over a Pond in Southern Bohemia* he wore shoes that were one size too small for him, and when he did this *Karlstein Scene* he hammered a quarter-inch nail into his heel through the heel of his shoe. While he was working on *Beech Forest Outside Litomyšl* here he didn't take a pee all day, and when he did *Horses at Pasture near Přibyslav* he stood up to his waist in a smelly bog. And he fasted three days before starting *From a Mountain Peak*.'

While Mr Burgán talked Mrs Burgánová moved her chair

in front of each picture, huffing and puffing her way up to the canvas and wiping it off with a wet rag, and every five minutes she gazed off in the direction of the explosion and said tenderly, 'The rascals.'

By the time the church bell rang noon, the brass bed had rolled clear across the room.

Mr Burgán pointed to the last picture and said, 'Our son calls this one *Winter Mood*, and before he painted it he took off his shoes, rolled up his trousers and stood observing the scene in a freezing-cold stream in the middle of January.'

'The rascals,' said Mrs Burgánová, and climbed off the chair.

For a while the silence was oppressive.

Mrs Burgánová pushed the brass bed back across the kitchen.

'The pictures ...e beautiful. They show deep feeling,' I said. 'But why did Jirka have to wear shoes a size too small for him? Why did he have to hammer a nail into his heel? Why did he have to stand barefoot in that freezing water? Why?'

Jirka's eyes were glued to the floor; his face burning with embarrassment.

'You see,' said Mr Burgán, 'our boy has no formal training; he makes up for it with deeply felt experiences. And, well, that's why we asked you out here. We were wondering whether our son should study in Prague.'

'Jirka, you paint your landscapes from nature, don't you?' I asked. 'Where do you go for those superb colours? The way you juxtapose blue and red! Why, the Impressionists would be proud of them! Where do you find them?'

Mr Burgán drew the curtain open with his sickle. A fine powder issued from the material.

'See that?' asked Mr Burgán. 'See those colours out there? Nearly all the pictures hanging in the kitchen were painted not far from here. Just look at that riot of colour!'

Mr Burgán held the curtain back so I could share his view of a countryside as grey as a herd of old elephants. As soon as anything moved, up rose long streamers of cement dust. A tractor pulling a reaper through a field of grey lucerne stirred up the sort of cloud that follows a cart on a dusty road. Two or three fields further on, a young farm-hand loading sheaves of rye seemed to be setting them on fire, so dense was the powder they gave off.

'Just look at those colours!' said Mr Burgán, the sickle quivering in his hand.

Up in the clearing an infantryman released the pin of his grenade and hurled it with all his might. The brass bed started back across the kitchen. For the first time Mrs Burgánová made no response.

'The rascals,' I said.

She put her hand on my sleeve and—her hanging eyelid drooping like a pancake—said to me in a motherly way. 'Not you. Never. We're the only ones allowed to call them names. We're not calling them names anyway; we're only blowing off steam. It's a game we play. They're our soldiers, after all. It's the same in your family, now, isn't it? Among yourselves you can do as you please—call your relatives names, tell them where to get off—but only among yourselves. It doesn't work with outsiders. Jirka and me, we're the only ones who can make fun of Father. Nobody else . . . But what do you think? Should our boy go to Prague? Will he do anything there for Czech art?'

She looked at me with knowing eyes, eyes with the power to pierce the depths of my soul.

'Prague is like a pair of obstetric forceps,' I said, looking down, 'and these pictures, they're no child's play; they're the finished product. If you ask me, he's got every chance of making a name for himself.'

'We'll see,' said Mrs Burgánová.

Mr Burgán opened the door and beckoned to me with his sickle.

'Our boy is a sculptor too,' he said, tapping the sickle against a magnificent plaster statue. 'Look at this. *Bivoj Without His Boar.*'

'Why, it's amazing!' I said. 'What biceps! Who was your model, Jirka? A weightlifter, a heavyweight?'

Jirka again lowered his eyes in embarrassment.

'Neither one nor the other,' said Mr Burgán, and pointed to himself with the sickle. 'Me!'

'You?'

'Me,' Mr Burgán repeated gleefully. 'The imagination our boy has! When he hears a tap dripping he sketches Niagara Falls. When he bruises a finger he runs and finds out how much a third-class funeral costs. Minimum cause, maximum effect,' he added with a wink.

'I can't get over how well you understand these things, Mr Burgán,' I said.

'Oh, that's because I'm from Vršovice,' he said, scratching his head with the sickle. 'Have you ever seen Shakespeare's *Troilus and Cressida*? Nearly a quarter of a century ago I had a walk-on part in it at the Vinohrady Theatre. In the fifth act the director needed two beautiful naked statues to decorate the palace. One of them was played by me painted bronze, the other by a girl painted bronze. During the fifth act of every performance we would lie motionless in the glare of the spotlights, with the stagehands ogling us—well, her—from above. And when *Troilus and Cressida* was over I asked the naked statue to marry me and she said yes, and the result is we've been living together for nearly a quarter of a century.'

'Is that your beautiful bronze statue?' I asked.

Mr Burgán nodded and smiled.

'The one that lay there with you during the fifth act?' I asked.

Mr Burgán nodded and smiled.

'How about letting in some fresh air?' Mrs Burgánová suggested.

Cement dust drizzled on to the rug.

'If you ever feel your nerves need a rest,' said Mrs Burgánová, 'think about coming and spending, say, a week with us.'

'But the grenades,' I asked, 'are they always like that?'

'Oh no,' said Mrs Burgánová, dragging a vacuum cleaner out of a cabinet. 'Only Monday to Saturday from ten to three. Sunday is so sad. The silence makes an awful racket. So we listen to the radio and Jirka plays his tuba all day. We can hardly wait to go to sleep because when we wake up it won't be long before we have our soldiers back.'

'Did you really both lie naked and bronzed on that stage? Really?'

'Really,' said Mrs Burgánová, waddling over to her husband and handing him the rolled-up cord. 'Father, go and vacuum off the aster bush near the wall, will you? I want to make Jirka's friend a bouquet. The rascals ...' she added tenderly, looking out of the window to the hill, where a small white cloud had formed just above the clearing. It was like a white hawthorn bush in bloom.

(*Translated by Michael Henry Heim.*)

Josef Škvorecký

The Well-Screened Lizette

All animals are equal,
but some are more equal than others.

George Orwell

When they threw me out, they allowed Lizette to stay. She got a clean bill of health, even though she had never taken a single exam in six semesters at the university. She hadn't even handed in her essays. They threw me out although I had passed five semesters including all necessary exams. But I was an element suspected of sympathies for the West, because everyone knew I played in Zetka's swing band. And, like a bloody fool, I showed up at the political screening session in coloured socks. Fendrych, the cross-eyed political inspector with buck teeth, stared at them throughout the session, and every time he asked me an important question—such as 'Are you descended from the working class, colleague?' or 'Do you believe in God, colleague?'—his eyes threaded the answer out of my socks, as if he were deeply offended by this symbol of bourgeois decadence.

Needless to say, I didn't pass. This same Fendrych passed Lizette, who was under no suspicion of harbouring questionable sympathies, and quite rightly so. There was only one thing in the whole world for which Lizette had strong sympathies: Lizette herself.

Obviously, I wasn't present at her evaluation, but I can imagine the scene quite easily: Fendrych stared, but not at socks or anything like that. No, I am sure that Lizette had put on her oldest blouse, which bore the marks of rough embraces and working-class ardour. I have no doubt that she stressed her father's proletarian occupation as a stagehand, though normally she referred to him as being with the National Theatre. They didn't question her about his political opinions, because he was a member of the working class; Lizette was thus saved from the need of lying. If Fendrych blinked at anything, it was at Lizette's majestically swelling bosom, or her knees covered with darned working-class stockings, which she skilfully exposed to view, knowing full well that they were worth a couple of good points. And so Fendrych passed that green-eyed snake in the grass.

And why not? He had been panting after her for two years, and she never totally rejected him because she never totally rejected anybody who might possibly be of use to her.

And so she stayed on. Many people declared that to their dying day they would never understand how this beautiful, wide-eyed bit of fluff could ever have passed a course in Old Church Slavonic, not to mention pasting together a doctoral dissertation. And on the surface it does seem incredible, because to this day Lizette isn't sure whether Masaryk is spelt with an 'i' or a 'y', but anybody with a drop of sense need only take a good look at Lizette for everything to become crystal-clear.

Even now, at thirty, Lizette is still a knock-out. In America she'd be photographed in Technicolor, posing for Maidenform lingerie.

Looks, plus a cunning as immense as her abysmal ignorance of elementary grammar, minus any consideration for others, minus the slightest trace of altruism, plus exemplary single-mindedness when it comes to her own person.

Take that business with Old Church Slavonic. Lizette showed up for examination at a time when Professor Marek did not expect her and, as she had ascertained in advance, he was alone in his office. With lowered eyes she confessed that she didn't know a single word of Old Church Slavonic but that she desperately needed a certificate of proficiency in order to pass her political evaluation. Professor Marek had intended to get furious, but he looked at Lizette's bra, then higher, into her green eyes. There, he drowned.

And he wrote out a certificate for her.

It cost her a few trips to the suburb of Hřebenka, where Professor Marek lived with his wife and three children. During those trips she had to listen to his life story. In the course of the last journey he confessed to her that he, too, was bored to tears by Old Church Slavonic, and he offered her safe passage in all exams up to the doctorate, in return for occasional sexual favours. But Lizette was sparing with this kind of merchandise, and since she no longer needed to worry about her exam she went into reverse and backed out of the garage.

In similarly debonair fashion she conquered literature, Russian, Marxism, everything.

I happen to know, because Lizette had a soft spot for me in her heart, which mellowed to the tones of a tenor sax. That may seem like a violation of natural law, for a stone is a stone; I guess Lizette's heart was simply a special kind of stone. It happened when we played in Vlachovka. Her heart started beating in sync with my solos and after the concert I got to know her well, that green-eyed snake in the grass. Yes, she belonged among a special group of beautiful women, a group that's now dying out; Prague is becoming integrated. Lizette left in time: she slithered out of Prague all the way to Rio de Janeiro, God help her. But even if she were to slither all the way to the moon, in her heart she'd remain a snake in the grass.

As far as Lizette's doctorate goes—well, that was a bit more complicated. After carefully surveying the situation she decided to specialize in psychology, because she correctly pegged Professor Zajc as the most approachable of her teachers, from a strictly human point of view, that is. She also set her sights on a certain classical philologist, a scholarly young man whose knowledge in the field of female studies was strictly theoretical. Lizette provided him with his first opportunity for practical, preliminary sexual research. Her dissertation was finished within three months, and it was such an outstanding and inspired piece of work that they asked her to add a historical introduction and submit it as part of her application for the position of associate professor. Lizette contented herself with the doctorate.

For she had other plans.

Mind you, that classical philologist never got his own doctorate. After Lizette threw him over, he took to drinking and behaving in a scandalous manner, and in the end they fired him as an incorrigible bourgeois. He now works as a bouncer in a night-club in Ostrava.

While I was fulfilling my military obligations, Lizette's career progressed, though rather modestly at first. She got a job teaching Marxism at a Smíchov high school. Most of her fellow graduates had to become maths teachers in the provinces, but Lizette made the timely acquaintance of someone influential in the Ministry of Education, whose name I forget.

By the time I'd finished my National Service, she had become programme director at the Centre for Folk Art. She'd appear in the Alfa Café bedecked with gold and precious stones. She had met someone high up in the Ministry of Finance, and her family was well prepared for the fiscal reform.

As one might expect, Lizette's goings-on did not endear her to everyone, and there were growing numbers of fellows who hated her and voiced nasty insinuations about her whenever they could, but as soon as they found themselves *vis-à-vis* Lizette and her bosom, they were bewitched once more into silent adoration.

Communists, non-Communists, Jews.

Fraternal equality.

Even Jan Vrchcolab, a promising poet from the Youth Organization, fell for her. Lizette's bra blinded him to such an extent that he began to confide to her his ideological dreams and doubts. Which she promptly passed on to me. She had a liking for me, that snake in the grass, though she wasn't too generous with her favours and in the end she sent me packing, too.

Whenever Vrchcolab was to write something for *The Youth Front* magazine, he consulted Lizette first. She gave him her advice. And because Lizette, like a true woman, shifted her moods and opinions with astonishing aplomb, Jan Vrchcolab's opinions changed accordingly, often making a complete about-face. *The Youth Front* readers lapped it up. Thus, via Vrchcolab, Lizette exerted a profound influence on the youth movement.

Of course, this was a secret.

Actually, no matter what ideas Lizette came up with, deep down they all focused on one thing: Lizette herself. In that regard, she was remarkably consistent and loyal.

She kept changing Vrchcolab's views just out of boredom, for the sake of fun. Many people started to scratch their heads, trying to puzzle out Vrchcolab's philosophy. In vain.

Whenever she put some especially amusing notion into his head, we'd meet at the Alfa Café and enjoy the joke together. And we would collaborate on new nonsense to pump into him. He liked to sound off in public about every new cultural or political event, and he was unaware that he'd become a dummy for a pair of ventriloquists.

His remarks, regularly reprinted in *The Youth Front*, stimulated polemics and weighty discussions. Various socialist-realist theoreticians analysed and expounded Lizette's bebop profundities, giving rise to a virtual new literary movement. Some articles were published in the Soviet Union; from there they were taken over by *L'Humanité*, then they appeared in *The Masses* and *Mainstream*. In this way, Lizette's influence extended across the Atlantic.

We developed an appetite for this kind of amusement, and began to target various prominent persons: via Vrchcolab, we accused them of cosmopolitanism, bourgeois nationalism, Zionism, Mendel-Morganism, formalism, kowtowing to Western culture. We branded them as henchmen of Slánský or Tito, lackeys of naturalism, Freudianism, idealism, spiritualism, opportunism, revisionism, surrealism; we denounced their fluency in English. We carried on our campaign in private, at meetings, in the course of political evaluation sessions, and to some extent in the press.

Naturally, Vrchcolab suffered the consequences. He is still suffering.

In the end, he managed to help place Lizette on the preparatory committee for the Sofia Exposition, and thereby his usefulness to her came to an involuntary yet definite end. Lizette's contribution to the preparatory committee proved predictably disastrous. But before she bowed out, she fulfilled one requirement set by the committee's director, Comrade Borecky: he asked the women employed by the organization to order, at state expense, three dresses from the fashionable Rosenbaum couturier, in order to represent our country abroad in a proper manner.

Lizette was so keen to obey this directive that she ordered not three but six dresses from Rosenbaum's.

She screwed up whatever she touched, but the director became fond of her all the same. He called her 'our Lizzy', even in front of the press. As a result, one young woman reporter, who had been kissing Borecky's ass in the hope that he would get her a job at the ministry, was encouraged to do an interview with Lizette for the forthcoming exposition, presenting her as a typical Socialist woman of our day.

Well, the reporter made quite a hash of it, but nobody knew at the time.

Before leaving for Sofia, there came a directive from above that the unduly overgrown staff was to be cut by a third. They threw out Maršíková, who had been putting in two hours' unpaid overtime a day. They threw out Behmová, who had organized all the pavilions dealing with industrial machinery, light as well as heavy. They even threw out Tatyana Letnicová-Sommernitzová, who was political officer and supervisor of the Workers' Brigade.

History repeated itself once more: Lizette went to Sofia. She took along all six Rosenbaum creations, in addition to various items to trade and exchange. The cases of Ríša's double bass and my tenor sax were filled to overflowing.

You see, we went too. Zetka's Swing Orchestra. That was the only thing Lizette managed to do right. When it came to gags and practical jokes, you could always count on Lizette.

And so we introduced the folk music of the oppressed American blacks to Sofia. We ourselves weren't oppressed in any way, although we were given strict instructions by the

Ministry of Culture. Night after night, hundreds of male and female Sofians stomped and swayed on the floor to the sounds of Benny Goodman. Lizette was among them, accompanied by various swains and later by a tall, blond man from the Bulgarian Ministry of Culture.

He was also the one who started calling her Lizette. Her name was actually Lidmila, but she had all sorts of nicknames: Lída, Liduše, Líza. That handsome Bulgarian called her Lizette, and it stuck.

After a few days they took off for a seaside resort. Of course, that was against regulations—the exposition was under strict discipline—but did that matter to Lizette? What a naive idea.

She joined us in Budapest, on our return trip, and she was escorted by a new admirer. He looked like an undercover policeman. The devil knows what he was, but with Lizette anything was possible.

She had brought back with her a TV set, a silver fox cape, a Persian rug, a calculator, two cameras, a gold watch and some six ounces of gold jewellery. Also, six metres of Chinese silk with a pagoda design, but she sold it because Prague was overstocked with that particular item.

And she got away with it. The other women, each of whom was returning with one nylon nightshirt and two litres of maraschino, gnashed their teeth in fury. They hated her. Pokorná actually denounced her, but the report dissolved somewhere in the secret files of the Ministry of the Interior.

In Sofia, before she turned her back on the exposition and whizzed off with her blond companion, Lizette managed to bewitch the deputy director, Řeřich, an extremely influential figure in education. He blazed up like an Olympic flame.

He arranged a public appearance for her. In the name of Czech women, she addressed the children of Bulgaria on the occasion of their new school year, and her speech was carried by all the Bulgarian media.

Back in Czechoslovakia, it was cited in the press.

She and I had composed the speech early one morning in the exposition dance hall, under the influence of heady Bulgarian wine.

Fortunately, nobody pays any attention to such addresses, and they are promptly forgotten.

Lizette, however, was not forgotten. No sooner had she returned to Prague and put in a claim for an additional three thousand crowns in expenses, than Deputy Director Řeřich made her assistant editor of the State Pedagogic Publishing House. The favourite candidate, an experienced pedagogue, was suddenly discovered to be a dry intellectual of bourgeois origin, with insufficient Marxist erudition.

In comparison with Lizette's proletarian background, this was a serious shortcoming.

And because Lizette didn't have to start from the bottom, her deficiencies in elementary grammar never came to light.

But there is one thing you have to hand to Lizette: she never forgot old friends. Trusted translators, employed for years by the publishing house, were dropped and translation assignments were distributed to Lizette's buddies instead. I benefited, too. With the help of a pocket dictionary, I translated from the Russian some poems of Mao Zedong, as well as a handbook of criminal law.

Lizette never learnt of the disastrous consequences.

At a writers' congress, she met a man from the Foreign Ministry. A month later she was made cultural attaché in Rio de Janeiro, instead of a fellow named Hrubeš who had been studying Portuguese for five years in expectation of the assignment.

I know, it sounds unbelievable, the mind rebels against it, and yet it's a fact.

There are many mysteries 'twixt heaven and earth.

Political evaluation, class origin, Socialist zeal, merit, are one thing; generous bosom, shapely behind and green eyes are another.

Like time and eternity.

I don't know how you feel about it, but I would never dare weigh one against the other.

Anyway, Lizette, that snake in the grass who left so many in the lurch—including me—is now in Rio, sitting pretty as cultural attaché.

I expect that one day she'll become the first woman president of this country.

And then at last we'll have real Socialism.

(Translated by Peter Kussi.)

Jiří Gruša

Chapter 1 from
Doktor Kokeš Mistr Panny
(Doctor Cocker, Virgin Master)

Honking Horns

There they were on Joseph Square, in the city of Prague, Marian Cocker and his father, Charles, sitting in a line of cars waiting for the lights to turn green. Father was crying, his eyes blurred with tears as if from make-up, though these were ceremonial tears. They dripped on to the leg of his trousers, tailor-made as usual, soaking into the Madeira and into all the other food stains from occasions less meaningful than today's luncheon celebrating the appointment of Dr Marian as associate professor and the publication of his *Divorces in the Eyes of the Judge*. Every so often his father's jaw would involuntarily drop to release a stream of saliva. This embarrassed the son (it made him feel as if he himself were drooling), so he turned the other way and saw a woman passing their car, her arms full of chrysanthemums, dressed all in black with a poodle, also black, at her heels. The woman, more handsome than her dog, stepped off the edge of the kerb, then stopped in mid-step to wait for the lights, her rear end wrapped snugly in black velvet, and on seeing the prance of her Lippizaner legs Marian suddenly realized that he had been in that body once.

'Turn this way so I can be sure it's not just my agitation,' he ordered her. But it was her dog that turned to face him, its eyes like blackcurrants, in its mouth a blossom from one of the chrysanthemums. Then things started moving and all the horns behind Marian Cocker began blaring, insistent and shrill. 'Go,' he barked at his father, but then he saw the shine of saliva flowing from the corner of his father's mouth on to his chin and then down on to the Madeira stains, away from the white that was flooding his eyes and draining his face, which was now so pale a green that no shrieking was loud enough to drown it out, not even Marian's calls for help. And finally it dawned on the son that he would have to engage the handbrake, move the body aside and take over the steering wheel.

Father collapsed on to son, his head thumping against the window; on the other side eyes bulged and necks craned, blurred and useless. Jesus Christ. The son sped off, flashing his lights and honking his horn all the way to Doctor Shtet's, who feared it was too late but nevertheless ordered the body to be brought into the operating room and laid on the table.

One of the nurses in the hospital on the riverbank said, 'It's no use.' But Shtet thought otherwise: 'Let's give it one more try,' he said and administered a shock. The body moved.

And so did Marian.

First to the place where it had happened, to Joseph Square. The doors to the Capuchin church yawned open, the flames of the candles at St Jude's feet as chilly as icicles. Marian was sure he'd seen the woman come in here with her dog, but all he saw now was an encephalitic selling elastic waistbands for long johns, offering his wares under a statue of St Thaddeus. Who would take anything from a hand like that? People pay so they won't have to touch it.

People like Marian. Oh, what aversion he feels, and yet suddenly he finds himself holding a rolled-up piece of rubber, and he turns around and weeps. As if only now was he seized by the fear of mortality and his body's realization of it.

Until now nice and cosy, he's been peeled out of the pulp.

He had, for instance, x! (the symbol for the act of sex) with one Anilinka, that was at 7.45 p.m. And before that, at 5.20, he had had to put his father on the train to Ch. And of course then he'd got . . . no—his appointment with Robus. Here in his office in Cattle Market Square. Comrade Robus deals with cattle more or less, and this is where he intends to forsake his Natasha. Magda Smotlak is the name she was born with, though back when she was still his juicy-Russki, back when she had his buns in the oven, he called her Natasha. Today he no longer calls her anything at all. He simply signs power of attorney over to Dr Cocker, who will now assume responsibility for the rescindment of the little ones.

'Here you go,' he says, as if he were sending the doctor to the local knackery. The chair creaks under the bulk of his anal flesh, the little table chatters. 'What do you say, Doc? I mean, here she is writing me up, my own wife writes reports on me, and by what right?' Robus tells Dr Cocker, the devil's advocate, in Cattle Market Square. He doesn't find it fair that he should be one of the *reportables*, of that he is certain. This is the only certainty he's got in fact, and he's infuriated Natasha dared to do such a thing. 'Roast her for me,' he pleads, though only with his neck and the fatty blood running through it, 'pulverize her.' Marian breathes in the scent of the request through his narrow nose, inhaling its glow, and with an assenting, silent smile he begins straightening out the pens and pencils on his desk as if he were already sorting things out.

In fact he is only making another note in his diary, his sharpened pencil point scratching 'Filial Gratitude as Reflected in the Law', a lecture written down for 11.15 a.m., with a lofty Cockeresque introduction about an Eskimo tribe whose supplies run out at the end of the winter, forcing them to leave their elders to the mercy of the cold, until they die what is said by some to be quite a comfortable death.

'Well then,' Dr Marian says fervently, 'so much for the child–parent relationship. This, my friends, is the mirror of our culture, and woe when it is the lawyer, not the poet, who must speak of such matters!'

Except that in the middle of his tundra, left to the freezing cold by the one who sired him, Dr Cocker somewhat stutters; the Lundi, Montag, Lunes overview scratched into his leather diary has come unglued, and from platform no. 3 train 0048 is departing without Charles Cocker, and even though it is truly and demonstrably 5.20 p.m., Dr Cocker—counter to the original timetable—is weeping. So it happens that long after 8 p.m. Anilinka, a student at Charles University—though only in theory, for her main occupation is tenderness—nervously crosses the studio apartment Cocker has managed to find for her and, seeing no other option, dials another number.

'Lee honey, not right now—I'm feeling so down about my mortality,' says Marian. Because he is obsessed with describing every one of his feelings, he intends to make a note of his grief, and so he will write:

BLACK WOMAN AND DOG

It was death, it stands to reason, in combination like a centaur, though a female one: part mare, namely, Edith Talanc, who taught me German at high school; part Jana, who is now dead. I was on my way to meet her at the Green Tree pub; I was fifteen, and a twelve-ton truck passed me on its way to Hrádek, travelling the route between Ch. and Hrádek, the one they used to transport cement to Ráječko so they could build the dam that's there now. Jana was standing under the green tree, under the linden whose branches still gave refuge to coachmen, when the diesel stench of the truck passed me by. I held my breath to avoid swallowing, and in that state, lungs on hold, I saw the wobbling axle, saw the enormous wheel peel away from the right-hand side, and saw Jana—her back to me and the truck, that is, turned away, gazing into the valley of death—squashed. All before I could take another breath.

Dulcimer, Jana's poodle, was the first to react, letting loose with a wail so human that mine seemed nearly out of place by comparison. And so I became a widower, cement mush pouring towards me out of the tipped-over truck like grey manure, like a giant cloud of lead that had broken loose from the sky and plummeted to earth, where Jana lay sliced in two like the flowers I shot for her with my air rifle instead of picking them, tumbling towards her, heads bowed. 'This one too!' I had shouted, standing in our garden, and the tulip had doffed its cap to Jana, paying his respects, before referring her almost lovingly to the fantastically accurate marksman.

So there she is now, lying in front of me, sliced in two, her mouth full of blood. The driver has leapt out of his cab and is carrying over a plank with wheels, the one he lies on when he needs to get under his truck. Meanwhile my mouth is stuck tight to Jana's, and though her blood flows out of her and into me, there is no breath, no soul that I could swallow for a time and then return that her body might revive and be again mortal in unison with mine.

Lord . . . do not shoot through this flower, for I have smelt of her and even in death she will be mine.

I press my mouth to hers as I longed to do when she was living, and sometimes even did when she was feeling especially submissive, and I gag on a mouthful of her blood. It dries as it streams down my neck, under my shirt, and the driver says, 'Lay her down here!' On the roller, he means, the roller for bodies laid out flat on their way into the crematorium ovens, puffing smoke even as we speak. 'She's gone,' says the driver. And he trembles at the sight of her beautiful corpse, then covers her up with a crumpled sheet of plastic from under the seat in his cab.

So that's the upper half of my centauress. The lower half, then, was brought to me by black Dulcimer, the dog who followed me away from the Green Tree like the widower I was. My grandmother, Theresa Odette, opened the gate for him and told me I shouldn't have taken him with me.

'Why not?' I said.

'Because he's constantly in mourning.'

'But Dulcimer is a happy dog.'

'He can't be,' she said. 'He has a strange wariness about him. May God console you, Marian.'

I was fond of Theresa Odette. She had a soft spot for me because she believed that I would be a gentleman. Which for her meant a dragoon lieutenant, the man who sixty years ago left her, the beauty queen, to my grandfather. When it came to Dulcimer, though, I didn't pay her any attention and drifted off with him at my feet. We slept the way fuses blow, in other words, before long our eyes were again wide open and weeping for Jana: him sobbing and panting with his tongue hanging out; me staring stupidly at the stain from a green aphid I had squashed expressly as it tottered in from the garden. The next thing I did was compose a poem for Jana (I already had the first stanza, so actually all I had to do was finish it):

No more, Jana, of your spurning
For now that you are fixed eternal
My hand, too, extends in yearning
Like that of the angel nocturnal
Who weeps on to your stone
A rain so soaked with soot,
While you, oblivious, alone,
You shall not budge a foot.

One such angel stood over Janá's granite tombstone, a grieving sandstone angel, his right hand extended at chest level as if to say, 'Sshh, be quiet!'

I wrote more stanzas still on the back page of my notebook of vocabulary for German class with Edith Talanc. But then she ordered me to translate: 'Siehst du den schwarzen Hund im Staat und Stoppel streifen.' Dulcimer had run away from home again (all he had to do was make it to the yard, because no matter how carefully I wired shut the spaces in the gate, he just jumped right over it) and was now sitting in the little park across from our school, where he could be seen from the classrooms. I didn't know 'Staat und Stoppel', so I had to write the words down in my notebook, and I also had to carry Talanc's compositions home for her. As I carried them in my arms, about half a step in front of her, there again was Dulcimer leading the way. 'Der Kreis wird eng, schon ist er nah,' said my teacher.

And then, in her kitchen, 'So, you've lost her.'

She meant Jana. And she knew because I had attended the funeral as the groom in black, the black bridegroom to go with the white coffin.

'And you're a poet.'

'Yes,' I nodded, since I couldn't imagine lying to my high-school German teacher.

My voice was timid—but curious too.

'Wait,' she said and walked over to the window where a reseda plant was blooming. She tore off the flower and stuck it into the lapel of my black bridegroom's jacket.

'It looks good on you.'

I set up for the poem. I could sense that something was going to happen, but I didn't know the right word for it.

My hand, too, extends in yearning
Like that of the angel nocturnal,

I said in the kitchen with the white cupboards and the blossoming reseda, as the cultivated hand of Edith Talanc ran from my knees up towards the spot that had once separated me from Jana and was now determined to join me with a totally unknown woman. From the clock behind Edith the cuckoo popped out. Six times it bent down towards the place I would have liked to peek had I dared. But me: tears. They flowed into me so that Talanc couldn't see them. I was sad and I knew it, only there inside it was cosy and warm, a looseness like when a fever ends and it feels so good that despite my weakness I feel like I could fly.

I walked out of her house into the street and saw a ditch running alongside it. I was so relieved that I hopped zigzag back and forth across it, until the edge gave way and I vanished into the hole. And there again above me was that dog.

Gaping and panting.

And this is the lower half of the centauress: ass slightly angular, though high-set and delicate.

Unbreakable C, also slightly higher up, the majestic legs of a race horse.

In the days before he met his centauress, Cocker had been Dr Immortal: a little angel in robes, with a palm branch in his hand and a star upon his forehead. AD 1949 in the Bliss theatre, which belonged to the Cockers but was in the process of being expropriated. For the time being, though, they still had performances, and Marian sang merrily in his child's soprano as he hovered above the grotto of Bethlehem suspended from the ropes.

The audience was filled with moistly shining eyeballs.

'My, what a handsome child,' remarked the refined lady

next to Marian's mother, without realizing whose son the angel was.

'Truly a beautiful boy,' said Medel the fag. And even though Marian's mother knew what Medel was, she shed 333 throat-choked tears over the words of praise from seats 332 and 334, her tears flying like 333 thrashing thrushes over 333 thorny thickets. She certainly did, for Mrs Thea Cocker has the ticket with the seat number on it pinned to her chignon and tucked away as a keepsake in the Cocker family's Biedermeier chest of drawers.

'Gloria in excelsis Deo,' the young Cocker lilted. His body reported to him nothing of the floating and sinking that now gulp him up and swallow him down as the adult Dr Cocker, being, as he was, airborne in his immaculate corporeality, yummy. 'Cantus firmus,' he sang out in a canary-like voice, at that moment firm in both song and body, in contrast to his wobbliness of today.

They applauded him, hands fluttering, and Cocker in his immortality bowed down to them, the star on his forehead shining out into the hall like an ear doctor's mirror. The only ones who envied him were the mortals—for instance, one particular mortal by the name of engineer Matolin—even though it was they who had the leading roles in the dramas of the honourable Mr F. Jamnik, *Lawrence the Martyr* and *The Lepers' Comforter*, and acted as if they were thrilled to die; nevertheless they looked askance at this angel, who with such ease and puniness concerned himself with nothing in particular, instead simply declaring glory from on high and waving to the hall with his human hands, for he had spotted his human mother, who was waving back and applauding. She applauds, they applaud, for it is clear that this fluttering of hands and this streaming sound of course belong to him.

'Yow! What do you think you're doing, Mr Matolin? You've stabbed me right through my sandal!'

The sword-wielding Mr Matolin, however, replies, 'Wipe that smile off your face, kid. This isn't the National Theatre.'

But then the angel's sobbing tears join his mother's, and the hall, splotched with weeping from both sides, begins to soar, to swell into sparkling crystal, let us behold its beauty.

And it is also sweet, for Theresa Odette and his mother, Mrs Cocker, are waiting for the angel by the dressing rooms with a box of EGO brand sweets from Klaban's—eucalyptus lozenges and fine sweets assortment—and they feed the angel and tell him stories about the chocolates they used to eat in the days before the war, and they promise those same chocolates to him. One day that day will come, that chocolate day, that is, with no more stinking cabbage, slag and ashes, and they tell him all about that day, sweetening him up and saying 'success', a word the angel will remember in the following combination:

a) alighting *ex excelsis*;
b) pain in the foot stabbed by the sword;
c) Klaban's fine sweets.

'Yes,' says Theresa Odette, 'I know those too. They're sweet at first, but then in your mouth they turn sour like lemon drops. But anyway, it's great when you do something people like, you can tell, and that makes it good for you, too. I was wearing a white dress and I made a wish at the cross— it's always the prettiest girl who gets to make the wish. I made that dress myself, and the band walked to the cross and I said it, and then again in front of the tavern, at the Green Tree. And after that we danced.'

'Which dance?'

'The shake,' she said. Marian pictured quivering aspic, which made him laugh. Very hard. But the truth is that Theresa Odette really had been a beauty queen, and a dragoon lieutenant named Daphnis stepped up and asked her to dance the Halley's Comet. And on the dance-floor he had asked her if they might someday dance the Halley's Comet together in Prague at the Yokohama coffee-house where they had a bona fide Chinaman waiting on tables, and he asked her to whisper her honourable name, because if she did, he would 'make her happy and she would not have to grow sour in an office somewhere and her sweet lips would not have to whisper any dry numbers and her splendid teeth would not have to nibble on the end of a pen'. So that's how it was with Theresa's immortality, she still remembers, and as she feeds her grandson Klaban's sweets she can hear the musicians from that day long ago and she's positive they're playing Halley's Comet.

Meanwhile Dr Cocker sees his adversary Matolin the leper and he's glad, for in the doctor's vision no Comforter comes to heal the engineer, and those plasticine boils he so eagerly and hideously stuck on himself before the performance, and which Marian had initially admired, now eat away at his face until it is so repulsive that even the people in the leprosarium sit as far away from him as possible.

'I tell you, Mum, that man is such a jerk. He leant his sword into my foot just as I was waving to you.'

'You mean . . . you were waving to me?' sobs Mrs Cocker.

'Don't be silly,' says Dr Cocker, 'who else would I have been waving to?'

Or else he is still more immortal (again Dr C), for he is *soaring*. He has taken off his cassock and decided to be a Czech poet. Today he heard three funeral-loving widows in the choir of St Barbara's launch into song about a lute without braying even once:

To speak not is impossible,
My lute I take in hand,
For love it is impossible,
Let me sing to beat the band . . .

I shall find myself such a lute, said Dr C, and he lifted off from earth. At first he had trouble staying in the air, but just past Venhoda's bakery he discovered he could move smoothly at a height of about twelve inches above the kerb. He then maintained a constant height, manoeuvring with ease around the blossoming acacias. They smelt of perfume; night was falling. The sound of the evening bells, the murmur of leaves turning their lacklustre side up.

Cocker gazed about and heard the 'C' bell, the worldly ding-dong-ding of Mr Hemele up in the belfry made of girders, the one that took the place of the oaken one, which was so fiercely buffeted by a shock wave in the war that its splintered shingles murdered hens as they raced from the air raid and the old copper bell cracked with a smack, like an apple split in two. The new one is cast iron. Whenever anyone dies, the cast iron sounds the death knell and Hemele is he who tolls. He pastes up the obituary notices, unties the ringing rope, and threatens death to all who hear. But otherwise he softly rings in the summer, the summer and the soaring. Leaning his prosthesis against the fence of Odette's cross, he follows Marian's flight and jingles his bells; and he says to himself: If he can fly like that, maybe he could get my leg back for me. By this Hemele means his original leg, in whose place he now has a wooden hoof that clomps against the pavement when he walks.

'Bring it back to me, pet,' he says to the boy as he lands, 'or else find me another.'

'Alas,' says Cocker, still quite distracted, 'I haven't any left. And anyway, the one that I had wasn't yours.'

'I would have made better use of it, though.'

'No, you wouldn't. It was already dead.'

'It would have come back to life if you'd prayed.'

'And how about if I blow on it for you?'

'How about it?'

'I don't know,' says Marian, 'when you drink so much and all. Odette says . . .'

'Who says, preacher man?!' And Hemele clip-clop rushes headlong at Dr Cocker, who is suddenly very much grounded, no matter how he waves his hands.

Nevertheless, the truth is that Cocker had been the owner of one human leg after the air raid in forty-four, but they took it away from him. 'Give it here,' they said, 'and we'll cremate it on the giant gridiron at the dairy.' As they were carrying it, though, Mrs Tlamsa recognized it as her husband's missing limb, wrapped it up in a large mourning shawl, and had a special chest nailed together for it.

Entry in the diary of the mortal Dr Cocker
(in the column marked 'Lundi'):
1) phone Dr Shtet,
2) meet Robus,
3) Anilinka.

Re: 1)

Marian calls Shtet, doctor to doctor:

'So how does it look, doctor?'

'I'm afraid that your father . . . clinically he's already dead, do you understand?'

'Is it . . .?' says Cocker.

'*Irreparable*? Yes. It's been a full twenty-four minutes. I've been searching the literature for a longer interval, but no luck.'

Dr Marian then watches Charles Cocker for the same twenty-four minutes, standing by the bed where Charles lies as if already carved into the tombstone. Like that, his body laid out straight and stiff in its contours under the covers, and in that stiffness folded like the drapery of sarcophagi, eyes wide open in light softened by blinds and flickering with contraptions that house tiny green deities who manufacture death with lights and numerals and pour out endless lengths of paper covered with a curve of physical lyrics. Eyes open, 'fixed in unseeingness' (Dr C quotes from one of his early works) and yet seeing right through the doctor or anyone else who chances to step into view; shadow in his eye sockets but a slight sheen on his countenance. Breath detectable only from very nearby, while surrounding his mouth something quietly blissful.

'No!' says Dr Cocker, for that would mean that death is *full-being* rather than non-being, that would mean that we fear death in order to devote ourselves halfheartedly to a life that is from the standpoint of full-being an absurdity; just imagine, if we were to realize what bliss death really is, it would make life impossible: no one would put up with the drudgery!

Re: 2)

Not even Robus?

What bliss maintains this substance in drudgery, that is, in motion, if 'die Bewegung = Daseinweise der Materie', a mode of existence, right, Talanc? It wasn't you who gave me that to translate, it was the ones who made—brr—a Dr out of me. And in fact weren't they right? Overflowing with the categorical non-love that drives them from within, they charge after the fruits of their deeds. And yet even as they pine for them, stirred and shaken, they feel good in the flow. There's a thrill in it, too, a perfect thrill that makes you forget. Occasionally it excites even me to sink into it, especially when I see them dealing with substances of a lower specific gravity; there are laws for dealings between one body and another, but between non-souls . . . oh, I just don't know, and look, Robus across from me behind the T-shaped table in the director's office is squirming. He's agitated by the fact that there's something I don't know, he doesn't like that:

'All you ever do is beat around the bush, Cocker, twisting and turning like meat on a skewer. I'm not going to bite you, you know.' He bares his teeth. 'Flies aren't my style, so what do you mean you *don't know*(?).' I say I don't know whether he should get a divorce under these, shall we say, circumstances. He says, You say circumstances when it's nothing but a couple of threatening letters from my wife; I say, It could hurt you. And he laughs and laughs until there's so much smoke that he gets up and turns on the fan. Robus is a maniac for ventilation. He's always wearing a shirt with loud stripes, sleeves rolled up like a butcher's, and still he sweats, and it's getting chillier and chillier.

'I think you misunderstand me, Doc.' He opens the cabinet where he keeps the drinks. 'A couple of years left till retirement, my position is rock-solid . . . I'll take care of the lady myself. All I'm asking you to do is put up with looking at her.' He leans over and pours out a drink into two glasses, *stakany*, he calls them.

Anxiety gurgles in his stomach. I whisper to him that I came here by car, but he gives me his calling card (that makes number four) and tells me just in case I should give a ring. The vodka reeks as I raise it to my rising entrails, although it seems to slake my thirst as it moves downward. I focus on the warmth as Robus hunkers down, his neck more purple than ever. His skull, split in two then healed into a groove, is frosty with microscopic sweat. I stare at it, trying hard not to ask who gave him that scar, that nasty scratch on his skull that runs all the way down to the top of his spine. It changes colour like what's underneath, which was meant to be split in two and is now a magic eye, a crack in the interior, Robus's receiver, and I have to tune it like a hi-fi if I want to touch it.

So we're talking about a transaction, he says, and he asks if I heard. I hear and obey, I ought to say.

'Do you know the word "escheatage?" ' he asks, his pothole losing its colour for a moment. 'You make her a proposition . . .' he slugs down the rest of his drink and slams the glass on to the desktop. He's holding it in his fist so the punctuation is clear. 'All you have to do is persuade her to buy the house.'

'If I understand correctly, then, it's to be an offer.' He says he intends to settle the Robus couple's joint property.

'The house isn't yours,' I say. He compliments me on my response, pours himself another drink, and says that the house belongs to Bertha Samuel, an elegant Jewish lady. He takes from his private drawer a bulging folder, a hanging file, and hands it to me. His potbelly combined with the T-angle of the table prevent him from reaching all the way, so I have to stand.

The only label on the folder is the number

666

and in it: archival blueprints, stamped by the mayor's office in AD 1910 and lettered in calligraphy—in itself something of a work of art: an undulating loggia protrudes from the façade in the frontal projection, the window-sills stand out, and there is a roundness to all the profiles. The vertical floor-braces look almost like statues and the surrounding metal-work forms a tulip, doubtless green in reality, just as the glazing on the window casings must be green as well—the blue-green art nouveau colour scheme of the home of Aron Samuel, industrialist (according to the description below). The folder also contains a detailed, unsigned appraisal of 'the above-mentioned real estate' to the tune of an incredible 74,000 crowns. Also excerpts from the evaluation of the city surveyor, the approval both of Parks and Forests and of Gardens for the removal of the ancient vegetation (granted retroactively), as well as a declaration by the

chief architect and the Historical Buildings Administration
that the building is not of special interest, and most importantly (written on octavo, without any institution's
letterhead) a physician's statement on the health of Mrs
Samuel, the elegant Jewish lady, describing her condition as
'irreparable'—Marian has heard that once today already. At
the bottom of it all is Robus's petition of settlement, according to which Mrs Robus, after consideration of all credits
and debits, is entitled to precisely 74,000 crowns, and so Dr
Marian, as expected of him, looks to the petitioner to ask if
he considers that a generous offer.

'Yes,' says the lawyer, 'most generous,' and splashes some
more vodka into Marian's glass.

'A little soda water,' Cocker requests. Robus brings it over
and it's as cold as a compress.

'The lady, if I am not mistaken, is still alive.'

'Not only that, doctor, she still lives there.'

'I confess,' Cocker stutters, but Robus stops him with a
Robus joke: 'Now, now, Doctor, no confessions; the rap is too
heavy for that; a king keeps his silence. Trust in the voice of
experience.'

I do trust, or, in other words, I ask with the voice of experience when Bertha will be passing away. And he says soon, a
month at most.

Hmm, and the waiting period is extremely active, so active,
in fact, that it could be murder—pure perishment (Marian
notes this in his diary before going to see Anilinka).

Re: 3)

He makes no note on Anilinka in the monologic person,
for he is writing, even if without ever really nearing the end,
an essay on her entitled 'Essay on C', in which Anilinka is
transformed into C, which signifies her thing down there,
though it could also be him, Dr Cocker, reduced to that
dimension. As a concept it's a vague monster, but as C it's a
coat, a cape, a convertible.

'Enough gobbledygook,' says Anilinka, 'in general, I

mean.' She thinks in general, she is educated, she uses *The State and Revolution* to prop up her couch.

And she's beautiful too, her eyes like jewels, her face long and thin, as if plated with gold—no one can figure out why, but the glitter and smell are the same.

Her mental hand (Dr C's label for this sort of hand), its fingers slender, though pointy not angular, and palms as smooth as sea shells, her . . . face with its protruding cheekbones, like those of Botticelli's maidens, illuminated with animation from within, yet worn from handling on the surface. The long neck of a porcelain teapot. And a voice that floors and anchors Marian—it was she who first made him aware of the feminine ending: the '*la*' attached to the past tense of a woman's verb in Czech. And so now 'C' has to be constantly defined by what she *did*: *šla a nesla* (she walked and she carried), *byla* (she was), *žila* (she lived). What is now, *miluju* (I love), can be said without telling man from woman, as is true for what they are *going to do*, but every action already performed is immersed in the difference between them—it's a *la*-world and in it she sits on the throne. Blonde-haired, a distinctive ripple in the middle of her upper lip—the sign of a strong sex drive? (see page 37 of Cocker's 'Essay')—eyes of equal distinctiveness (again s.d. = sex drive), the centre of the pupil below the imaginary axis, a strongly protruding lower eyelid, and of course that thick upper lip, so loved for its fullness, for bulging with something that is constantly in shadow.

'To deceive an idiot is bliss,' Anilinka says in high Czech, for she intends this thought as the motto for a coat of arms. But Marian says, 'I serve him and therefore do not deceive him.' To which Anilinka (with her large lower lip): 'You should be used to it by now! Being here, I mean. Otherwise it'll kill you.'

Marian: 'He makes me feel as if I've puked, I don't know anyone else like him, he's got an aura—perishment, as you call it—but he fascinates me, he's authentically pure—that's him: distilled spirits.'

In her (that is, in Anilinka, from the third preface to 'Essay')

In her with my hands. Especially and with my eyes too. Between my fingers a seeping dampness. Hold to it: hold it. Beasts either withdraw or make themselves scarce (viz., Dulcimer, already with that Talanc woman). They differentiate. In other words, I leave it to open and close on its own, while I perish into the world, utterly content. Like the time I was walking barefoot across the carpet and stepped in the wet spot where she had been lying. It froze me in place and I was so turned on (and also so cold) that I started to cry. But if there's any such thing as a declaration of eternity, that was the first reading of it, and if eternity has a magic circle for the uttering of incantations, that was surely it.

(Translated by Alex Zucker.)

Sylvie Richterová

Fear Trip

Mother has come to tell me she has given birth to a black baby. It was black as a shadow and immaterial as a spirit, and it vanished before her eyes like an apparition. Yet she had seen it. It was born of her, it came out of her, she beheld it and now she feared dying from it. As she told her story she clutched her hand to her head and rubbed her temples and neck; she was frightened. I wanted to comfort her, tell her she was in no danger. I sought convincing proof, circling the shelf that suddenly housed paintbrushes, oils and solvents instead of dishes. I went into the next room, where two women I had never seen before were boarding up the door and windows. I turned into a black baby and vanished.

It was the time when Blind Narcissus started appearing more frequently. I knew he was the most frightful being one could ever meet, but I was unable to give him concrete human form. He took on all human forms, that is, he appeared in all human forms, including my own. He was most frightful in the morning before the sharp imprints of past encounters had transmuted into the approximate grip of everyday encounters.

Knowing nothing of beginnings or ends, he staked his life on identifying differences and forms. His other means of cognition were induction and self-pity.

He resolved to retire half a minute earlier each night than the night before, and half a minute earlier the next night and the night after as well. Within a month he had increased his sleeping time by quarter of an hour, within half a year by one and a half hours. By the end of the six-month period he had become so attuned to time, so at one with it, that he completely ceased to need a timepiece and stopped winding the cuckoo clock in the kitchen and the watch on his wrist and the Swiss alarm clock on his bedside table. He went to bed on time to the second.

He would leave his eyelids open for a minute; never moving his pupils, he could see the darkened room and watch the objects disappear, the furniture and walls, the ceiling and its long-bulbless lamp, watch them fade away, stars by day, landscape by night. He would lie with his hands resting on the pillow under his head, fingers crossing over the crown, thumbs brushing against the skull. His back and buttocks adhered evenly to the mattress, his thighs and calves likewise, the knees diverging slightly in such a way as to make the ends of the soles come together, the right instep lean lightly against the left and the heels, sloping gently outwards, touch the inside of the bed. He would observe his body like a perfectly sealed system of electromagnetic waves, its undulations rising from the rib-cage to the head via the neck, suffusing the skull and moving down through the forehead to the face, then back to the neck, where it split into two streams and travelled on along the shoulders to the arms and hands. The route to the hands led along the inner arms, which rested on the cushion facing up, the right-hand current passing into the left-hand current and vice versa through the crossed fingers and flowing on beneath the skin, pressing down on the cushion to the shoulder blades and emptying into the back. It then slowly, warmly descended the back, passed through the buttocks and calf muscles as far as the tips of the toes, and after seeming to rest for a while in the soles proceeded to rise again through the shin-bones, knees and inner thighs. Leaving the sexual organs in peace, it arrived at the abdomen, where the cycle came to an end. It lasted fifteen minutes, after which he would drift off and finally sleep. He never remembered his dreams, though their reality cannot be denied.

He was going on a protracted car journey. He took along a travelling bag with toilet articles, a change of underwear, a freshly ironed shirt and a fairly warm sweater. Once behind the wheel he did not think of the goal of his journey; he merely moved slowly with the flow of the urban traffic. A shabbily dressed, unkempt old woman ran into the road at an intersection, and he nearly hit her with his right mudguard. He had to pull the wheel to the left and slam on the brakes, which he did mechanically and with perfect composure, just as the light, which at the last moment he had decided to go through, turned red. The woman came up to his left window and began yelling something incomprehensible at him. Clearly she was calling him names, and her voice sounded menacing until he closed the left window. When the light turned green again and the other cars started moving, the woman limped out into the traffic. Soon she was in front of his car again, dragging along so sluggishly that he seemed likely to miss the next light as well. She made some clumsy gestures taunting him to go, go on. When at last he started up, all the pedestrians' eyes were on him and he had the feeling they were all of them—especially the women and children on the pavements—waiting stealthily for him to pass so they could race under his wheels.

The moment he reached the main road leading north out of town and increased his speed, a flock of geese ran out into the road. He braked lightly and cursed; in the rear-view mirror he saw a white wing flapping slowly in the road, like a butterfly whose membranes have lost their powder yet tries to fly. The stone saint standing on the village bridge with open arms and outstretched cross seemed on the point of leaping into the middle of the road. Fortunately the village was deserted, but there was a dog racing down the slope where a flock of sheep were grazing. It reached the asphalt just in time to meet the bumper; the clear crunching sound could only have been its skull.

A shiver went through his whole body. He slowed down, even though the road was now going through the open countryside. To his right a coniferous wood climbed the hill; to his left ripe grain was rippling. He regarded the golden reflection of ears of grain in the sun as one of the wonders of the world. Even while gazing hopefully at the wheatfield, however, he realized he had no idea where he was going. It will come back to me, he said to himself, staring ahead at a point on the horizon where the road turned black. Before long he made the black spot out to be a crowd of people, a parade or perhaps a procession. He frowned, braking almost to a crawl. The parade moved forward slowly, gathering more and more people. It was led not by a priest but by a seedy-looking old man. Their eyes met. Or rather the old man's eyes dazzled him and the old man cast himself on the dusty road. The crowd then split in two, as if making room for the car. He hugged the left bank so as to avoid the body lying in the road. Just as he passed it the onlookers started stretching out on the ground. He could see their faces flashing by, close up; they were frightful and frightening, twisted with a resolve he could not fathom. He stopped the car, switched off the engine, and covered his eyes with his hands. This can only be a dream, he said to himself. And indeed, when he finally managed to open his eyes and look round, there was no trace whatever of the curious parade. Only the smooth furrows of dust gave continuing evidence of the chilling encounter.

He started the car up again and set off. Just round a bend, where the coniferous wood ended, the sight of a body falling under the car flashed through the windscreen. He had no time to brake or pull the car over to the side of the road. The body of a man in a grey suit, his tie askew and the contents of his briefcase senselessly scattered over his chest, lay in the road. It was flat, thin as a pancake and every bit as lifeless. He slammed his foot on the accelerator and took off at top speed. On and on he drove, self-willed faces flashing past his windows, flattened corpses lining the road behind him and later in front of him as well. He would zigzag, brake, go into reverse, turn on to country roads and come out suddenly on broad cement motorways. Bodies and faces rolled mercilessly under the wheels of the car, as if seeking satisfaction of a sort. At last he let go of the steering wheel and leant back, as if hoping to peer at the sky through the tin roof.

Having finished writing his dream about people flinging themselves under his car, I put a pink mohair sweater on over a pair of navy-blue trousers, combed my hair, made myself up and left the house, relieved. It was dark out and pouring with rain. I ran to my car and got in, started the engine, put on the heater and slowly took my place in the row of cars moving through the waterlogged city. At the traffic-lights by the river I turned left on to the bridge, when suddenly the darkness before the windscreen was rent by a white human face. I failed to hear the screech of the brakes; all I heard was the dull thud of a body first against the car, then against the asphalt. It is true that the thin little wisp of a man of indeterminate age bounced back up from the ground in a flash. It is true that he sustained no injuries and that he bore the dream-like name of Thyme. Though it is true.

Night crawled towards day through a dream, and only the watchful morning stiffness experienced death. Windows. She groped her way along her dead desires, thinking of evening, night and midnight. Her eyes were heavy and her body was giving in and out.

She had something else to take care of that evening, something else to see to; it was a matter of life and death and she had been postponing it all day, but she couldn't remember it, she kept putting it off, it was always a matter of life and death, though it never became clear until the end of the day. She groped her way through the day with the feeling that it would turn up at its end. When her body started giving in and out. She believed that what would turn up at the end was true; she feared that the truth would not turn up until the end.

The thing is, people basically want what they already have, but in a better format.

My end is peaceful, quiet, free of anything dramatic and drastic, he would say to himself as he lay down on his bed five minutes earlier than the day before. All people had vanished from the cities; houses and objects were untouched. And it was a large city, an enormous city: it could have been New York, but it could have been Paris or Berlin or even Moscow. It had a modern business centre with skyscrapers, glass buildings, grey residential areas, streets, squares and parks. Plants were untouched and unharmed; they grew peacefully, as did flowers perhaps. Nor was it lacking in offices, banks, shops and hotels, to say nothing of grimy industrial outskirts or Metro entrances; there may even have been a river somewhere in the vicinity. Not a single window was broken, not a single car overturned; there were no corpses lying anywhere and no encounters.

Adam and Eve were strolling along a broad street, avenue, boulevard or Strasse or prospekt. He was about twenty-five, tall and swarthy, with light hair and a light beard, blue eyes and a pacific disposition. Eve had to have been on the far side of thirty, but she looked young; she was slender and had soft, smooth skin and a sad look deep in her eyes. When she smiled it turned into serene affection, which she passed on to the man and a boy of approximately ten who could have been their son but was not, and in fact could not have been their son because the three of them had not met until recently, which was long before, and had been travelling together ever since through the vast empty city.

They pulled along a wooden cart fitted with automobile tyres and a canvas hut, that is, a tent in which they kept the few things they needed. They needed so few because they could always stop and take any useful or useless article from any shop or flat. At night they would go into a private house with a luxuriant garden; everything was neat and tidy inside, the furniture and appliances perfect. Yet they touched nothing: they did not turn down the bedspreads, they did not open the china cupboards, they merely sat quietly at the kitchen table and laid out their own paper plates and ate tinned meat they had brought with them and stewed fruit from their own reserves. After supper they would drag in mattresses and blankets from the cart and lay them out in the spacious entrance hall next to the library, from which they never removed a book. The boy would inspect the nursery with its toy trains and dolls and building-blocks and robots and wind-up cars, but he never touched any of them. In the morning they would drag the mattresses and blankets out to the cart and gather up the paper plates and empty tins and throw them in the half empty dustbins at the gate. The cart moved noiselessly on its rubber wheels: they always walked on level ground or slightly downhill.

One day they stopped at a large department store and went inside. They spent quite some time in the baby-wear department, piling their wire baskets high with nappies, shirts, sweaters, tights and woollen pyjamas. Eve was no longer slender; she had a big stomach, she was pregnant and the baby was due any moment.

Having loaded the new supplies, they headed for the hospital, and after passing through long, bright corridors they entered the delivery room. The man and the boy helped the woman on to the bed and stroked her hair and arms.

It's a boy, the man said in amazement, rinsing the newborn baby in the bath they had prepared for it. A boy, the last woman said softly, and she closed her eyes.

In the morning she finally got back on her feet and started walking. Walking like stamping. Well, not really: she watched her shuffle her way to the bathroom. I had not yet lifted my head from the pillow. Well, not really: I jump out of bed, my eyelids go up and she goes up with them. Consciousness does not drag behind the body or the body behind consciousness or where would we be. The third concept attracts me the most; it has the most life to it. I gave it a nod behind my closed eyelids, in the morning, when I failed to get back on my feet.

If my fears were justified, if my fears were truly justified, if *my fears* were justified, my fears are most probably justified, if they were, they are most probably. My fears are.

While waiting, she went through various slow and deliberate movements. She picked up objects, pressed them firmly into her palm, clung to them with her fingers, then put them back with precisely measured movements or in other places or simply laid them down, though with great care. She removed some cherry stems with smooth, easy tugs, chewing the cherries slowly but without smacking her lips. She spat the stones on to a plate, which she drew up to her mouth for the purpose. Once she found she no longer felt like eating cherries, she waited in painful anticipation. Waiting is a form of illness. Or rather, what causes waiting is an illness. Though in this instance it amounted to the same thing: she was waiting until she awakened from her morning stiffness.

She put the bowl of cherries back into the refrigerator without their stems. She placed it gently in the lower container, using both hands, and shut the refrigerator door without slamming it. She went into the bathroom to wash her hands, rinse out her mouth and—why not—brush her teeth. A neatly squeezed sliver of toothpaste lay on the toothbrush, and the waiting got no easier; she feared it would end only when she relented. She rinsed out her mouth with lukewarm water and rinsed off the toothbrush. She changed the water in the vase, grateful to the flowers for needing fresh water. She was less grateful to the cat for wanting to eat, though she patiently cut up a piece of lung, which is not easy to cut: she had to sharpen the knife.

Blind Narcissus is ironing the curtains. Glassy eyes. Talkative. Make sure you dust the white door with a wet rag twice a week, there are no two ways about it, it's got to be done, and don't use a detergent, it will harm the paint, and don't forget that dust tends to gather in the indentations and there are always loads of fingerprints around the knob, and remember the doorframe, doorframes get dirty too, they get full of dust, especially next to the knob and up at the top and down at the bottom, where you can't see, make sure you dust the white door with a white rag twice a week, there are no two ways about it. She came from Munich and thought it absolutely essential to convince me that when my daughter is raped I mustn't report it to the police or any other official body, I must hush it up and take personal revenge on the perpetrator, in other words, get my friends to beat him up, if I have any friends, that is, to beat up the perpetrator when my as yet under-age daughter is raped. Five to eight years from now, say. Or douse the rapist with vitriol myself.

Because firm conviction is the greatest certainty. That should be a book title.

For the first half year he did not need to alter his daily routine in any way to accommodate his new regime: he did not need to curtail or exclude any of his usual activities; he merely began to move with greater speed and efficiency, to organize things better, to avoid wasting time and procrastinating. For the next half year he abandoned several habits like reading newspapers, going to the pictures and making such minor daily purchases as fresh bread, milk and the like; he increased the efficiency of the shopping process by driving around on one Saturday morning a month, when he did not work, and laying in an ample supply of groceries that did not spoil easily.

The bedtime ritual was swift and mechanical; it would not in fact have been a ritual at all had she not performed the washing of the apple. From a basket of shiny apples she would choose one, wash it and place it in the centre of a white china plate on the bedside table. Beside several books that gradually took turns. But the apple was the centrepiece. She would puff up the pillow and lean it against the head of the bedstead, sit down on the bed and make herself comfortable, pull the quilt up to her breasts, open a book and pick up the apple. She would bite into the apple slowly, chew, then bite into it again and chew. Three hundred and sixty-five or -six apples a year, gnawed and swallowed night after night, core, brown pips and all. It was her only habit, but she clung to it with the fidelity of a lover or, rather, with inveterate tenacity.

There were yellow, red and summer green apples; there

were Jonathans, pippins, russets, Granny Smiths and name-less varieties picked up from under trees. She would glance into the book as she ate, but what she mainly, chiefly, saw was that she was in the bedroom all by herself, that she was there all by herself even though she was not in her bedroom, even though she had moved and now had another bedroom, she ate the apples all by her lonely self, biting right through the peel, as if to say, Yes sir, I'm really eating those apples. Two or three times a year she actually said to herself, Yes sir, I've eaten oodles of apples and I'm going to keep eating apples, night after night, all by myself. And she would smile, as if symbols unnoticed by anyone in this life meant something. Otherwise the tree would stop growing.

They were female phantoms and somewhat reminiscent of tantric figures. Their bodies were assembled from the oddest elements implanted, embedded, ingrained one into the other. They were not symbolic figures, however; they were made of spare parts, scraps of machines and mechanisms of various sorts, steel perhaps, but alive. The one closest to him opened at the bottom, her whole body then opening like a mouth, like a shark's jaw, like the lips of a sea anemone and revealing her innards all the way to the womb. He reached out to her body, to her fantastic figure, uterus, anemone, shark's jaw—all open.

The disgust and horror that overcame him lasted even after he had opened his eyes, even after he had shut them again. A wall of rainbow-hued tiles surrounded him on three sides. He moved closer, the better to examine the strange pastel boxes, and discovered that the construction consisted in fact of letters. There were addresses on the envelopes, all of them his. He removed a light-blue envelope from the top layer of one wall, opened it and pulled a white rabbit out by the ears. There was another white rabbit in the next envelope, which was green, there was a white rabbit in the pink envelope, in the yellow envelope as well, and a white rabbit in the white envelope. Indeed he pulled a white rabbit by the ears from each of the envelopes, thus having gone through the entire set of rainbow building-blocks. The three walls were then white and still standing. A fourth he did not see.

On mouse days, days more marauding than a malady advancing minute by minute through the veins, on days of endless starts in the direction of dead eternity, she longed for night to come as soon as possible.

Evening was the morning of hope, morning the evening with a crescent moon on the wax. She would start prudently anew by watering the house plants scattered in pots all over the flat, gulping down something fresh as she sprinkled them from her watering-can. Then she would make breakfast and gaze at it with satisfaction: the milk and butter white, golden honey and golden apricot jam, a yellow egg or yellow orange, red tomatoes or a red round of salami and strawberries already all red. A high, marbled, yellow-brown cake with scalloped edges and icing sugar. But most of all bread-coloured bread. Until breakfast the day held promise, and she held on to it while rinsing the flowered plates and cups under the running water.

I lose days like teeth.

The anxiety that life will resemble this day, all life will be like this day, death will be like this day. One must work doggedly to change one's days. Exchange them for what? For not being afraid. Because death will definitely resemble them. Because life resembles them like peas in a pod, every day.

At the last moment.

Then it comes back over and over again, that last moment. The powerful surge of a possibility more sensed than known, the certainty of the last uncertainty, without strong words. Splitting evening into midnight.

It makes its way from all distances to the threshold of the bed. (I know that beds have no thresholds.) A single necessity emerges, as clear as if lit by lightning and as empty and persuasive as an embrace. It is how and in what direction and does not add on why.

I think, I am saved, and just then my eyes close and I fall out of the picture. And so it goes night after night with the frightful regularity of definitively final things.

I would hold on to it if I opened my eyes at a time when I could no longer open them. That sentence is not meant to refer to death. To say something with absolute certainty and not be mistaken. Question mark.

It forestalls death. Or, rather, does not court it.

It insists with ever-increasing intensity on the interconnection of all words. At first the labyrinth seems impossible to follow to the end; it seems to have no end, insofar as this is not the end. But once words are interconnected, the path will no longer move from word to word.

He managed only occasionally to seal the shutters and devoice the walls and secure a bit of silence and hear what his lips had uttered with difficulty, with great effort, with the help of closed eyes. He was often short of breath. Today he lay motionless on the bed, managing not to stifle the words that circled about him and landed from time to time in his mouth or heart or even in his hands or on the tips of his fingers. When the phrase 'the peace that gave rise to the song' settled in for a while, he ceased dying of fright (like a fish). Noise could hurt him no more thereafter, though it was unlikely to be heard by anyone but those closest to him.

Thus what he would say when interrogated by the police was extremely important, as were the opinions he would voice on Czechoslovak television, the articles he would write for Paris papers, the challenges he would make in Polish pamphlets, and the answers he would give to the Russian émigré who runs around Rome on Saturday evenings, horrified at the realization that the world which could no longer be called free was having supper and would go on doing so.

He stood in the middle of his room, where all that was left was a table and chairs and a filing cabinet in which he kept documents, old reports, bills and receipts. And a new flower trivet with a blue hyacinth on it. The bookshelves, which had once covered two walls, were gone, all the walls now being covered from top to bottom by close writing. Like the inside of the Pinkas Synagogue, whose white walls are covered with names in black and red, all names of Jews who perished during the Second World War. The overall view is that of a uniform pattern, comfortingly regular and recurrent, the view from up close that of infinite incisions into living worlds, each of which is unique in the flicker of the name it hears and answers to. Human consciousness expands and merges with each of the worlds, making what was unknown one's own.

He went over to the wall, whose very whiteness illuminated the dark letters, and saw sentences jump out at him from the dark arabesque.

I've told you many times that the first light we saw would be from a shot signifying the end. Because my perception is as futile as our rejoicing over having answered a question that begs to remain unanswered. The cultural programme consisted of songs by a chorus of blind children on the balcony under a banner reading Truth Is the Apple of Our Eye. Reality is created only in the memory. Perhaps only he believed that sentence, and if so he was plainly mentally ill. But the idea of being mentally ill did not particularly upset him; he was much more frightened of being—in addition to mentally ill—wrong. People who speak do not know; people who know do not speak. And I am grateful to the moon for including me among those on whom it shone.

He lifted his head and looked out of the window into the night. He did not see the moon through the narrow opening between the roofs and sighed. He looked back at the walls covered by close writing, but could no longer recognize a single letter. The words and phrases had turned into a flowing whisper too soft for him to make out; the dark lines slowly clustered into black blotches, enlarging and expanding over the wall like dangerous cracks, then merging, fusing into black silhouettes of human figures. Not outlined on the white wall, however: each silhouette was in actuality an opening, a passageway for one person.

He leant his left arm on the table top and saw his mother in a grey skirt over a freshly laundered tracksuit. She was squeezed between wooden huts on a beach lit by a weak bulb and was disconcertedly examining a green, two-piece bathing-suit. The flowerpot with the blue hyacinth that she picked up from the flower trivet with both hands turned into the black massage device Father tried to shave with in the small room of a cheap Parisian hotel. Meanwhile Grandpa was ploughing waves in the turbulent sea with mighty strokes of mighty arms. Having reached the shallows he stood up slowly on Grandma's ladle, which then like an endless lift raised him towards the horizon. The sea gradually filled Father's septic tank, which was connected with the municipal water-purification plant. The tank's walls were transparent, so he could watch his sister, mother, father, grandfather and grandmother through them.

Anxiety is lying in wait for me, or am I lying in wait for it? The nuts I remove from the narrow cellophane packet one by one, the sugar-coated peanuts I crush energetically, almost spitefully, between my teeth. I'll come to the end of them soon; the packet will be empty. And anxiety will overcome me when it is empty. In fact, it took hold of me a while ago or has been around for ever; it was definitely here a while ago when I noticed how few nuts were left, that the packet was half empty. Though I'm starting to feel I've had enough: they're too sweet; they don't tempt me any more. But the more upset I am about coming to the end of them, the faster I cram them into my mouth; I can't wait to get to the last one. I gobble down the absolutely last nut and all hell breaks loose. Once I've crumpled up the packet I'll have to pull up blades of grass, chew on sorrel stems or tell myself, They're only peanuts. Or tell myself, I don't like peanuts. Or tell myself, Big deal! Peanuts. Or tell myself, Peanuts have nothing in common with anything else on earth that runs out too. That runs out too.

And why the affection of a lawn planted with daisies for tears. What must sorrow go through to be pure. What must joy go through to be pure.

Still, the first joy she felt for the first daisy she ever saw must have been pure. It condensed into a tear which is dripping on my solar plexus like the deadly drops of water on the heads of walled-in adulteresses in the Spielberg catacombs.

He stood facing a cloudy glass cube approximately two metres high. He could walk around it on three sides, the fourth side being wedged into a sky-blue wall running both to the right and to the left of it and merging with the clear blue air. The walls of the cube were cold and smooth. He walked around them, then returned to the front wall and moved back a few steps to examine the entire cube. He observed his own face and body before him, saw himself as in a mirror. Yet it was not a mirror image: it did not correspond to his movements, it did not follow his glance from head to foot and was even dressed differently; moreover, it looked better preserved than he remembered himself from other mirrors, healthier somehow. He was less surprised at seeing himself than at standing face to face with himself and failing to tally.

Alive as it was, the figure had something glassy about it; it gave a three-dimensional impression, like a slide projected on to a screen. He moved closer to the wall and began running his hands over the image on the cube's surface. It was as smooth as the side wall and every bit as cold. He breathed a puff of air on to the right cheek; it did not condense on the wall. Yet the surface did seem to be disturbed, to have dissolved somewhat, and a moist spot appeared on the cheek. He breathed a puff of air on to the left cheek and again felt the cool surface warming and changing. He raised his arms and placed his hands on his forehead, and it too was warm. Once more he stepped back and examined the figure carefully. There could be no doubt it was himself: besides the form, which had pierced him to the marrow, something far more definite and unequivocal linked him to it.

Once again he inched his way up to the figure, this time pressing his whole body against the outline of his body. He felt the cold surface giving way, ebbing upon contact with it. The pervasive quality of his body encouraged him to press even closer. He moved up several centimetres until the right side of his face, chest and trunk and his right arm and leg merged with the left side. He was glad when he realized what had happened; he perked up, like a person who has just learnt something new and important about himself. He felt it with his entire being, and a name for it suddenly came to mind: sense form. He could no longer see his own body and could not say he saw anything, but it was clear to him that whatever he was in was shaped like a large goblet, arching slightly inward in the middle and broadening somewhat at the top and bottom. Energy, spurting in from above, flowed down to the lower pole, then came back up along the walls. An enormous vase and living source of sun. By taking one more small step forward he entered the field of energy and filled his body with it, and it was happiness and life and the word love had never had so full and radiant a sense to it before. He knew that if he stepped out of the cube he would never again see his own form on its wall. And that he would wake up without ever again measuring half-minutes or minutes or hours and without pulling white rabbits out of letters and without being titillated by gaping phantoms and without having dreadful people run in front of his car. And that he would never need to sleep again.

Pure, warm tears flowed from his eyes, washing off his face and neck and chest. He dipped his hands into them and wet his forehead. Then he slowly leant back and lifted his right foot so as to take a step away from the cube. But he was unable to: there was nowhere to go. Pressing his back against the solid wall he could move only forward. In that direction there was a dark, almost pitch-black tunnel. Which might lead somewhere.

If joy is to be pure. And if sorrow is to be pure. Chestnut blossoms, mad candles. Japanese cherry-tree pink in May many years ago. Why can't I look at them without coming unhinged? Is it a memory of the past or of the present? The songs of birds always the same in all parks and the rainy morning in New York on the last Sunday in August evoke the same mental processes as proceeding along a wet wooden fence on the outskirts of Brno. I had to pass the fence and take Fifth Avenue to Forty-Second Street to discover that. Or maybe not.

And which place allows me to do so. To determine a point in space I need three points already defined. Or to enter another space.

I still think tears are closer to joy than any other emotion. And he will never sleep again.

(*Translated by Michael Henry Heim.*)

Ivan Klíma

Tuesday Morning

A Sentimental Story

On Tuesday, at about nine in the morning, the phone rang. I invariably answer by giving my name, but those who are calling me don't usually give theirs. It's understandable: the tappers who listen to all my phone calls know full well who is speaking at *my* end, but they don't have to know who is at the other. Sometimes, though, it happens that I don't know either. This time the voice at the other end seemed quite unfamiliar. 'Lída here. Forgive me, but could you tell me what your profession is?'

'My profession?'

'Yes, that's right, yours.'

'Are you carrying out some research that you want to know this?'

'No, I just want to know if I've got the right man.'

I seemed to detect a slight foreign accent. I hesitated for a moment, wondering whether I hadn't heard the voice before, after all. 'Well, I have several professions. . . .'

'It *is* you, Mirek, I recognize your voice,' she interrupted joyfully. 'I'm here for two days and I'd like to see you.'

'Where have you come from?' I asked, her voice suddenly seeming more familiar.

'Just now from London, but I live in New York.'

'I see. Where are you calling from?'

'I'm in that hotel just round the corner from Wenceslas Square. In a narrow street. I think it's called the Alcron. All these hotels . . . I get them mixed up. You know which one I mean, don't you?'

I said I did.

'Can you come?'

'Now, this minute?'

'If it's not inconvenient.'

'OK. I'll be there in an hour. What's your name these days?'

'I'll be waiting in the lobby. You won't have any trouble recognizing me—everyone says I haven't changed a bit.' She gave a hearty laugh like a real Prague girl, and then I really did know who she was. It must have been at least twenty years since I'd seen her last.

I met her when I was in my second year at university, and I had by then had my first story or two published. Although a little younger than I, she had already been married for over two years, or at least that's what she told me. Fortunately, I never saw her husband. Nor any member of her family. She never let on where she lived, and I did not try to find out. She worked in a small bookshop in suburban Vršovice. We locals knew it as Myšík's Bookshop, even though it had been nationalized some years previously and Mr Myšík sent to work in the coal mines. But that is where I got to know her. I first went there to look at the books, then at her. I have almost forgotten what she looked like, just as I no longer remember what books I bought there. I think she looked fairly ordinary, blue eyes, perfect teeth like Monica Vitti's (whom I didn't know at that time, not even by name), and she wore golden earrings. I didn't like the earrings, but those blue eyes aroused my desire.

I felt I had to gain her confidence, somehow. Once, when we were alone in the shop, she went into the back room and brought me several books which had long ago disappeared from the shelves. They included Hemingway, Steinbeck and Maurois, an oasis in the parched desert of available reading matter. With those few books she doubtless did far more for my knowledge of modern literature than all my professors at the faculty, but at the time I was not yet able to appreciate that.

When I had browsed in that shop for perhaps the tenth time (by now I knew the titles of all the books on the shelves and on the counter by heart), I plucked up the courage to ask

her what she did after work. She replied that she hurried
home to her husband, but then added that she was sometimes
free at lunch-time.

Next day, and again the day after, we spent the lunch-break
strolling in the nearby park. I don't of course remember what
we talked about, but I am sure I must have tried to impress
her with my literary triumphs, and undoubtedly I also
preached to her about our new society, being at an age when
one is still capable of enthusiasm for revolutionary ideals and
violent change, and when that which fills wiser souls with
horror, or at least with dire foreboding, is dismissed as mere
teething troubles not worth worrying about. I wished to convince her that we were living in wonderfully exciting times,
when the revolution had liberated working people and put an
end to exploitation.

Had I but known it, I could have have saved my breath
because, unlike me, she had come to know our wonderful
revolutionary times from the receiving end. Her parents had
had their shop taken away from them, some of her relations
had been imprisoned, and she herself was not allowed to
study at the university. Some liberation!

In those days I also had pretty definite views on what a
woman whom I might love should be like, and what rules
were to be observed when falling in love. I was absolutely
convinced that it was not the done thing to fall in love with a
married woman, for instance, so that had it been left up to me
we should never have got beyond discussions of politics and
literature.

We had known each other for about two weeks when she
suggested that we take a walk in the direction of Bohdalec.
She had two hours off for lunch, and this didn't seem enough
for such a long walk, but she assured me I was wrong. We
would get there in a quarter of an hour, she said.

At that time Bohdalec was still a wilderness on the edge of
the city. On warm evenings it was doubtless the destination
of many a courting couple who had nowhere else to go to lie
in each other's arms. I had no idea that one could go there
with the same intention at high noon. And, true enough, we
got there in a mere twenty minutes. The place was deserted

and silent as the grave, the silence only broken occasionally by the sound of a railway engine from the distant Vršovice depot.

From our high vantage point we could see the marshalling yards, and I remember to this day the sight of those railway lines gleaming in the sun, with the locomotives being shunted along them, looking unbelievably tiny at this distance. I was about to sit on a sunny slope and carry on pontificating about Maxim Gorky or the gradual withering away of the state, but my companion, with an assurance that betrayed a thorough knowledge of the local geography, led me further along the forest path, past a low barbed-wire fence, all the way to a spot where the fence had been broken and where she indicated that I was to follow her into the fenced-in area. There, in a clearing so small that it felt as if we were in a ship's cabin, we lay in the grass and kissed and then, before I even had time to recall my moral principles, made love.

My initial reaction was one of shock at the enormity of what I had done, and perhaps even more at what *she* had done (after all, she was the married party). I fully expected a torrent of tears or reproaches, but she seemed quite calm, her face showing every sign of contentment, possibly even happiness.

I did not have a girlfriend at the time and so I soon overcame any scruples I may have felt, letting my lust rather than my principles be my guide. We repeated the excursion to Bohdalec two days later, and after that almost daily except when rain or the regular processes of the female body prevented it. Our relationship had but the one purpose, or, in other words, it was monothematic.

We never met except at lunch-time, never went together anywhere else, neither to the cinema nor to the theatre, not to an exhibition or a restaurant. The streets through which we walked, or rather ran, were always the same, as was the spot which was our final destination. We called it our little room. And that's what it was. I cannot tell whether anyone else used it at other times of day. On a nearby building site I found a notice with the inscription

NO ENTRY
Trespassers will be prosecuted

I nailed this warning to a tree next to the broken section of the barbed-wire fence, thus increasing the odds against our being discovered in our hiding-place.

It was not exactly a comfortable little room, needless to say. No roof over our heads, no water, running or otherwise. We had no blanket or sheet. Only my raincoat, which I always, rain or shine, took with me, much to my mother's surprise, and spread out underneath us. While she started bringing along a large silk scarf with which to cover my nakedness (hers being covered by me), though at critical moments it invariably slipped off and revealed all.

We had exactly seventy-five minutes for our love-making. We talked in the intervals. But somehow it didn't seem appropriate to hold serious conversations about the meaning of life, and this eliminated me as an equal partner. And so I mostly listened to her brief accounts of what she had done the day before, what she had cooked for supper, how Joe, her husband, had again been nasty to her, how she visited her brother. For all this talk, she revealed next to nothing about her family or her past. Her deceased father had been a bookseller. She had some relatives living in America. They were very rich and she made out it was a foregone conclusion that one day she would pay them a visit and not come back. I learnt nothing much about her husband, having no idea what he looked like or what he did for a living. Sometimes he cropped up in her conversation as an illiterate boor, sometimes as a gentle and cultured companion. He could have been an engineer, a mechanic or an architect. If I asked her straight out, she would only laugh and say it was better for both of us if I didn't know. In the end I began to believe that her husband was engaged in some important official and therefore also secret work, and this lent the whole affair an exciting *frisson*.

On one occasion, she told me she had spent last night in the night club at Barrandov, where she saw a dozen famous film stars; or again she said that on Sunday they had driven down to South Bohemia at the invitation of a former industrialist who threw a grand dinner party. Which industrialist? It didn't matter, I wouldn't know him anyway. It could all have been true, but then again it probably wasn't. As if former industrialists were in a position to give grand dinner parties.

One day—and I was frequently to recall this particular conversation in the years to come—we did get on to a serious subject. She asked if I wouldn't prefer to live in another country. I couldn't understand why I should want to. Well, she said, if for instance someone I loved lived there? What if *she* were living there?

I said that she lived *here* and that I was glad she did, because I loved her and I loved this country. I went on at some length about one's fatherland and the culture in which one was born. She listened, or so I thought, with interest, even with some emotion. Later, at home, I tried to fathom what she might have meant by her question, and I was startled by a sudden premonition: her husband was a diplomat (that would explain the cloak of secrecy in which she enveloped him, as well as his contacts in high places and their participation in posh dinner parties), he was about to be posted abroad, and she would of course go with him. This prospect made me feel so sorry for myself that I could hardly sleep that night, and the next day I put several questions of my own to her which I considered extremely subtle, with the intention of discovering her husband's identity. She, however, saw through them and left me as unenlightened as ever.

That summer my parents and brother went away on holiday and I was on my own in the apartment. On the very first day I tried to persuade her to come to my place, extolling all the advantages of a real room as compared with our 'little room' in the woods. She refused, saying someone might walk in unexpectedly. She felt safer in our usual spot. Also, there what we were doing didn't seem so much like adultery because she couldn't get used to me, nor was she 'so aware of me'. It seemed that to be aware of someone was more sinful where she was concerned than making love to them.

What about the evening? I wanted to spend at least one

evening with her, to embrace her in the dark without having to hurry or look at my watch.

Oh no, in the evening she had to be with her husband. And so we continued our excursions to Bohdalec while my apartment stayed empty. Well, at least it was a nice, warm summer. Only once were we caught by a sudden shower, and I still remember the sensation of the unexpected rain licking my bare bottom, cold and wet. And once a small child disturbed our solitude. I heard a rustling in the grass and, raising my eyes from her face, saw the kid standing in the bushes just a few paces away. It could not have been more than five years old, and I could not make out if it was a boy or a girl. For a fleeting moment we stared at one another. I made a hasty attempt to cover myself with that ridiculous scrap of silk, but the child turned round and fled, crying loudly.

Only then did she open her eyes and look up. But all she said was: Oh well, a small kid like that can't read—so the notice didn't help.

As the summer gave way to autumn, the weather turned very cold, and it rained all the time. I no sooner spread my raincoat on the ground than it was soaked through; also, I had to clean the mud off surreptitiously at night so that my mother wouldn't see. Our 'little room' had come to the end of its usefulness. I visited her several times at the bookshop, buying books I didn't need and trying to lure her to the cinema, or at least to come and have lunch with me. She declined everything. The winter would pass, she said, and in the spring we would go back to our nook in the woods. I tried to get her to promise, afraid that she would forget all about me long before the spring. No, she kept repeating, I was not to worry, we would definitely meet again.

A few days later I went to the shop and she wasn't there. For a long time they wouldn't tell me what had happened to her. Either they didn't know themselves or they thought I was an *agent provocateur*. Then, at last, the new manager hinted that she had gone 'over the hills', which was the term people used about someone who had fled the country.

I could not believe she had done it. It was as if she had died, and throughout the following spring I found myself frequently glancing anxiously at the barometer to see if it would be warm and dry enough by noon to lie on the ground in the woods.

A year or two later she sent me a postcard from the USA. The message was so impersonal that if she had not addressed me as 'Mirek' I would not have been certain that it was from her. There was no return address, and in any case who knows if in those days I would have had the courage to write to her.

Now, at the Alcron Hotel, I of course *didn't* recognize her. Strangely enough, she recognized me. She rose from her leather armchair and came to meet me, smiling. She still had teeth like Monica Vitti's, but instead of the earrings I had disliked she now wore large golden hoops; round her throat she had a golden choker. 'Hi, Mirek,' she said, and kissed me.

Her make-up was so flawless that you could not detect a single wrinkle on her face. She was, if anything, even more appealing than I had found her all those twenty years ago.

I sat down in the armchair opposite. There was a drink on the little table between us, and she asked if she could order one for me. But I couldn't drink as I had come by car, and anyway it was up to me to play the host.

'As you wish,' she said, smiling again and looking at me intently. Or was it—I wondered—a provocative look she was giving me? She told me she was visiting Prague with her husband. He was here on business and had a very full schedule, so that she was free until late that evening.

'Not just at lunch-time, then?' I asked.

She smiled.

'And your husband . . . is it still the same one?'

'Same? What do you mean?'

'I mean Joe.'

'Joe?' she asked, puzzled. Then recognition dawned. 'Oh, him! I think I invented him, you know. Or did I? I just don't remember. My husband is American,' she explained. 'He's in the grain business—and beans and things. Terribly dull, but you get to travel a lot. And the money is good. I can visit Europe every year if I want to—or Australia for that matter.'

'And you enjoy it?'

She shrugged. 'Well, it beats selling books, I guess. Wouldn't you say?' And again she gave me that certain look. 'But what about you? Are you married?'

I nodded.

'Any children?'

'Yes, I've got children.'

'Two?'

'That's right.'

'Boy and girl?'

'Here, you some kind of a clairvoyant? Or have you made inquiries about me?'

'*Everybody* has a wife and two kids,' she said. 'And half of them have a boy and a girl. How old are they?'

I gave two ages which weren't exactly right, but who cared?

'And tell me, are you unfaithful to your wife?'

'Of course not,' I said.

'Of course you are. *All* men are unfaithful to their wives. And we to our husbands,' she added. 'You and I don't have to pretend, do we.' She talked as if we had last seen each other only a week ago. Perhaps it was because she had already had a little to drink. Or maybe she had mastered the art of rapidly bridging the distance between herself and another person— at least in conversation. That is an art many American women excel at, preventing themselves from seeing that they never actually get close to anyone.

'How's life been treating you?' she asked, leaning toward me. 'You haven't changed much, you know. Your hair is as thick as ever.'

'Quite right,' I agreed. 'My hair's doing just fine.'

'And you, how are *you* doing?'

'Fine,' I said. 'Like my hair.'

My reaction confused her, and she changed tack.

'Such beautiful weather here. In London, it rained and rained. We spent two whole days cooped up in the hotel, just ventured out in the evening to see a musical. A dreadful show, somewhere in Piccadilly. You know London, of course?'

'Yes, I was there seven years ago. I even went to the theatre.'

'You know what,' she said, 'I saw a play of yours once.'

'Really?'

'At home, in New York. I kept an eye out for you, thinking you might be there for the first night. But you didn't show.'

'No, it's a little out of the way for me.'

'Maybe, but it would've been worth it.'

'Also, I don't have a passport.'

'You don't have a passport?' She did not understand.

'No, they took it away from me. Not just me, many people have had their passports taken away,' I explained. 'Writers, journalists, politicians, and so on. What was the play like?'

'In New York?'

'Yes, the one you saw.'

'I liked it. A critic said it reminded him of Dürrenmatt. You mean to say you can't leave here, you can't travel?'

'Well, I might be able to, but that would mean leaving for good. Then they just might let me.'

'Well, why don't you?'

'I've already told you—I'm doing fine.'

She shrugged. 'You still believe all that nonsense you used to spout?'

'The answer to that question was in my play. Didn't you get it?'

'Yes, I got it. That's why I can't understand you.'

'Well, we lead such interesting lives here,' I said. 'And a writer has to be a bit of an adventurer, you know. He gets bored if nothing much happens, conformity destroys him. Living here, I sometimes feel like a character in a thriller: cars with dimmed headlights, people tailing you wherever you go, searching your house. When I go to a friend's funeral, they even photograph me with concealed cameras, which aren't all that concealed, either.'

'You *have* changed to some extent,' she said.

'Have I?'

'You were always so terribly serious. In fact, you didn't talk so much as preach. You didn't seem to have the slightest sense of humour.'

'Oh, that's just self-defence,' I explained. 'Against the absurdity in which we live.'

She gave me a quizzical look, but as usual when I was supposed to give a more detailed description of this absurdity, I felt a growing distaste which prevented me from explaining anything, complaining about anything.

We each of us have a few relatives and friends whom we are fond of and for whose well-being we fear. We go through life trying not to think too much about the inevitability of death. In this country, however, it is not only death that separates people; they're separated from one another, while still alive, by fear. And those who decide not to give way to it don't have an easy life. Some of them are driven into exile, just as Lída was two decades ago, and it is unlikely that I'll ever see them again, or if so, then not for many years. If we live that long. And what about those who remain behind?

I have a friend, somewhat younger than I, who during his student days was considered the great hope of Czech philosophy. Today, he is working as a night watchman. In the Institute of Philosophy. How about that for an example of our special kind of absurdity?

My former chief editor, a literary critic by training, has for seven years now been employed washing shop windows. Another friend, a well-known philosopher, is digging tunnels for the Metro. The theatre director who dared put on my last play (last of those that could still be staged, that is) is serving a prison sentence; apparently he committed the crime of sending some scripts abroad. And so on and so on . . . They have managed to silence the noblest and most creative spirits, raising the most spiritually impoverished and the most servile writers and philosophers. They have pulped tons of books, forbidden dozens of films; the censors have scoured the libraries, abolished news about the world and are doing their best to shut out foreign radio stations by jamming their broadcasts. They have bastardized the language to such an extent that it no longer resembles the language of our forebears. They have abolished churches, theatres, magazines, publishing houses, scientific societies and cultural associations—yes, they have even torn up the city's ancient cobblestones.

All this, and much else, is absurd enough—particularly when you consider that we have been at peace for several decades—and at the same time insignificant when compared with Siberian labour camps, mass executions in the aftermath of diverse revolutions, the gas chambers, or the Hiroshima bomb. And the real absurdity resides not so much in the individual details I've recounted above as in their duration, their agglomeration and daunting repetition, in the way they have managed to penetrate every nook and cranny of our daily life. In the end you become used to the absence of decent magazines and journals on the bookstalls, you get used to everyone everywhere celebrating some foreign revolution, you become accustomed and inured to all this so that you no longer take it in—but then one day, as you are about to catch a train, you wish to buy something to read on the journey and, after long deliberation, select a dog breeders' journal because you think that here at least there is a subject they can write about without humiliating you. So you open the *Canine News*, and there on the very first page you come across yet another wretched article about someone else's glorious revolution. This is when you get a fleeting glimpse of the utter nothingness which has you at its mercy; you as much as your dog. Trouble is, all this is incommunicable. Dante was wrong when he thought that the inferno and purgatory could be described. No, all you can hope to do is describe individual torments. The most cruel thing about them—their endlessness—cannot be imagined but only experienced.

And so all I said was: 'You have a choice: either you set fire to yourself, or you make fun of it all.'

'The Czechs always prefer to make fun,' she said.

'Not all of them.'

'Oh, I know, Czechs have also gone to the stake for their beliefs, or immolated themselves in protest. But hasn't it occurred to you that there is a third alternative?'

'What is that?' I asked, even though I knew what she meant.

'Simply to get out.'

'I guess I'd be homesick. Are *you* never homesick?'

'Sure I get homesick at times. Now and again we get together with some other Czech exiles and reminisce about the golden city.'

'And what about me? Do you ever think of me?'

'As you see. *And* that spot of ours. You know which spot I mean?'

I nodded.

'For some time we lived in Detroit, not far from the railway tracks. Whenever I heard an engine hoot I thought I was dreaming. Sometimes I do dream about that place. *You* don't even have to be there, not necessarily. I just dream about the wood. I'm lying there in the grass and looking up at the sky.'

'There you are,' I pointed out, 'I have the advantage of being able to go there whenever I feel like it. If I feel nostalgic.'

'*Have* you been there? Since that time?'

'No, why? You see, people only dream about places they *can't* visit. But I drive past there often. The wood is still there.'

She leant towards me then and said in a low voice: 'How about us two going there? It's almost noon—it would be just like old times!'

I looked at that carefully made-up face, at the expensive dress which came from heaven knows which fashion house, and tried to imagine her lying in the grass in the woods at Bohdalec. Still, it was *her* idea . . .

Outside in the street a June sun shone in a cloudless sky.

'I'm so glad I found you,' she declared as she sat down next to me in the car. 'I have always wanted to go back there with you once more.'

I turned round as we drove off, trying to spot the vehicle I knew must be tailing us.

'Who are you looking for?'

'Nobody.'

She leant across and kissed me. 'Doesn't it worry you to be shadowed like that?'

'Not in the least,' I said. 'In other countries this sort of treatment is reserved for the most prominent people.'

'But do you have to put up with it?'

'Yes, if I want to go on living here.'

'And you do—you want to go on living here even though they treat you like dirt?'

'It's home, isn't it,' I said wearily. 'A man needs to belong somewhere. Does that make me an eccentric?'

A red Fiat had now been behind us across at least five intersections.

'Can you get into trouble for taking *me* out?'

'No, I shouldn't think so.'

'Oh, good. I wouldn't like that. Do you mind if I take a swig?' She pulled a small flask out of her handbag and poured a shot into a tiny tumbler. She offered me one, but this was hardly the best place for it.

'I haven't told you how *I* live,' she said, and started to fill me in on the details of her existence. Apart from their sumptuous New York apartment, she and her husband owned a whole island on Lake Michigan, where they had a luxurious home and two splendid stallions. They also had a house in Switzerland, and something in Hawaii . . .

The red Fiat dropped away and we were now being followed by a white Volga. But then, there was always one car or another following you on a busy city street.

I asked her which countries she had visited, and she gave me a run-down of her travels on several continents. She must have spent a fortune and expended an incredible amount of energy, this girl with whom I used to make love in the woods at Bohdalec. Had she denied herself just a fraction of her extravagant way of life, the money she would have saved could have enabled one of my many former colleagues to live and carry on his calling instead of eking out an existence as a navvy. She might even have done it, but why, if she did decide to devote some of her wealth to charity, should she give it to a Czech intellectual? Why not send it instead to India and help feed a child who would otherwise die?

We crossed the old railway bridge and turned into a bumpy country road with small family houses strung on either side.

And then we were at our destination. She turned round in her seat, pointed to the back of the car, and said, 'You've got a blanket back there. Aren't you going to take it along?'

I turned round now and saw that we were no longer being followed. Or, if we were, they had stopped before the last bend to keep out of sight.

'Should we?' I asked.

I reached out to pick up the blanket. How ridiculous, here in what was now a built-up area.

A man in a check shirt came striding past us, heading towards the wood, his hands in the pockets of his jeans.

I spent some time trying to fold the blanket so it would resemble a large handkerchief.

We were surrounded by high-rise apartment blocks, the once empty plain having been transformed into a building site. Two heavy trucks loaded with earth trundled along the rutted road that led past our wood.

'Tell me,' she put the customary question, 'what do you actually live on?'

'My foreign royalties.'

We had reached the wood and were walking along our old path.

She looked quite out of place here, in her high-heeled shoes and her fine clothes in which only yesterday she had strolled along Oxford Street.

'Will you find the place?'

'I'll try.'

From the building site behind us came the noise of a crane, and someone giving orders to the workers in a raucous voice. It occurred to me that perhaps this wasn't the right path, after all. Maybe they had felled some of the trees, and those that remained had grown out of all recognition.

'I can't understand why you insist on living here when you publish your books abroad.'

'*Where* you publish isn't really so important,' I told her. 'Rather, what you write about.'

'So, what *do* you write about?'

'About all this!' I said.

The barbed-wire fence was of course no longer there, nor

the warning notice. The bushes had gone, too. The wood was completely transparent now: we could see right to the other side, where several old-age pensioners were sitting on benches, enjoying the sun.

We turned back. 'Maybe that wasn't the right path,' she said. 'Let's try to find another.'

'All the paths are wrong. That spot doesn't exist any more.'

'Come on, surely we aren't just going to give up!'

'You shouldn't have left.'

'But I had to!'

'Why?'

'I just ... I just couldn't live here.' She stopped and stretched out her arms. We embraced and kissed. Someone was coming up the path behind us, the man in the check shirt and jeans, a professionally nonchalant look on his face.

'Have you ever thought of me?'

'I thought of you a lot that time when you disappeared.'

'I wrote you several letters but never got a reply.'

'I only had one card, that's all.'

'Really?'

'That's nothing unusual,' I explained. 'They simply stop your correspondence.'

We returned to the car.

'How about going back to my hotel?' she suggested. 'My husband won't be back till late tonight.'

'You sure?'

'He took a plane this morning. To Brno, I think.'

'It's not exactly a good hotel for that kind of thing,' I objected. 'I'm afraid they keep an eye on all the guests. And the rooms are bugged.'

'You're kidding!'

'I'm not, I assure you.'

'But that's incredible!' She was again sitting next to me in the car. 'Well, why don't we go to a different hotel?' she said softly. 'We can sign in under a false name, if you're scared.'

'No, we can't,' I corrected her. 'Whichever hotel you go to, you have to leave your passport or identity card at the desk. They'll take down your name and send your particulars to the security police. It's not that I'm chicken, I just know the drill.'

'Well,' she said after a while, 'you're not exactly the great adventurer you made out earlier, are you?'

How could I explain to her? I just said, 'Look, we never used to go to a hotel in the old days, so what's the point now?'

She was silent.

'I'm sorry,' I said. 'Sorry we couldn't find the right place.'

'Still, I'm glad you took me up there, just the same,' she said at last. 'I'll remember our trip. You know, I guess I do get homesick sometimes. When I'm on my own at home. It's a huge house, twelve rooms. And I'm often alone, just me and my dog.'

'No children?'

She shook her head. 'The house can seem terribly empty, even though it's full of objects. My husband collects primitive art, and so we have walls full of masks and shields, embroidered skirts and totems. We have people in quite often, and then we talk about all sorts of things—about art and literature, and what they've seen on their travels. We drink beer out of cans, or gin, but then the next morning, when I wake up . . . well, you know how it is.' She gestured with her hands, took a handkerchief out of her handbag and dried her eyes.

When we got back to the hotel I suggested, 'How about having lunch together? Would you like that?'

'No, we never did that before either,' she replied. 'It wouldn't make any sense.'

I agreed.

'I guess this is the last time we'll see each other,' she said. 'I'd like to ask you something, may I?'

'Sure, go ahead.'

'You don't think you wouldn't be able to make a living abroad, do you?'

'No, I don't think that.'

'Nor that you would be less free?'

'Hardly!'

'And you said you think they'd let you emigrate?'

'Yes, and I also told you why I didn't want to.'

'Oh, come on, those weren't your *real* reasons. Can't you tell me why you really don't want to leave?'

I hesitated a little, then said, 'No, I can't.'

'Do you know yourself?'

I could have repeated that it was because this was my country. Because here I have several friends whom I need just as they need me. And because people here speak the same language as I do. Because I'd like to go on being a writer, and to be a writer means also to stick up for people whose fate is not a matter of indifference to me. At least to speak up for those who perhaps are less able to do so than I am, to give expression to their desire for freedom and a more dignified existence. All this I can do here, where I grew up, where I became part of whatever is happening and can therefore understand it, at least to some extent.

The freedom that exists out there, which I have played no part in creating, could hardly give me satisfaction or happiness, just as I couldn't hope to feel the sorrows of those people. I would feel that I was wasting my time. I could have said: Because I like to stroll over the cobblestones of one or two Prague streets whose very names remind me of the city's history, which I know and understand. But equally I could have said: My country is not to be found any more, it has vanished, just like that spot in the woods. Most of my friends have left, or are preparing to leave. The language I love is daily being violated by every means at *their* disposal—and they dispose of many and varied means. So all that remains is those few Prague streets. They have changed the names of most of them, and they'll probably change the rest before they're done, and they have let the city go to the dogs. They are even tearing up those cobblestones; rumour has it they're being sold for the construction of dykes in Holland.

It so happens that life often presents you only with a choice between two kinds of suffering, two forms of nothingness, two varieties of despair. All you can do is choose which you think will be the less unbearable, or even the more attractive, which will allow you to retain at least a modicum of pride or self-respect.

I could have given her so many reasons for and against, and still she would not have been able to understand. And so I preferred to reply by saying, 'I don't know.'

(*Translated by George Theiner.*)

Jiří Kratochvil

The Orpheus of Kénig

in the distance I saw the rainforest like a green expanse of
volcanic rock, like a depository of large emerald
cowpats steaming purple into the rosy-coloured dawn, I
slowly sank on all fours and, rocking back and forth,
I made the strange sounds Zalanha had taught me,
through which man invokes the spirits of the forest
before venturing into its depths for the first time, and I
didn't know if I had remembered them right and if
I imitated them faithfully, because the only response was
the screeching of parrots, as if I were entering a large
aviary or a circus tent, and when I finished the ceremony I
could do nothing but sit down and wait for my Indian
guides who, to be sure, took their time, and so I waited
almost till night, and I tell you, all that time I was hassled
by some insects that mostly looked like copies of Edward
Stoward's abstract sculptures, and then I saw my guide
and heard Lennon's 'Yellow Submarine' playing on a
miniature tape-recorder set like a filling in the decayed
tooth of a smiling Yurimagua Indian

It happened at the beginning of those crazy years after the
entry of the Warsaw Pact armies, sometime in the autumn
of 1971. I was sitting in a pub in Kénig, reading a note from
some slut who was appealing to me, yours respectfully, when
on to the table fell Bucek's shadow.

Show me, he said, and held out his paw. That girl must be a
great medium. I've been looking for one like that for ages.

Are you out of your mind? I laughed at him. She's just some ordinary cow.

But Bucek was already clutching the note, mesmerized by the handwriting, caressing its every flourish with his eyes. In the end I never found out what the slut had been trying to tell me. Most likely she was in need of some services which are not normally available even for her own kind.

Find out all you can about her. And he stuck the note in his pocket and off he went.

It must be said here that I let Bucek get away with a lot of things. He must be the most eccentric creature I've met in my entire life. And so, without delay, I got him all the information I could find out about the slut.

Her name was Marta G, and she was the daughter of some Party bigwig in Brno.

That complicates the situation but doesn't change it, said Bucek. She's the most sensitive medium I've ever come across. I need someone just like her. Without her I wouldn't dare go into it.

When she was thirteen, I went on, Konrad Däbbler used her as a model for his shapely masterpiece, *The Source of the Svratka River*; today she's twenty-one and she's a student at the Law School. She's had two abortions and a brief affair with someone who shall remain nameless. Martička belongs to the 'healthy core' of our golden youth, that prominent tribe whose members have been lately calling themselves Elephants and who hang out at the Continental Hotel, the International, the Grand and The Little Eye Patisserie.

Enough, said Bucek. Now introduce me to her.

And so I started handling Bucek's courtship. I got him a denim suit which made him look like a feeble-minded hunter, and I took him by the hand to the Continental where the Elephants were whooping it up like there was no tomorrow. But Martička was not among them.

Sit down, Bucek, I said. I'll have a look around to see if I can find her for you.

And I ordered a toothpick for a fiver to give him something to chew on.

But Bucek was at home only in a real pub or buried in his

books. In the Continental he felt like a pregnant camel in a boxing ring. He couldn't shake off the impression that everyone was staring at him. And he dealt with it as best he could. For instance, by sticking his left hand under his right armpit, stretching his right arm across to hook it round his left side, and twisting his legs together under the table like two deranged reptiles.

Bucek could sit like that for hours. Last time he did it was at the wedding of one Vrát'a Sedláček who had chosen Bucek to be his best man, and, having first prised him away from his books or flushed him out of some dive, brought him round and fixed him in the middle of the wedding table from where there was no escape. The guests babbled at Bucek from all directions, forced him to laugh at their stupid jokes and poured some vile peppermint piss down his throat. And as time passed (reminisced Bucek) my bladder got full, but I couldn't muster the courage to go to the lavatory because there was only one and it was permanently besieged. But shortly before midnight—and before I could do anything about it—there was a blast of spontaneous psychokinetic storm which relieved not only my inner tension but also my bladder.

It started as a minor disturbance in the wine glasses, then, as if on cue, all the pictures on the wall began to swing from side to side and the power in both chandeliers waxed and waned until eight lightbulbs exploded, scattering glass everywhere. From there, events took off: the crockery on the U-shaped dinner table began marching forth and the heaviest objects in the pile of wedding presents—one TV set, two fridges and three vacuum cleaners—began to levitate, soaring up to the ceiling, where they remained suspended as if in the grip of an enormous magnet which in turn switched itself off, sending everything crashing down. And above all the clatter reverberated a piercing roar, the voice of the poltergeist, the tormenting ghost.

At that time (we mustn't forget that Vrát'a's wedding took place in March 1965), nobody knew anything about spontaneous psychokinesis (until 1967, when the Freiburg Institute published its famous report on the incident that took place in the law chambers of the Bavarian town of Rosenheim where a similar spectacle was unleashed by the nineteen-year-old Annemarie Sch.), and so no one had a clue that Bucek could be the cause of this nuptial pandemonium.

When (at 8.42 p.m. on 2 November 1971) I finally brought Marta after a three-hour search, I cast my eyes at the spot where I'd left Bucek and saw him sitting there all twisted round himself, his face showing that unbearable tension I already recognized, and, to top it all, I could detect the peculiar smell which Bucek never mentioned but which I now safely identified as the ominous sign, the diabolical incendiary—and I knew at once that we were in trouble.

As if to confirm my suspicions, the glasses and bottles on all the tables throughout every floor of the hotel suddenly clashed with a clank, loud and clear. At that moment, Bucek broke out of his torpor and leapt up, upsetting the table. Run, everybody! he yelled pointing with all his arms to all the exits.

Everyone turned round to stare at him but by then hell had already broken loose.

Several minutes later we were speeding away from the wrecked hotel in Marta's little car and she was casting passionate glances at Bucek from the steering wheel. Psychokinesis happened to be a fashionable topic among the Elephants just then, and no one had ever before thrown such a wonderful fireworks display in Marta's honour.

And now a few words about Bucek's project:

When, in 1971, the process of 'normalization and consolidation' had gone too far, Bucek said: Enough is enough, and came up with the idea of transporting the whole of Czechoslovakia to Amazonia. He cut out the shape of the republic to scale and placed it on a map of the Amazon region so that its eastern tail touched the Mato Grosso, while the muzzle of its dog's head sniffed at the Porto Velho. I pointed out that he'd failed to consider the Trans-Amazonian highway (it wasn't marked on the map), and that he'd completely forgotten about air traffic from which anybody could snoop into Czechoslovakia as if it were a chicken-pen, which meant that the Brazilian government would waste no time in deporting us. He then took a long time shifting the cut-out this way and that, trying to squeeze us into the Amazonian rainforest. He was utterly fascinated by the six hundred thousand square miles of forest land pitched against the piddling fifty thousand of our suffering homeland. In the end, he (reluctantly) gave up and became more realistic. A city like Brno, for example, would disappear in the Amazon like a ring in a duck's stomach. But even that was a project of some magnitude, especially if we consider that under no circumstances could Bucek count on using psychokinesis, which is really good just for smashing dishes, exploding lightbulbs and levitating wardrobes, TV sets and fridges. He had no choice but to resort to the classical method, that is, to deconstruct the city like an enormous jigsaw puzzle and smuggle it into Brazil in suitcases, handbags and briefcases. Provided, of course, that at the same time its substitute was transported in the opposite direction, all neatly packed in items of luggage. It might be best explained by giving you a concrete example. Take the Dietrichstein Palace at the Green Market: every stone removed from its walls would be immediately replaced by an exact copy, so at the end of the transfer the Dietrichstein Palace at the Green Market would be a fake, whereas the original would be standing somewhere in the heart of the Amazonian rainforest. The same goes for everything else, until one day the city of Brno would be nestling in the rainforest, while in its place there would be a manufactured replica. Of course, all that transportation, the swapping and switching, would have to be carried out unnoticed. The success of the whole operation would depend on its being totally inconspicuous. The complex organization of such a transfer would, of course, require the skills of a world-class genius, and Bucek certainly fitted the description. You see, we had already decided not to doubt his unique abilities, otherwise the whole thing would make no sense.

Thanks to Martička's party connections Bucek managed to get on a package tour to Vienna and never came back, leaving me with Martička on my hands. She was a luscious girl, despite her propensity for the above-mentioned elephantilism, but I slowly got that out of her head.

I lived with her, heeding Bucek's strict instructions not to let her out of my sight so that I could be in constant receiving mode, because there was no telling when he would make contact through her. Where there's no contact, there's no command, they used to tell us in the National Service, and I thought that applied even more in the case of transporting large cities.

It happened for the first time on a sheepskin rug Martička had brought along from her papa's residence, in a situation I would describe as contact of body and soul.

Martička was busy making various ugly noises I was already getting a bit fed up with (for me, love is a quiet garden slightly past its prime or perhaps a gentle breeze whispering in a wheatfield), but then these noises surprisingly turned into a babel of exotic languages among which I managed to identify a knot of Portuguese and Indian syllables—like when you pop a cork and at first there is a murky, frothy flow which quickly clears up—and this is what I heard:

casiqui só e de tapajos santo siltt virrur stle mallttuc lnev lezett kodyyz ilhade marajó tefe xxzet tthen I wokke up andd abovve me I ssaw an Indian face with Zrzavý's painting of the Piazza San Marco daubed on it with pigments and vegetable juices, and I looked for the signature in the lower left-hand corner, but just then the match went out and you can't imagine how peeved I was 'cause I didn't have a single match left! and so I had to wait till sunrise but in the morning the buggers returned from the river with their little faces freshly scrubbed; I thought I'd chosen my Indian guide but it was he who'd chosen me, and I had no idea, until it dawned on me that he had designs on my kidney, he probably needs it for some ritual purpose and so he's prepared to accompany me while he's waiting for his opportunity, but because I can't do without him in these parts I have no option but to accept it; or yesterday: we were going through a rainforest arcade in a canoe, a kind of tunnel made up of vegetation, and suddenly I look up and see bunches of sleeping bats hanging upside down from the dense canopy of branches, what a fucking experience,

going down the river in a convoy of seven canoes
carrying all my measuring instruments, everything one
needs to build a city in the rainforest, and the Indians
are keeping up this monotonous drone—or is it singing?
hrrtl tlqeemqeeing, how am I supposed to understand
this stupid lingo—their polished chrome-domes glowing
in the twilight

After a while I became more experienced with this state and
I knew that, no matter what, I mustn't disturb Martička if I
didn't want to switch off her medial reporting and disconnect
Bucek's telepathic broadcast. And so I would carefully reach
for the tape-recorder and put it near her lips, and then I
would just hang in there. After each letter I poured Marta a
drink, though she had no idea what it was for.

The moment Bucek finished dictating his letter (in the
heart of the Amazonian rainforest), Marta would go out like
a candle, not a syllable of those profound lines left in her, and
she would wake up into her usual dippy chatter which was
what I had to put up with in between Bucek's letters.

(Many of you, darlings, have shown an almost touching concern for detail, wanting to know whether it will be necessary
to transfer the city with all its bits and pieces, including, for
example, the notorious Brno sewer system. In our 'Letters to
the Editor' we also return to the question of transporting the
citizens of Brno. Dear reader from Julianov, you ask which
citizens are going to be transported and which are going to
be left in the replica, and whether relevant lists are being
compiled. We cannot exclude the possibility that in the end
some list may be put together for purely technical reasons,
but have you given any thought to the appropriateness of
such measures? Finally, we've also had several inquiries from
readers in Fučík's district regarding reimbursement for some
large state companies in Brno.)

we set out downstream the Black River (Rio Negro)
towards the central Amazon, and what an incredibly

exhausting journey it was, brightened only by the cries of neurasthenic animals echoing above those eternally melancholy swamps, and where the Rio was not navigable, we were transported on the backs of the amphibious *Titanus giganteus*, a true superinsect which, for reasons unknown, migrates to the Amazon through its tributaries at this time of year; and the way they treat animals here would make us blush: the Indians wash themselves with the blood of a freshly slain tapir, and the sight of a tiny tot being bathed in blood makes a particularly strange impression, the child then runs around splashing blood like a chunk of meat fallen off the butcher's hook; from the moment I set foot on Brazilian soil I'd been hearing the incessant hum of the greatest of all rivers, and now I've finally seen it: a huge uprooted tree was floating down the Amazon and in its branches shone the eyes of dozens of leopards like bright blossoms, the guide told me the river was a good five hundred feet deep here, then asked for a coin to throw in, and we watched it glide slowly in the turquoise waters until we could only sense it as a faint ripple of light criss-crossing in the immeasurable depths; at that moment I heard a deafening noise and, looking up, I saw a swarm of helicopters travelling from Puerta Yacucho to the Misty Mountain (Cerro de la Neblina); the Indians explained that it was an international scientific expedition of surveyors, biologists, entomologists, botanists, zoologists and archaeologists who were flying to the as yet unexplored ring of table mountains on the border of Brazil and Venezuela; I got worried about the level of air traffic in this part of the Amazon but one of the Indians assured me that this encounter was exceptional and the statistical improbability of it happening in this very spot had been calculated by computers as 1:96,8756—in other words, high enough for me to rely on; but now let's get down to business: we've finally achieved some results! listen everyone, and especially you, Kája, yesterday we staked out the space where we're going to put the city of Brno, we worked our asses off but it's done! it's going to

stand here, on swamp and mud just as it did once upon a
time (Brno, derived from the Old Czech *brnije* = mud, in
its adjectival form *brnem* which means 'city built on
swampy ground'), shame we haven't got telepathic video
yet, so that I could send you a picture of the very spot
where we're going to put Kénig, our native Krpole, and
when I say staked out, we're talking sixty-foot poles,
and over that area we're going to erect an ingenious
construction to hold a stainless-steel net into which
we're going to lay the city like a baby into its nappy, you'll
soon be able to appreciate the wonderful location I've
chosen, away from all roads, ideas and bad intentions,
where the sky-blue Morpho butterflies emerge from the
impenetrable vegetation and the large brown *Brassolidae*
flutter up from the river to meet them, where caymans
loll peacefully by the river banks, their docile eyes
reflecting the starry night and the obscenely yellow
moon, and the Atta ants travel along the routes they've
been treading for thousands of years, each carrying a
moist leaf or two, or a couple of green shoots—but now I
can see that one of them is in fact carrying my fork,
another a spoon, the third a knife, the fourth my map of
the Amazon, the fifth has a tie in his clutches, the sixth a
pair of gloves, the seventh my socks, I run after them
clapping my hands and shouting: Hey, you fucking
bastards, hey, you clowns! but they pay no attention, they
don't react to sound, and so I just watch them leg it up a
long liana joining two rainforest giants, with the cutlery
and map and tie and gloves and socks and all, and my
shouting brings the Indians running with their long
serbetana blowpipes, but the fork is already disappearing
in the crown of the tree and the spoon and the knife,
socks and tie catch up with it in no time

We found Bucek in a tiny room stuffed with books, trav-
elogues on the Amazonian rainforest and frivolous novels
from Brazil. He hadn't gone anywhere, and all his telepathic
missives were being dispatched from this very room—from a
distance of only half a mile, only two streets away and not

across continents and oceans as we'd believed. Pinned up right above his head was a full-colour page from an illustrated weekly, depicting an anaconda swooping like a monumental shadow over a family of white bunnies.

First I went up to the wall and tore the picture down. The floor was covered with empty tins and the air was stiff with stale smoke from cheap cigarettes. In the time he'd been there, Bucek had grown a vulgar moustache, and as I looked at him I felt one of the greatest disappointments of my life, which almost matched the shock I suffered when, at the age of sixteen, I saw a girl from my class, a painfully fragile and pure love of mine, in the arms of a loathsome old man.

Don't spit around here, complained Bucek and quietly picked up an orange watering-can to sprinkle a strange, weedy plant in a little pot.

Can you give me something to drink, Bucek?

Not on your life, he whispered. All I can give you is a punch on the nose.

I was itching to hit him but I thrust my hands in my pockets, turned on my heel and walked out.

When I got home, I sat on a chair staring at the wall for a while, then grabbed the keys and went down to the cellar, where I have stashed a demijohn of cheap wine and a bottle of strong spirits. Already, on my way down, I could hear that wild rumble, but I thought it was just my own anger, and as I put the key in the lock and opened the door I barely had the time to step back, and then I just stood there gasping, flattened against the wall.

Come, I'll draw you a picture, said Bucek a little later, as he tried to show me how the city is suspended above the swamp in a gigantic skeleton construction, a basket of reinforced concrete. What you heard was the river, and I can tell you that in some spots, including right where you live, the city hangs over and touches the water surface. What you saw was the Amazon.

And if I haven't told you yet, this is a story about the power of love. Shortly after the above conversation with Bucek I realized that I had no idea where my prominent slut was. I searched for her everywhere but she'd disappeared off the face of the earth. It took a fortnight before Bucek let me in to the true state of things. She simply had not been included on the list of transported persons. And in such a case there was nothing he could do to help. It dawned on me that I had no choice but to return. And I was in luck because our Mother Country had just then decided to grant all refugees a generous amnesty. I applied for repatriation through the Czechoslovak embassy in Brazil, accepting all their conditions, going through the whole humiliating rigmarole, at the end of which I was reunited with my slut. And there was no greater love in the world. When we split up two months later, I knew that there was no way back.

One morning I was standing in Malinovsky Square, watching a crowd of people rushing from the bus stop to catch the tram, when I suddenly had a stunning vision: a dense cloud made of thousands of butterflies descended on the crowd, covered it and mingled with it, and people were mixed with butterflies like poppy seeds with plum cheese. I knew what it meant: I missed the Amazon. But, as I said, there was no way back.

Another day, on another occasion, I suddenly realized that the city I live in is a mere replica and that everything I touch is just as unreal. And I knew I could never accept that.

Sometimes I dream of huge concrete orchid blossoms floating on the swamp and of the mighty Leviathan tossing in the rushes. I could talk to you about my technicolour dreams for hours. But what's the use?

In this unreal world even dreams are paltry and insignificant. The Elephants in the Continental have been replaced by the Boars, hustlers as young as nine and ten hang around the hard-currency shop in the Yalta Arcade, and the beer is now sour and expensive even in our pub in Kénig. Our lives are nothing but substitutes, and our city is a denture spat out of a filthy mouth. Whose, I dare not say.

(*Translated by Alexandra Büchler.*)

Zuzana Brabcová

extract from the novel *Far From the Tree*
The Slaughtering

*Once upon a time in Bohemia there was a flourishing trade,
which, it seems, is now defunct: they took a child, cut its
lips, cracked its skull and shut it in a box to stop it growing.
In this and other similar ways they created highly amusing
and extremely lucrative monsters.*

Jean-Paul Sartre

Hands. Hands covered in. Hands covered in blood. You
fattened a pig, you took a mallet—and that was it. Mr
Zámek knew, Mr Zámek was there. Mr Zámek, blood of
Ivan's blood.

The uninhabitable world was slowly peopled with psy-
chiatrists. They donned glasses, and began to probe me, while
respectable Dad in slippers anxiously prayed in waiting
rooms.

'Draw a tree,' one says, shoving me a piece of paper.

'Ah yes, every dream has its own umbilical relationship to
the inscrutable . . .' another says, citing that master of masters
Sigmund F, as I allow the possibility of a flood in coming
years, and—looking at my tree—he places it vertically.

'Not like that, please.' I react with annoyance and correct
his view. 'It's just been struck by lightning, you see . . .'

My 'faintings', my flights below the surface remained unexplained. In vain did others enlarge my diagnoses several
times over, in vain did they send reconnaissance teams crawling down my nervous system. With technical aid my heart
only confided to paper more of Dad's meaningless squiggles.

I was fit and well, and my parents were unhappy, for they wanted an answer: my incomprehensible health hung them on a question-mark's noose.

I was fit and well, my IQ was severely subnormal (bordering on the animal level) and yet I did not despair. Sometimes, it's true, I faltered. Especially in Czech classes, when it was not I who stood in front of the whole form on lovely legs and read out brilliant essays, not I but . . .

Slavík warbled on in the hushed silence. I want to write a novel (no more postcards to saviours), I want to name every living soul, even if I do border on the animal level. I want to write a novel about water, about beautiful Bohemia, my own land, that paradise, and about a great big sad pig-slaughtering.

'Excellent, Janáčková, go and sit down. I am touched, really touched . . . Comenius would have been proud of you, Janáčková, I'm sure. Do you see? Even that scoundrel Dzurisko in the back row is touched by it,' quavered Slavík, seeing off Kate with a smile as sticky as a warm boiled sweet. Damn it. About a pig-slaughtering—and that's that.

'And this is my home,' declaimed Kate. 'This is the land whose soil the great Teacher of the Nations felt in his hand on that day in early February 1628 when he left it for ever.'

The pig's head drags on the ground. One slash from top to bottom is enough to show you the anatomical hell inside . . . Mr Zámek knew, Mr Zámek was there.

'Ivan, Ivan, no!' I cried out in my sleep. Too late: Mother magically appeared in the doorway and felt my brow over anxiously, to open it up and gaze inside. For a split second she glimpsed the clarinet in my body and my body on the floor of the presidential box. Just for a split second, but that was enough.

'I really don't like you seeing that Zámek boy. You'll get yourself involved in something.' Unlucky choice of words, I think to myself coldly, retorting even more coldly in spirit, 'How could I not get involved, when you explained sex to me at the age of fifteen, using butterflies as your example . . .'

We make love often. We make love wherever we can. Mostly at Leather Adèle's. Leather Adèle, sweep of hair across the forehead, pays us no attention, engrossed in her water-divining. Her room with a window over the Vltava . . . the dim balcony . . . neighbour Franz, one-time circus act . . . all this formed a back-drop, Ivan, entirely overshadowing the tiresome business of going to school. That spring you announced categorically, 'Why waste time? Why carve graffiti on the desk out of boredom? I already know how to lie with my feet towards the epicentre, safely shielded by the Communist daily.'

Finally, without any obvious connection, you added, 'Though I must say, sometimes I think of Gagarin's bones up there,' and you gazed at the long-ago-painted ceiling of our temporary lair.

Still, Kateřina Janáčková continued reading her essays out in class, even through high school, and my envy grew. I got low marks for Czech. My sentences, unlike hers, were underdeveloped, basic and off the mark, and they never managed to touch that scoundrel Dzurisko . . .

'So this is your last chance,' the other promptly remarked, fastidiously lifting his patent-leather shoes from the damp carpet.

Maybe he's discovered something, I thought. Maybe he's finally got through and the one on the other end of the line has confirmed that most of the American continent is under water. It wouldn't surprise me, Joseph; Lord, wipe them off the face of the Earth, if you repent that you made them . . . But the analyst said nothing; he got to his feet and motioned me to the door.

The clack of patent-leather shoes behind me. I return down long corridors to my damp cell, mentally adding a new picture to my album, Řeháček sitting proprietorially on top of the biggest skyscraper, gazing down into those murky waters, gazing down, his ginger head shielded with an umbrella, just as blithe and immoral as ever, only instead of slippers he's wearing ordinary boots. America never became the extension of his room. And his chimneysweep Dad? Lucky no more; did you ever see a chimney on a skyscraper?

The door shut behind me, the spyhole opened and closed. I'm cold, Josie, I'm endlessly, damply cold, and somewhere far away boundless America, land of shattered opportunities with rockets at the bottom, milk and honey, dollar and rust, stupid chimneyless country deadened with rain. Řeháček was the first, then others took their turn.

Weird people started hanging out at Leather Adèle's. Some recited their poetry about lanterns spewing light, about Prague New Age golems, about the siting of atomic missiles in Europe, about failed copulations. One novice tried reading in a gas-mask. Leather Adèle tossed one egg after another into boiling water, stirring the surface sometimes with a spoon, to discover what awaited our generation in tomorrow's bright dawn.

'This is Věra, vicar's daughter. Ever since she was five she's been writing her autobiographical novel but she's still at the prenatal stage.' Ivan would introduce me to new arrivals.

Since everyone talked, I too tried to talk about Grandpa Václav, in the hopes of stumbling over a root. No one listened. Scoundrel Dzurisko in the back row wove chewing-gum into my hair out of boredom.

'Beer, bum and cops!' cursed Leather Adèle—perhaps she'd just seen our picture in her circles—and she chucked her egg into the Vltava. I slowed down the shot and followed its trajectory for a long time, till the river swallowed this spherical angst.

Mister Franz, former circus act, often came and spoke of the Soviet Union, a land of fascination, revealed with an animal whiff of sawdust.

'One day, folks,' he cleared his throat, 'I'm riding in this tram from one end of Moscow to the other, packed, like here, to the gunnels. On Yasnopolyanskaya two lads get on, all in black, and—would you believe it—with a coffin. They pull it up on to the platform, and squat down on it—nowhere else to sit. I say to myself, here everything is possible, much like the circus: a mast up to heaven, whiplashes, queues for corpses, revolutions, coffins—' he waved a hand and touched his red nose, perplexed—'so I stare at the two lads, as we ride through the snow-covered city, I stare at this prime gag, they on the coffin, cool as cucumbers, the rest gaping out the windows, clearly accustomed to all such sights ... We reach the terminus. I get out and watch them curiously as they huff and puff away under their burden. Christ, it's quite a weight, I tell myself, and then it hit me, what I hadn't realized up till then—that was no empty coffin.'

The weird people reacted with nonplussed silence. His punchline fell on deaf ears. I think of the incommunicability of Grandpa's bones crossly wedged in the ground. I don my gas-mask and crack the shell, in order to break out finally on the pages of my novel from the prenatal stage.

Ivan pours the vodka and drinks with Franz to his glorious past. He's stopped noticing me. From a certain point, if wanting to stroke him, I've retracted my claws, and that's bad, Doctor. I hang on his lips. I hang in his sky like Gagarin's bones. Nothing else exists, no mother-steppe, Katy in the thunder of crop-spraying aircraft, nothing, not even Austria, that leviathan land which gobbled up rust-haired Řeháček, not even language—sweet, venomous husk; there is only Ivan, sprung from the earth, his life behind the scenes of the derelict theatre. I could not know of the others to come, but I managed to divine something from Adèle's hydromantic pursuits. I observed the Vltava from her window: one reality looming over the river, another, deformed, wobbling shakily on the surface.

These evenings were endless. I wanted very much to be alone with Ivan, but Adèle's visitors showed no signs of leaving. Moreover, that nut Cyril fastened upon me. 'Do you know it's all so boring in the States?' he bawled at me. 'If there's any history, it's happening here between Aš and the Tatra Mountains.'

No good trying to explain that my severely subnormal IQ made me unfit for his spirited utterances, so I watched Ivan across the torrent of his words, his ever-changing face, with and without the mask, with the shadow of the clarinet across it, a three-dimensional face full of tracks, which besieged, enthralled, and sacrificed me to delusions.

'I love you,' I felt like telling him, even though I knew there was no more time for banalities, 'I love you,' I tell him, smiling at half-daft Cyril. 'In Washington I slept with Elizabeth Taylor, in China they proclaimed me a god.' He raises his voice to a threat: 'You don't believe me? They built a statue to me.'

A wretched generation. Autistic. Alcoholic. Riddled with debt. Moodily, unambitiously Eastern. Matter-of-factly, acceleratedly Western. Anchorless, oceanless—I love you. Are you here, Josie? Are you here in the darkness? Why did you keep putting off the moment when I'd open the door and notice the others?

Still with the warmth of your palms under my sweater

I was hauled here through the sea

Why more interrogations? Why a need to continue? One day the surface will also cover this building. And then ... Seagulls. Fish. And in the bowels of one of them I, fish in the water, I in the fish, and inside of me a shot of Cyril, his eyes piercing: 'Give up Ivan. He won't stick around anyway. You know, his Dad ...'

I don't follow. I want to ask, but someone rings the bell. Adèle goes to answer. 'Those ambitious film makers are here.' She shrugs her shoulders distastefully, and returns to her vessels.

They start showing their film. I don't get it at first ... Greasy people round a table stuffing themselves stupid. Head of a pig on the ground. One slash from top to bottom ... Hands. Hands covered in. Hands covered in blood. Somebody swung a mallet—the animal stumbled. The pig blinking merrily at the camera ... Still I don't quite get it ... A slaughtering. An ordinary village slaughtering. Only backwards. From bursting tummies to the hog skipping blithely about the yard.

'That's really dire,' Ivan yawns.

'Let's get out of here.' I cravenly exploit my opportunity.

We end up by the Vltava. Some early-evening drunk has vomited among the swans. It's spring, it's May. The Nation for Itself, turned to pillars of stone on the other bank, still harboured my fakir's semen. We hopped up on the rail.

'Sometimes I'm just horrible, eh. That's with all these rivers burning. You don't believe me? Two kilometres up in flames near Karlovy Vary. A bloke and a girl like us were sitting on the bank, he chucks away a fag—and up it went.'

Ivan cast his cigarette into the Vltava with an expansive gesture. It hissed, but that was all.

'River burning, river burning,' he droned out of tune. 'I can't imagine,' he started up again, 'you know, May, lilac and that, it makes you think ... thirty years ago it was the end of the war ... The other day I went to the cellar for some potatoes and I started imagining quite vividly that it was the black-out, with bombs flying overhead. My stomach really turned. I had to get out of there quick.'

'Ivan, do you want to leave?'

'Don't be stupid, Věra. If there's any history, it's happening here between Aš and the Tatra Mountains. That's what Cyril says, anyway, isn't it?'

Suddenly a falling sensation. Some knight passed with an Alsatian and took off his head. The future will be different, he brayed at me by way of a greeting. Into what spindles have you spun me, legend? Who cut me out of Grandpa's map and stuck me here, into reality, its contours so ominously clear?

We reached the Strahov hills, retracing the footsteps of Joseph K. Our steps rang out across the supercity, glassy and emptied of people, till finally we arrived at our destination: down the long corridor I saw eyes, a pair of remembering sharp eyes, and yet these were not the eyes of the hundred-year-old doctor, though they bordered on the animal; they belonged to a thousand-year-old ferryman, who never knew death. These eyes had travelled down the generations, from body to body, from face to face, like the tip of an illusion, like God's side of a coin, like ancestral longing. If Jews believe in the thirty-six just men, required in every generation for the survival of humanity, then these eyes, Josie, were surely some kind of condition laid down by God. They had travelled, till they reached down the long corridor to Mr Zámek, the Strahov stoker. And Mr Zámek knew. Mr Zámek had to know, because he was there.

'When my father wants to talk about himself, he always says "we". If I want to say something about my generation, I only talk about me,' said Ivan, somewhat inappropriately;

like me he was awkward in the presence of his own blood, perhaps because that blood in blue overalls ruled over fire so God-supplantingly, perhaps because it had intimate knowledge of black-outs in cellars . . . nothing at all could be read just now from the water of either.

The ferryman went up to the control panel, with its seductively glowing coloured buttons, and smiled insidiously. 'They're numbered, you see? You only have to press the right one and a whole Prague district goes up in smoke.' He went glum. 'There were times I was strongly attracted to the idea. Times dead and buried.'

He steers about the boiler room, Ivan and me obedient behind him.

'This is the pressure gauge or manometer,' he shouts over the roaring boilers. 'When they arrested me, I only had a Bible on me. With cheap colour prints . . . it could only happen to a non-believer.' The hags of Fate, despite their nasty ways, began to prance on clashing cymbals in a quasi-hieratic trance. 'Do you hear me? Do you hear me, son?'

Your overalls, sir, billowed like a sail. The boiler room, one crackpot's yell on the limit of hearing, floated out to sea. We followed after, we followed blindly after, but Ivan, your son, heard not a word.

'This big rudder is the armature. The one in patent-leather shoes turned out my pockets, and when he found only the book, he started leafing through it disappointedly. "Do you know, Mr Zámek," he began jovially, "who Jesus Christ was the son of?" Without waiting for an answer, he gave me a triumphant look: "Why, Herod of course, Mr Zámek, Herod himself. It's clear as anything. Herod had all the innocents slaughtered, in order to get rid of the heir to the throne. Do you get it? I didn't get a thing." (This, he said touching a mysterious vessel, is the expander.) "So this was discovered," eventually I managed to utter, "by our Prague secret police?" '

Ivan crouched in the corner. The Fates crept into the boilers. Strahov went quiet.

'That's a story from one of your books,' I said as softly as possible, but the echo cruelly amplified it.

'Really?' The blue sail went limp with embarrassment.

'Along with another. After seven years they let you out. You're walking along as if on thin ice, breathing deeply, the colourfulness of objects seems unbearable. With the Bible under your shirt you entered the first pub, and there you opened the book for the first time: "And God saw that the wickedness of man was great in the earth . . ." '

'You shouldn't have signed,' came a voice from the corner.

' "And it repented the Lord that he had made man on the earth, and it grieved him at his heart. And the Lord said . . ." '

'Dad, you shouldn't have signed . . .'

' "I will destroy man whom I have created from the face of the earth . . ." Suddenly someone put his hand on your shoulder. "Come along with me." You'd experienced this once already. Dully you snapped the book shut and hastily drank up your beer. Outside, you looked round in vain for a black Volga . . . the other, frowning all over, lifts his eyes to the sky: "Do you see it too, or am I just so pissed drunk?" The sun in the sky. In the sky hung the sun, a great blind sun in eclipse.'

On thin ice, deeply, unbearable . . . Yes, Josie, I seem to be unbearable. I want to drown, I want to sink beneath the surface with shame, but I am very consciously on guard, like the Spartakiad crowd up there, overhead, in the dust of the Strahov stadium. Comenius definitely wouldn't have been proud.

'You're right. Sometimes I really don't know what I've made up and what actually happened. It's my age . . .'

A sudden flash of regret against a blackboard's background, regret for entirely different fathers. At that moment, perhaps because it lit up our Malá Strana window too, the pencil in my respectable father's fingers instead of the commandments began to write crazy, oddball words, and instead of parables shaman-like zigzags and squiggles. The priest's sermon altered to a hornèd babble. Mr Zámek was old as Jericho and like some melody-I-don't-remember, like Gagarin's bones, he was old as the eyes of the ferryman, for whom death always got off the hook, and those eyes, whose bearer

he was, those eyes now—mother, smile, steppe, hold me—
fixed themselves upon me: 'I'm told you're writing a novel.'

Ivan's grin ran across my back.

'Yes, it's about a flood.'

I shake and expect a stream of questions, to which I am
accustomed from others, testing my fraudulence.

'Did you make it up, or did it happen?'

I can't believe it. To make certain I pass him a piece of
crumpled paper. On it a tree, plucked from its roots, in the
process of decomposition, on the threshold of carbonization,
long ago struck down by lightning. He looks at it horizontally,
that is to say correctly. It is beyond doubt. Mr Zámek, Strahov stoker and writer, must have experienced drowning just
like me. Beyond doubt he must have read Ivan popular remnants of myths and passed with him through the looking-
glass. Maybe he even spoke to him as you would to a child.

'Why did you sign it?' Ivan barked again.

Funny to think: thousands overhead have just put their
arms by their sides. I don't get what Ivan is talking about. He
squats in the corner, the clarinet wedged like a fishbone in his
throat.

'You never told me . . . you don't care what'll happen to
me . . . empty gestures, that's your speciality . . .'

'Come on, Věra, I'll show you something,' said Mr Zámek
quite calmly, taking me by the arm, while up above in the
dust of the stadium eager mothers made a big NO out of their
bodies.

I stand in the clashing cymbals and gaze at Ivan in a trance.
I gaze at his eclipse and cannot believe it . . . do you see it too
or am I just so . . . 'Poor thing,' I want to say to him, even
though I know there's no time for banality. 'Poor thing,' I say
to him, smiling at the rudder of the armature. Claws out,
trees sold, rivers in flames.

I let him take the lead. His hand trembles in mine. The
once elegantly disgusted fakir yells out after us stale truths
gone sour. Then goes quiet. It was so unexpected that both of
us, the ferryman and I, turned at once. Ivan rushed angrily
to the control panel. The stadium above gave a sputter of
applause.

'Ivan, Ivan, don't,' I try to shout. Too late. His furious fingers start towards the buttons and there's no way in the world I can slow this image down.

'Visit Europe, while it still exists!' he roars insanely over the panel and rips at the scenery.

In the big bang of the end I tick off one district after another: Vysočany, Karlín, Libeň . . . and Ivan's fingers hungrily touch oblivion, just as they recently touched me . . . Motol, Smíchov, Vyšehrad . . . from a stormy surface like this, Adèle, there's nothing at all to be read, and Ivan, though he did not create, will turn to dust both man, and beast, and the creeping thing, and the fowls of the air . . . Holešovice, Vršovice, Břevnov . . . Mr Zámek, restrain your barking son, save your wrathful blood, universe in a universe universe in a universe universe in a universe between a tree and an apple . . . Hradčany, Old Town, New Town, Malá Strana . . . But Mr Zámek only absent-mindedly smiled and laid his hand on my head without an axis: 'Leave him to it, Věra; once I was also very tempted.'

Hand in hand we descend to the underworld. Scattered lines of Spartakiadniks slowly raise themselves from the all-weather surface, loudspeakers urge calm.

'This is the collector. It has pipes leading under the whole Strahov stadium.'

Gloom, damp, dripping water.

'Come on, don't be afraid. I want to show you something. I've got this enterprising colleague, Prkno . . . it was his idea.'

Still hand in hand we grope down the underground tunnel, held by the sudden unaccustomed silence, in which Ivan's hysteria has instantly evaporated. The stuck pick-up arm slid and clicked in the hush. Where's he taking me? The passage took a sharp curve. We follow it, this complete stranger and I. Stranger . . . I remembered Ivan once indecipherably mumbling between two heartbeats: 'Damn it . . . those dads of ours . . . Don't you find it idiotically unpleasant sometimes, sharing a flat with a walking legend?'

His large, weighty hand in mine, his thirty-years-older breath above my head. And finally—his sail. His sail, on which you may see the schematic sign of prison bars like the shadow of Jesus' crucified body on the Turin shroud. Concentration camp, Jáchymov uranium mines, dozens of square-ruled exercise books in drawers, and in them stories, ones which happened and ones yet to happen, circle within circle on the surface. Stranger, ferryman with age-old eyes, Prague heating employee, walking legend, which I was about to kiss in sorrow and shame, shame for my crassly unfinished novel, for that undischargeable tribute, when my nose was hit by a terrible pong.

'It was my colleague's idea . . . Prkno . . . he started with coypus, but it was too hot for them here. You're the first I've ever shown our Crispin to, Věra.'

At that moment, hardly a few steps away, something grunted. Then I finally saw Crispin; at the far end of the passage, in a little pen of wooden planks, stood an enormous pink pig.

'Bohemia was flooded by the sea in the Palaeozoic age,' said the man, said the teacher, said schoolmaster Slavík. Events after that took a swift turn.

We were sitting with Kate in the yard of our house, just in our slippers, feeling neither quite alive nor dead, a couple of days before her departure, piously reminding ourselves of crop-spraying aircraft and do you remember Granny, Kate, and the Bible-that-was-a-tree, and at that moment Ivan appeared before us, he sprang from the ground, and his eyes were like never before.

'What's happened? Not off to Jericho, are you?' I'd spotted the bag on his back. 'Believe it or not,' he spoke slowly, yet breathlessly, it was curious, 'I've just run away from the police station. They had me in for interrogation about Dad. And as I was sitting there—one tapping away on the machine and another, awfully like the chap in the Kufr the other day, opposite me—suddenly something snapped and I said: "I want to go to the loo." Another man appeared in the door. "Take him to the toilet," said my one to him. I went out, the policeman showed me the loo and went off to some office. Sheer carelessness. So I'm all packed up, bring me a map, so I can get out of here as quick as possible.'

I ran quickly for a map. Fortunately respectable Dad was at a meeting of Evangelist youth and Mum, where was Mum? Maps. I pulled out one drawer after another and found nothing but Grandpa's creations. Billowing orange oceans, South America next to North, the Eskimo eye of Greenland, the Soviet Union, a softly forward-moving flounder. Finally I found the one they rubbed our noses in in geography: horribly realistic, because, Grandpa—I look to see the scale—such is the world.

We search with a finger for a crack in the outline of borders. It's daft, so daft I won't be able to put it in my book.

'It's daft.' Kate was the first to come to her senses.

'Now or never,' Ivan commanded, and I began to feel I was in some absurd Soviet anti-war movie. 'Anyway, I've got no passport. I'll cross at Sněžka,' he said, and he did.

A few days later I got a postcard from the Krkonoše, a mountain's silhouette and in that silhouette a fakir's shadow, the sigh of a drunken-away clarinet, the mark of lightning on the inner wall of the chapel whose solemn reopening was daily approaching. And on that postcard the words: 'And this is my home. This is the land whose soil I felt in my hand on that day in early autumn this year when I left it for ever.'

Perhaps it would have been more effective to have sprinted, but I preferred to be taken up to Strahov by bus. Mentally I repeat the words, which, articulated backwards, are only a hornèd babble to appease many-headed Svantovít. 'Mr Zámek . . . Ivan . . . I have to tell you that . . .'

My finger touches the bell, an eye for an eye, a golden tooth across the crack of twenty years. Behind the glass door I see the scurrying of people with reddened faces, wreathed in steam . . . I don't follow what's happening . . . why doesn't Mr Zámek come to the door? I hold my finger tight against the bell and don't let go; come on, ferryman, I summon him up, come and haul to the surface that truth which is now hanging on the spinner of your reel . . .

Mr Zámek stands before me.

'It's you, Věra,' he murmurs with emotion, hiding his hands behind his back.

'We've just,' he adds, awkward and proud at the same time, 'Crispin's just been . . .'

I look at his hands. Hands covered in. I look at Mr Zámek's hands, which are covered in blood.

(*Translated by James Naughton.*)

Michal Viewegh

extracts from the novel
The Blissful Years of Lousy Living

I

Quido's birth, according to Zita's calculation, was due to take place during the first week of August in the year 1962 in Podolí Hospital.

By then his mother had completed twelve seasons of her theatre career, though she regarded the majority of her roles, which were mostly as children in plays by Jirásek, Tyl, Kohout and Makarenko, as embarrassing sins of youth. After all, she was in her fourth year of law studies at the University, and viewed being an extra in the Czechoslovak Army Ensemble at the Vinohrady Theatre as a mere game of little consequence (on the other hand, this did not prevent her from presenting the more or less accidental circumstance by which the birth of her child was to coincide with the theatre company's seasonal break as an act of self-evident professional discipline). Paradoxically, under the patina of her amateur histrionic zeal, Quido's mother—a one-time star of school productions—was actually very shy and allowed nobody except Zita to examine her. Zita, chief obstetrician at the maternity ward in Podolí Hospital and long-standing friend of Grandmother Líba, had known Quido's mother since her childhood, and tried patiently to satisfy her quirks by promising to rearrange the doctors' schedule so that on the critical day there would be no men in the childbirth theatre to attend her in labour.

Zita makes giving birth
in Podolí a painless mirth,

jingled Grandmother Líba over lunch. Even Quido's father's
father, Grandfather Josef, although *a priori* sceptical of all
things Communist, not excluding health care, naturally, was
willing to admit that the probability of Quido's head being
squashed by obstetrical forceps was somewhat narrower than
in other times.

The one element no one took into consideration was the
bedraggled black Alsatian that appeared on 27 July, on a
scarlet-hued sunlit evening on the banks of the river Vltava
just as Quido's mother was struggling to climb out of a taxi,
and which—after a short, silent bound—pinned her against
the warm façade of the house on the corner of Anenské
Square. The stray dog's intentions could not be described as
openly hostile—first of all the animal did not leave her with a
single bite, although enough was achieved by landing its
entire weight on her slender shoulders, snuffling all over her
face with—as Mother herself put it later in a less than fortu-
nate manner—'a rancid stench of long-unbrushed teeth'.

'Aaahhh,' yelled Quido's mother, having partly recovered
from the initial shock.

True to his word, Quido's father was waiting for her in
front of the Theatre on the Balustrade, and on hearing the
scream he immediately charged forth. He was not quite sure
to whom the panic-stricken voice belonged, yet it at once
planted in him a gnawing suspicion which he did his utmost
to ignore.

Aaaahhh! The scream of Quido's mother grew ever more
piercing, since by this point the dog's front paws were liter-
ally crushing her brittle collar-bones. Quido's father was
regrettably correct in his suspicion. His body stiffened, para-
lysed by some unknown force which he subsequently
managed to shake off as he set out towards the voice dearest
to him. Filled with wrathful tenderness, he sprinted across the
granite paving stones of the square. His wife, he assumed,
was being assaulted by another of those innumerable
drunkards whose company—ever since performing the role

of Hettie the waitress in *The Kitchen* by Wesker—she quite simply did not exercise caution enough to avoid, preferring instead to convince them of something or other. The very moment, however, that he beheld his wife on her last legs trying to fend off the enormous black burden weighing her down, he did something which in Quido's eyes for ever lent him a stature far beyond his five feet and six inches. In full flight he grabbed the nearest dustbin, lifted it up and with the bottom edge bashed the dog to death on the spot.

Later, Quido's mother confirmed that the dustbin had been full to the brim, which as a fact can be, I think, positively discounted. Still worse, however, is that a *conscious* part in the whole incident—and hence also the right of testimony—is claimed by Quido himself.

'Of course I am not denying I was then—like any other foetus in the womb—probably blind,' he maintained later, 'but I must have had a way of perceiving all this, because how else to explain my being so strangely moved every time I watch the dustmen do their job?'

Presumably in an effort to better Leo Tolstoy, whose memory allegedly reached the very threshold of his infancy, Quido ventured even further: for instance, he tried over the years to manifest to his younger brother—with somewhat chilling seriousness—his accurate recollection of that sombre Rembrandtesque image of the maternal egg attached to the uterine mucous membrane like a swallow's nest.

'For Christ's sake, Quido, you're such a bullshitter,' objected Paco, piqued.

'Omitting the dog incident, I must say, pregnancy is to every single foetus with at least an ounce of intelligence a sentence to unimaginable tedium,' Quido went on unperturbed. 'I deliberately stress the *intelligent* foetus—unlike those bare-skinned, semi-paralysed cave olm fish, as happened to be your case even a few days after your birth when I had the ill-fortune of having to endure the sight of your foul purple face. Perhaps you will at least be able to *imagine* the horrendous tedium of those two hundred and seventy utterly uniform days, during which the already awakened consciousness is condemned to the idleness of eyeing the foetal water, occasionally kicking the abdomen walls to spare them up there any unnecessary panic. Two hundred and seventy long days which a young intellectually minded man has to spend like an synchronized swimmer training for the Olympics! Two hundred and seventy days without a decent book, a single written word, unless I take into consideration the hardly original insignia engraved on Dr Zita's little ring. Nine months in an aquarium with the lights turned off. I spent the last three months just praying for my mother to take a ride on a motorbike down a bumpy country lane or send me a couple of deep drags on a cigarette, if not directly a double shot of white vermouth. Believe one thing, brother: that dog was heaven-sent!'

The first time Quido overtly demonstrated his impatience was shortly after his mother, now crying hysterically, had collapsed into Father's open arms. The dead dog, however, drew considerable attention from the incoming audience, and for Mother the mere thought of further scandal, this time in the form of a premature birth, was clearly too much. So she dried her eyes and answered all the concerned questions with a courageously beaming smile: she was perfectly, really perfectly all right.

'My mother,' Quido later maintained, 'would never in her life have excused herself to go to the ladies' room while in company, unless she could do so entirely unnoticed. And, frankly speaking, she always got embarrassed merely blowing her nose.'

To this most intimate shyness, which lent her an aura of girlish grace, Quido's mother owed the protracted bouts of sinusitis and cystitis, the so-called habitual constipation, and, since 27 July 1962, also the 'in-theatre' child delivery. The first contractions had already started when she took off her checked three-quarter coat at the theatre cloakroom, yet she still managed to resist Quido—under Father's hypnotic sideways gaze—until the curtain came down, but not a minute longer. As soon as Estragon and Vladimir had exchanged their concluding lines and a brief silence had fallen, as it usually does before the applause, the first plaintive cry slipped from Quido's mother, immediately followed by a whole series of them. Quido's father leapt from his seat and forced his way to the foyer across the row of stultified spectators, darting out into the open night to make with calm and poise whatever arrangements were necessary, or so he undoubtedly thought. Luckily, an elderly lady to the right of Quido's mother came quickly to her rescue: two people sitting next to her she charged with the task of calling the ambulance while herself trying to get the woman in labour out of the crowded and stuffy auditorium. Quido's mother clung to the woman with all her might, scarcely daring to entertain the thought of giving birth in full view of so many men while simultaneously—she claimed later—finding it discourteous to spoil the Beckettian ambience of existentialist despair by something as optimistic as giving birth to a healthy child. However, despite all her resolve she collapsed at the feet of her escort precisely when passing down the aisle below the stage—on to which she was lifted by two men. They put her right at the feet of actors Václav Sloup and Jan Libíček who, about to receive the applause, went stiff with fright. Apart from the dozens of women hurling themselves at the stage without a second thought for their evening dresses, in order to share some of their own experiences with the young mother-to-be, the spectators remained seated, probably assuming the delivery scene about to take place was part of the experimental approach to the staging of the theatre play.

'Water. Hot water!' shouted someone, to show initiative. 'And clean sheets!'

'Clear the auditorium,' ordered one of the two medics present, when he had finally jostled his way to the woman in labour.

'Go away!' he implored urgently, but nobody moved a muscle.

'Aaargh!' groaned Quido's mother.

Within a few minutes the auditorium was filled with the screams of a new-born baby.

'And so he has arrived,' declaimed Jan Libíček, in a sudden bout of inspiration which for Quido became almost prophetic.

'Godot, Godot,' chanted the enraptured audience, while the two doctors took the credit with modest bows. (Fortunately the nickname did not stick.)

'We are redeemed,' bellowed Václav Sloup.

'Quido is his name,' whispered Quido's mother, but nobody heard. From the embankment came the sound of an ambulance siren approaching.

II

'To put things straight,' Quido told the publisher's editor years later, 'I have no intention whatsoever of depicting the whole so-called family tree and persistently shaking its over-laden branches until some dead building contractor or Count Thun's estate keeper drops off to tell me who I am, where I come from and that Masaryk had the workers shot at!'

'We better leave Masaryk out of it,' said the editor in a conciliatory tone. 'Your grandfather on your father's side was a miner?'

'You picked on the right one,' Quido laughed. 'He wanted to be a hotel proprietor! You should've heard him! When they got an unexpected visit from Party headquarters in the Tuchlovice mines and it was too late to reschedule my grand-father's shift, the comrades decided it was better not to let him come out of the pit. While the other miners debated with the Party delegation, Grandfather, abandoned deep under-ground, cursed and banged the piping system in fury. The miners called him Cinderella.'

'That's good,' said the editor. 'But what of it . . . ?'

'Exactly,' said Quido. 'What of it . . . ?'

Quido's father was born highly intelligent into lowly sur-roundings. For twenty-one years, he confronted it day in, day out: the ever-unmade bed, the odour of gas and warmed-up leftovers, empty bottles and bird food scattered around. Directly outside the windows of their one-bedroom apart-ment on the ground floor in Sezimova Street, the drunkards would vomit as they left the adjacent Baseth restaurant. The dirty façade was often smeared with the blood of the gypsies from Nusle. Grandfather used to leave home early in the morning or straight after lunch in a miners' bus to Kladno; when back home he would pace up and down the room smoking, with the bird food crackling under his feet.

'Fucking life,' he often used to say.

On other occasions he would spend hours feeding the budgies or playing Louis Armstrong and Ella Fitzgerald records at full volume. Grandmother, a fur-coat seamstress, spent all her time at home sewing from dawn to dusk. Dragging her feet across the creaking parquet floor around an old clothier's dummy, her mouth full of pins. Quido's father did his best to stay out of the house. He and his friend Zvára would climb over the battlements at Vyšehrad. They played hide and seek in the carriages on the sidings at the Vršovice railway station. Sometimes they stayed overnight in the great hall at high school. Later they sat in the college library, as Quido's father wished, or in Demínka coffee bar, as Zvára wanted. They did voluntary jobs and two evenings a week Quido's father attended classes at the School of Foreign Languages. Coming home late at night and reading under the small desktop lamp from an English textbook which he propped up against the cage covered in budgie excrement, at times he experienced a feeling tantamount to that of reciting the words of a mysterious prayer.

At some point towards the beginning of the fourth semester at college, Zvára brought Quido's father a theatre ticket. To judge by the expression on Zvára's face, it was obvious that the girl for whom the ticket was originally intended had for some reason turned it down.

'What is it for?' asked Quido's father. 'Who wrote it?' He was not a theatre-goer and the play's title could not be expected to mean much to him. Still, he wanted to have an escape route in case the ticket proved too expensive.

'It's for a load of rubbish,' said Zvára as if seeking acknowledgement from the passers-by. 'Shakespeare, I guess, who else?'

But he was wrong. They were showing Lorca's *The Shoe-*

maker's Prodigious Wife. During the interval they met Zvára's former girlfriend, who introduced them to her companion, a slim bespectacled girl in a dark-blue velvet dress with a lace collar.

'And with no budgie stains,' Quido always added.

It was Quido's mother.

Three months later Quido's father won an invitation to the flat on Paris Commune Square. He noticed, of course, the size of the two rooms, the height of the ceiling, the French-polished concert piano and the many paintings, but he was most impressed by Grandfather Jiří's study: the whole of the far wall was lined with mahogany bookshelves holding at least a thousand volumes, and in front of them stood a so-called American bureau, also in dark wood, with a rolling, arched top covering a typewriter and other innumerable stationery items, including sealing wax, a family seal and a knife for opening letters.

'Do take a seat.' Grandfather Jiří motioned him to a leather easy chair.

'Would you object to some carrot spread?' Grandmother Líba hurried in from the kitchen to inquire.

'For over twenty years indeed,' said Grandfather with gloom in his voice and lit a Dux cigarette.

'I am not asking you,' Grandmother laughed teasingly. 'I am asking Mr Graduate.'

'I eat anything,' said Quido's father, being honest. 'Don't worry about me.'

'Don't worry,' said Quido's mother, somewhat ominously. 'My mother doesn't in the least.'

Although neither Grandfather nor Grandmother altogether abandoned their guardedness (after all, Quido's mother was their only daughter), the visit exceeded all expectations. Quido's father proved to be a young man of mild manners, who weighed his words with honesty. Eventually Grandfather came to find him a more sympathetic listener than most of the young actors, poets and scriptwriters who came there to read their own pieces, blaming Grandfather for the horrors of the fifties and spilling red wine on the table.

'Come again,' he said, rather curtly, as he bid him goodbye, though Quido's mother knew there and then that Quido's father had passed with flying colours.

III

'I was a premature baby, then,' Quido maintained. 'Both grandmothers were alarmed. When I was one year old I weighed fourteen kilos, but they went on making every effort to keep me alive. Even when I was five years old they continued, by means of chocolate-coated bananas, the struggle to safeguard my mere existence.'

Quido was the first grandchild for both families, and therefore was caught in a constant tug of war. All (with the exception of Grandfather Jiří) tried to outpull each other over who was to take little Quido to the zoo most often. For a long time, Quido thought that hippos, ostriches and kangaroos were domestic animals . . .

Where to go from the zoo but to a cake shop?

'What's that gorgeous smell, little Quidee?' grandmother Věra would ask.

'It must surely be coffee,' fat little Quido would answer in tones so mellifluous that everybody in the cake shop was overtaken by a feeling of nauseated dismay.

When Quido's mother introduced her son to somebody in the theatre, a note of defiant caution crept into her voice.

'Especially after one well-known documentary director asked whether she'd mind my performing in their forthcoming educational project about the advantages of hormonal contraception,' maintained Quido. 'However—I do realize—it was the only period in my life during which I received maximum affection in return for minimum reason. They simply loved me for who I *was*. Blessed days!'

Grandfather Josef would take Quido along when he went fishing, to a football match or to feed the seagulls.

'Here we go!' Grandfather hollered in the Eden Stadium.

'C'mon, scoff it down,' he called to the seagulls by the Vltava.

'Stay stuck, or I'll tan your hide,' he ranted when the writhing earthworm refused to be skewered on to the fishhook.

All of this would happen in a horrendous, and to Quido then inexplicable, hurry. When they were at home, Grandfather was already rushing to be at the football match as soon as possible; before half-time he was already racing to buy a sausage at refreshments on the outside terrace, and before they had finished eating they were already dashing back so that nobody could take their seats—and twenty minutes from the end they jostled through the cursing spectators on their way home. Grandfather rushed to go fishing and back from fishing, rushed to work and back from work, to the pub and back from the pub. The moment he reached one place, something drove him elsewhere. It took Quido a long time to comprehend the source of that inner restlessness: his grandfather was in a rush to have this fucking life over and done with as soon as he could.

Quido, unlike his father and grandfather, was fond of the little flat in Sezimova Street. He did not live there, but Grandmother Věra often took care of him, and so he did not have to go to day care. Instead, he could play with the soft furs, and there were three budgies flying about. Then Quido would contemplate how, while his equals in age were on some boring educational programme, he could lounge around on a sheepskin pillow, watching the budgies climb the smoke-stained curtains. Grandmother had them so well trained that she could leave the window open without having to worry about them flying away. They used to stroll along the window-sill and only when one of the thousands of noisy local pigeons swooped down to join them would they fly in panic back to their guardian, to settle on her head and shoulders. To protect herself against their claws, Grandmother used to fix empty pin cushions on her slip straps in the summer.

'When all three birds took their positions,' Quido maintained, 'two on her shoulders and one on the crown of her head, she acquired a symmetrical effect approximating an altar.'

What drove Quido mad, on the other hand, was Grandfather's habit of sharing his food with the budgies: Grandfather would first diligently chew up the respective portion of food, open his mouth wide—and the birds immediately landed on him and began pecking against his yellowed false teeth to claim what was theirs.

'Never in my life, not even in any of those blue movies,' maintained Quido, 'have I ever seen anything more disgusting than those three feathered heads awash with saliva, sliding their beaks intermittently into Grandfather's mouth full of beef sirloin in sour-cream and root-vegetable sauce.'

(*Translated by O. T. Chalkstone.*)

Alexandra Berková

extract from the novella
The Sufferings of Devoted Lousehead

... originally there is nothing—fields of force—waves, eddies—look, smoke: where is there any right angle in this?

The photograph shows two small apes: they hug each other tightly, feverishly, gazing into the lens with big questioning eyes. The caption reads: a pair of frustrated baby apes . . .—and muddled-up humanity still sings . . .

anyhow, there's another way of saying all this:
   once upon a time everyone lived in Paradise happy as cats—
   —they rolled in the smooth soft grass and lacked for nothing:
   they searched for beechnuts, basked in the sun, cuddled each other, tasted and mutually intertwined their limbs, frolicking and wrestling together—
   and the sun rose and set and divine energy passed from one form into another—
   —and that into another and that into another and so on . . .
   and everything living devoted itself to that flow, like the birds to the air and the fish to the waters—
   and one beast devoured another—and everything was in its place—
   and so it went on for about a thousand years and a thousand thousand years—
   and the Highest said to his most devoted angel, who was just then licking His toes: Be off to the rocks, lousehead, you're boring me!

—and within devoted Lousehead there was a clap of thunder—

he blackened on the spot like every guilty one—

and, understanding nothing, crawled off to the side to tremble;

and water for him is no longer water, grass grass, night night, or day day—

all has wound itself up into squirming anxiety: immobilizing—paralysing—stifling—rain falls in his eyes, his belly is full of snakes, and in his heart there is only coldness and dark and silence without echo, as he groans without response:

come burst my heart, let me crumble to dust—

eyes, trickle out into that dust—

black soul, abandon the body and never return; the sun shines on everyone alike, only above me is there a cloud, for the umbilical cord of His love has ceased to throb and there is no other nourishment, since I can no longer roll in the grass at His feet . . .!

. . . oh, Lousehead, Lousehead,

as long as the God of the Waters ruled over the waters and the God of Wind over the wind, as long as the God of Grasses dwelt in the grass and the sun warmed everyone alike, the world was free and easy—

—but for what, Lousehead, tell me that?

How can you know the light, without knowing the dark?

How can you know good, without knowing evil? eh?

you can't—you don't. Because you're an idiot.

I mean, you don't even want to know, Lousehead, admit it!

I mean, it was enough for you to roll in the grass at His feet . . . but it isn't enough for Him: for Him this is insufficient, He requires more; He wants to see a bit of action—change—evolution—results;

And He will help you in this evolution, for you are His chosen one! He wants to make you perfect, because He loves you, Lousehead, do you see? That's why in His infinite kindness he will let you experience many adversities: he will persecute you with grief and woe and hardship; he will drive you out of the mother's womb into a tempest of wrath—for you to overcome it; to make yourself better!—Is this not wondrous? He will visit you with suffering and pain, blood, sweat and tears . . .

—and are you glad? Lousehead? What?

. . . Oh—instead of offering up thanks you only writhe in the mud, you mouldy old cretin!

Lousehead set out on his travels: he was cast out and rejected; all right. Most likely with reason . . . Probably he really is—bad, otherwise it would all be pointless, wouldn't it . . . but he'll sort it all out: at last they've given him a clear picture of what is expected. And he'll show them; he'll go out into the world and show them he isn't entirely useless. That he knows how to try, to work and work to the point of complete self-abnegation. That he knows how to make sacrifices. That he can practise self-denial for the sake of others. Unstintingly. For ever. Until they come and say: Lousehead, you're really quite OK now. Come and be received among us again.

Yes: it will be so. Of course—he'll have to try hard. But he's not so badly off, really: at least he has a rag and a stick. And if he's lucky, he'll even find a bowl . . .

—We're a quite appalling society, really—just look at the number of sick already beaten to death by our merciless Samaritans—

but we're expecting Lousehead's arrival any day now—

in the meanwhile we alter the rules of grammar and treat ourselves with sensitive folk: squeezing out the marrow, digging out the pearls with a knife; helping ourselves simply as best we can: after all the gardener has to torture the roses when his knife forces them into flower; listen to how beautifully this unfortunate groans—and when I hurt him again: o-o-o-oh . . .!

Naturally we throw the pearls back in the sea, to keep them rare, and if any girls are too beautiful we kill them, foreigner; how else could we go on loving them?

Tortured children make such wonderful poets of course!—this one, for instance: he's a doughty songster; his mother never embraced him, his father rejected him—would you like to strike him blind?

Lousehead set off, knowing not where, but the country seemed friendly: tall pink grass wound itself about his ankles, clinging to his garb with tiny fingers, all three suns softly glided towards the west—above them rose a green moon with a soft swish. A blue-tinged breeze sifted the sandy dunes to the side of night, and silvery insects, gliding in airy eddies, buzzed their evening songs. The green sea, too, readied itself for sleep: boomingly it began to turn the water over and downward, till it faced the sky with white shells up—the sky black and low, because full of stars, as skies are wont to be, when magnificent.

... and everything was there, yes, everything was there: steep hills with tops lit by the newly rising sun—their greenery silken silvery—and the valleys steeply down amidst them: green-black—black-green—deep, cool and dark; yes, everything was there: peaks of hills, sky, clouds—space—light and shade—the sky's open embrace—and God: yes.

... everything around is so lovely—only Lousehead cannot see it: for he has just left Paradise and entered the dreadful country of men ...

And Lousehead came to see that the world, which gives rise to stories, wishes in its turn to be nourished only with stories, and he travelled on; narrator of that which he lived.

... and he came to the Northern Land. In that land wolves howl and the north wind blows and the houses are as far from one another as parents from their children. And the people in that land are taciturn and shy, with melancholy deep eyes.

They greeted Lousehead kindly and listened carefully to what he had to say. Some rewarded him richly. Others wept inconsolably. Others simply remained sitting or standing—and remained this way for many years and the children planted rambler roses about them. And others, when they heard the amazing tidings, tore their garments and went off to the woods to live with the wild beasts . . .

In that land at dusk the men sit down together in dark huddles and they silently drink. They drink until someone among them suddenly laughs out loud and falls to the ground. The rest go on drinking, until they also laugh and fall—and so on, and round in a circle, because those who fall without managing to laugh repeat the entire ritual as long as is needed for success, and those who succeed are so delighted that they long to repeat the experience, and so it is always hard to put an end to the ritual, indeed there are places in the Northern Land where it continues for whole ages uninterrupted . . .

And in that land there are also villages with large houses and in every house there is a mother and a son. The last son, who did not find the strength to leave. The son keeps to the house and the mother looks after him.

. . . for God is malicious, that's why! This is in return for all those toiling days and weeping nights, for all that endless waiting for the one who brought me here and promised to love me! and then you all ran away, all of you ran away and left me here!—but I shall keep the last one!! he is mine!! he shall stay with me—he needs me—can't you see? look at how weak he is, what would he do without me, poor thing?— come, come over here and show yourself, you want to go out into the world, don't you? somewhere far away? among strangers? away from your Mummy? yes? So there you are, you see, he won't even speak to a stranger—what would he do living among strangers . . . so be off and mind your own business and leave us be!

. . . the son stands at the side and looks elsewhere. He won't run off. He's in his shell of love and fear and limy tears; as long as he stays inside it, his mother will live. As long as his mother lives, the son will stay inside. It has been like that for years. There is no way out. And Lousehead saw that the world was very strange . . .

Nail in his bonnet—bee in his coffin:
Mud-block! Gold-tongue! Know-all!

Know-block! Mud-tongue! Gold-all!
Gold-block! Know-tongue! Mud-all!
intercede for us!

In the Southern Land people are noisy and energetic; dressed in bright clothes, they like to live out of doors, yelling at one another, whooping out loud and making rude gestures, insulting, sticking tongues out at one another and showing their bare bottoms to the great amusement of those present, who always gather in abundant numbers, laughing and clapping and taking sides, till they all get into a brawl and go to the tavern to drink it off—

—they drink together and sing and dance, embracing one another, calling each other brother—clasping each other round the shoulders, weeping tears because they are not good enough as brothers, and their love is not brotherly enough— and they stab at each other with knives—and whoever does not die, he falls to the ground and sleeps.

And Lousehead saw that there were many things in the world which he did not understand, and having discovered that meanwhile they had stolen his gifts from the Northern Land and his bowl and stick, he went on further and the world became ever more strange.

What do you have these golden pitchforks for, my old woman?

We worship pitchforks here, stranger.

Why, my old woman?

Why not, my young blade?

She has a point—thought Lousehead and nothing ever surprised him again.

The Islanders were very surprised to hear that on the continent there were also sensible human beings who did not devour their neighbours, indeed, they even managed without outside help to read and write and eat with a knife and fork.

Lousehead liked the Islanders. He liked them very much. More precisely—he liked them so much that he would have liked to be one of them: yes, Lousehead strongly and achingly desired to remain on the Island; it would have been lovely to be one of those calm, elevated, slightly bored individuals; he would also lead their elevated, unperturbed, self-evident existence—and the rest of the world could go to pot . . .

He had to mesmerize the Islanders. He would dazzle them with the power of his imagination. This time he would prepare his tale in advance, leaving out the everyday banalities, cheap jokes and tortuous anecdotes, and he'd avoid horrifying anyone unnecessarily. He would concentrate on noble speech and the magic power of imagery: for the Islanders nothing but the best.

It was five days before Lousehead dared to set foot in the market. Another five days before he felt himself ready to sit down beneath the arches on an empty potato crate; he sat himself down and rubbed his temples. He sipped a little water and began to speak. He had meant to speak of the finest of his journeys, but he soon found to his surprise that he was speaking about Paradise: about how they lived together with the animals in peace and friendship as various parts of one single great I; how it was quite natural to understand the speech of the trees and the animals; how some were stronger and others faster, one more agile, another more colourful, another the biggest of all—and no one was superior to anyone; no lion felt himself to be lord of the fish and ruler over their lives, no tiger hired dogs for his protection and wanted the worms to work for him, and if the leader of the pack was weak and incapable, the pack simply tore him to pieces . . . Lousehead spoke with great tenderness and love. The Islanders smiled politely. Lousehead told a noble story of friendship and strength—the Islanders smiled politely. Lousehead spoke at length and in detail of the battle with great fire—the Islanders smiled politely. Lousehead spoke of ceremonials of love: he described the festive air of the whole settlement, the beauty and desire of the young couples, the ardent breath of the fertility dance by the night fires and the wailing songs of mothers bidding farewell to children as they embarked on the path of adulthood . . . The Islanders smiled politely. Lousehead timed the action, heightened the tension, elaborated with suggestive detail and flourished well-tested points—and the Islanders smiled. Lousehead stopped, and the Islanders clapped politely. One Island woman rose and publicly confessed before all that she had found Lousehead's presentation most entertaining! And did you really live through all that? you don't say! it must have been perfectly ghastly! you poor creature!—but surely it's much better now, isn't it? it was really really good of you, really, really! thank you!—and now, excuse me . . . she smiled sweetly at Lousehead and vanished into the throng. Several others smiled at him encouragingly, they clapped him on the shoulder—and left also. Lousehead watched the Islanders parading up and down, smiling sweetly at one another, and he felt like bursting into tears . . . for the first time he felt on the Island what it meant to be really alone . . .

. . . it is written that free fluttering Angst cries out to be anchored . . . and too much desire is its own punishment: you long for a warming embrace? damned lump of pruritus?— you're just weak ugh a weakling ugh, and undeserving of love!

In the Land of the Best the best people live, who have simply everything, who know and are acquainted with everything. They are the best of nations, and this makes them truly and sincerely unhappy: ah we the best people, they say, have nothing to strive for and aim at, no one to compete with and nothing to live for, for our land is the very best and there is nothing to beat it, so wherever we go, we find nothing but hypocrisy and envy and beggary, because all the rest of you are living in countries worse than ours;

except that our old people, those who made this land the best, are old now, and our young, who ought to—etcetera— just hang about, because what is there to make a song and dance about, when life here, with all its misery, is still the best to be had on the planet—

—so many young people pay the devil with their lives for their dreams about an absolute other world, they sniff this devil, inject it into their veins and deafened with the beating of their own blood they cry out: hey, God, is this all you can do? didn't exactly bust a gut, did you, I expected more!

—and every day many boats and vessels come to our shores with thousands of immigrants from worse countries who know that what would take them twenty years of hard graft at home can be found here on a garbage heap;

—and every day two or three ships come to our shores with an ambassador or a king asking for spiritual aid, for financial aid, or for military aid, or simply to look the place over, stick around for a bit, and buy a few knick-knacks—

—for there's plenty to be had: curtains for windows so strong they make darkness out of daylight—lamps so strong they make day out of night;

non-alcoholic wine, decaffeinated coffee, sugar-free cakes, nicotine-free cigarettes and touch-free sex;

bullet-proof silk for wedding dresses;

we've artificial flowers which never need watering, artificial trees with artificial birds in their branches, women with perfect bodies and succulent lips; powerfully developed men with muscular embraces, multiple-speed with auto-switching, in a range of sizes and colours, with home delivery and energy source in the price;

We offer a variety of fast exits, instant far-removers and get-the-hell-out-of-herers; illusifiers, amnesiators, stupefactors and plenty more, multicolour and bright, designed for the use of all those who do not know how to kill whatever time is left . . .

You want to be perfect, laughing on the beach like those handsome hunks in our leaflet? come over to our fit-centre!

You want to regain your originality, calm assurance and awareness of personality? come over to our fat-centre!

Buy our black-line vehicles for night driving and our silver-line vehicles for driving in the early dawn beside the ocean and our dead-line vehicles for one-time use only!

We also have many accessory appliances, which make your life so wonderfully simple: they knit, they sew, they cook, they wash, they roast, they fry, they launder, they clean, they shop in superstores, water your flowers, phone your parents, play with your kids, discuss your husband's work with him, go to the sauna, or the masseur, exercise and never age: they are

self-repairing and self-renovating, self-cleaning, self-disman-
tling, and they throw themselves on the junk heap;

we have many highly valuable services here which simplify
your life: we've read it for you—we've travelled it for you—
we've lived it for you, we've eaten it for you;

You can phone for a woman, submissive, lascivious, phone
for a man, brutal and tender, phone for a mother, loving and
kind, who sings lullabies for a premium, phone for a father,
full of understanding, who values your work and trusts you;
you can phone for a total friend, in whom you can absolutely
confide, and a bringer of good tidings, who will confirm that
your mortal enemy has gone bust, his son's out robbing, his
wife's in the gutter, but your shares keep going up and up;

And many other wonderful items have we here, and yet we
are very, very concerned, because we feel the enormous
weight of responsibility for the fate of the world, as it staggers
along clumsily behind us, so we can't enjoy our wonderful
toys properly . . .

Mesmerized by the dazzling brightness like a child in a
department store, Lousehead said to himself; ah well, I don't
have to understand everything in this world, do I—and he
went on his way.

Missus: I've seen Him! I definitely know it was Him, it was
terrifying, He had the shape of a fiery ball, He rolled me into
the grass, I was very, very frightened, I was so afraid! I waited
totally stiff with fear for what would happen next—in case
He did something to me—it was awful—awful—

Reporter: What happened next?

Missus: Nothing—All of a sudden He vanished. The fiery
ball was simply gone—so I got up and I went home.

Reporter: Were you burnt or scorched or anything?

Missus: No—not at all—well, not much. Actually I don't
know, it was a long time ago. It just simply vanished. He
vanished. It was Him, I'm certain of that.

Forty-year-old: I saw Him too—I was just going down this
street with my wife, early one evening, and suddenly I looked
up: and it was raining smoked mackerel. My wife and I were
totally amazed. How come, we said to each other, how come

it's raining smoked mackerel? Isn't it a bit odd? Because the sky was cloudless, you see—

Reporter: And then?

Forty-year-old: Well, as I say: the flowerbeds were full of smoked mackerel, the lawns too and the pavements and balconies and roofs. I'm certain it was Him.

Workman: I'd just got into the bath one day—and suddenly I looked: and I saw a snake in the bath. About thirty metres long, maybe more. I said to myself, what's this supposed to mean, eh? what's a snake doing in my bath? it's not another assault on the unions is it?—and all of a sudden it reared up opposite me—with a head like a horse—and sort of horns on it as it were—and it looked at me with its great big yellow eyes—it was quite clear to me at that moment that if I didn't get right out of there, things would be bad, that bath was his. At least for the time being. So I skedaddled out of that bathroom—at a rate of knots!—well—and when I went back a week later the snake was gone. There was only a kind of special whiff left behind—I don't know how to describe it— like disinfectant? rotten apples? I can still smell it now— it must have been Him, it's clear to me, I'm certain of it . . .

Schoolmistress: I believe I was also honoured by the presence—at the time I was just taking my class through the park over there, it was a Wednesday morning—about twenty-five years ago—we were just walking along that path over there, when a man stepped out of the bushes. Shabby, unshaven, in a long coat—I thought—you know what—I was simply scared—and with the children present too—but he only looked at me sort of sadly, very sadly—then he turned round and went away. I'm certain it was Him. I'll never forget that look of His . . .

Man with a beard: Come on, please, what's all this nonsense? these days every child knows that Lousehead doesn't really exist! he's a mythical figure! an abstract idea, like a white unicorn, the devil or Socialism!

Nobody contradicts the man and nobody takes his part. The witnesses who have just finished speaking look patiently to one side with a sense of benevolent superiority, waiting politely for the man to finish. The reporter steers the camera towards the centre of action, the sound-man holds the microphone under the man's chin, the cameraman films it all.

Man with a beard (into the silence): Wake up, people! No saviour is coming to save us! No one suffered for us, no one will pray and intercede for us! We have to suffer and achieve everything by ourselves!

Crowd: (murmurs its dissent)

Bald person: look 'ere, you, belt up!

Man with a beard: Let's just go and talk about it some more; once we've discussed it together, you'll see we'll come to a better understanding!

Woman from the crowd: Nobody gives a shit about you!

Crowd: (murmur of assent)

Man with beard: (falls silent)

(Between ourselves, the professor is a fool. We who secretly worship Lousehead, opposing the official orthodoxy of the Virgin, we know what we know . . .)

Another witness: I think at present He's only watching to see if we deserve to be saved. I had a cat once—with her I could absolutely feel how she used to study me. Watch me. Always behind me watching what I was doing and where I put something and what I was eating and sticking her nose into everything—well I really got all worked up about it— and how furious she was with me if I had a drink!—till one day I came back a bit early from the pub, and I caught her reading: she was staring at the timetable, leafing through it with her paw, as if she was looking for something. The minute she spotted I was watching she started to stretch herself and lick and behave like a cat, but I'd seen it perfectly well!!! and I know very well it was Him! it was Him for a dead cert . . . because that same day she scarpered off somewhere—I suppose she'd found her connection . . .

The cameraman goes round the witnesses with the camera on his shoulder, the film-crew girl powders their noses, the crowd thickens.

The Little Land is actually just as large as most of the rest, but somehow the belief has taken root locally that it is small and that what it produces is also small: its thinkers think small thoughts and its people make trivial things. From time to time this myth is effectively maintained in the interests of foreign powers, it is passed on from father to son, and the people of that country feel that they are small and regard their history as futile. This is so ingrained that on greeting each other on the streets they say: hi, what a bloody awful nation we are, have a nice day.

And so it is the custom to pass over as utterly without interest anything that was ever a success, whereas great attention must be devoted to every failure: the newspapers comment on anything of the sort in great detail, always reaching the same conclusion: 'but of course it was only to be expected that by international standards we would come off badly, do we ever do well in anything? after all, we are only a small nation.' And the men of that country sit around in pubs honouring lost battles, and nodding their heads contentedly: so you see, it hasn't rained again for three weeks, what a bloody awful nation we are ... and old women, returning homeward at dusk with a full cloth-load of grass, say before the setting of the sun: did you ever see the like, such a bloody awful parliament, I really dunno why we're such a bloody awful nation ...

And when election time comes, they say on the village green, dunno if I'll bother to go and vote, dear, I mean to say, there's no point, all the same rogues and bastards and defenders of the interests of foreign powers will get in again—but there you are, you see, we're just such a bloody awful nation ...

... and when the rogues and bastards and defenders of the interests of foreign powers get back into parliament more or less without any difficulty, the people say, as well they might: well, didn't I tell you, again it's all the same rogues and bastards and defenders of the interests of foreign powers, I dunno, we're just such a bloody awful nation ...

And so there are no greater glories in that land than the glorious anniversaries of martyrs' deaths and the even more glorious anniversaries of battles lost.

... but in all the people of that land there is anxious unease and pain and longing for something better—so they befriend one another a lot and support each other and slander each other and hurt each other and silently drink together and loudly sing and philosophize at length on the absurdity of existence and passionately argue about how to help the world—and then they all look forward with tremulous anticipation to the future, undoubtedly splendid, because inevitably that day is nearing when the Little Land will rouse itself to great deeds and knock spots off all the great nations . . .

That land was nothing but perpetual chaos and clamour and bustling activity and chuckling and tears and mournful silence, because nothing was ever settled once and for all, all was in constant flux—but Lousehead, God knows why, liked it there; maybe it was because the people there weren't as elevated as the Islanders, they were more like him—and maybe because he was pretty exhausted—anyway he got the idea it mightn't be a bad thing if he just stayed there—

so he set off straight away for the market:

I'm the site administrator—who are you?

A narrator.

Narrator of what?

Stories.

Nobody's interested in that around here.

You are not interested in tales of distant lands?

No. Nobody's interested in nowt round here, seeing as we're such a bloody awful nation.

Oh just leave me be, good man, Lousehead said encouragingly, I'll have a try and we'll see how it goes.

Five drachmae up front, said the site administrator, and he grabbed the coins and left.

Lousehead sat down in the shade of a linden tree and waited for an audience to gather. After a while a stranger came up and said: I'm the site administrator, and who are you?

I'm a narrator, but I have to point out that, if you're not a fraud, the one who claimed to be site administrator before you is.

That's all right, he's my deputy, this one said, gimme eight drachmae or clear off.

So Lousehead paid up, because a couple of layabouts were standing around, and though they didn't sit down, they were showing a certain vague, non-committal interest.

Then another site administrator turned up and three more after him—still, by now there were a few more layabouts who'd just happened to pass by, so Lousehead began:

I have travelled through many lands and experienced many remarkable things; of these I am about to tell.

Numskull: Wot for?

Lousehead: I am a wayfarer and narrator. I have travelled through many lands and—

Numskull: That's nothing, that's crap, I found a dead bloke in the willows once.

Gaptooth: It's a fact, I can bear witness.

Numskull: Yeah. Him over there can bear witness.

Specs: Leave him alone, let him finish.

Lousehead: As I was passing through the Land of Turquoise . . .

Numskull: Wot's turquoise?

Gaptooth: A battle-axe.

Specs: Rubbish, you're thinking of a cuirasse—It's a type of breast-plate, made of iron.

Woman in the crowd: Turquoise is a colour, in't it?

Numskull: Shut your face!

Lousehead: They called it the Land of Turquoise because of the rare green-blue mineral which formed the bottom of its great transparent lakes, where silver fish darted about in the limpid waters.

Numskull: Piss them, and their lakes.

Specs (to Numskull, kindly): Shut up.

Gaptooth: While we're on the subject—has the sludge pump been round this year?

Numskull (to Specs): Look 'ere, gimme a break, gimme a break . . .

Specs (to Gaptooth): OK, OK.

Someone in the crowd: Shut up, for Christ's sake!

Numskull: Who said that??

Specs: Let it go, it's all right, cool down . . .

Numskull: Then what's he fucking getting at me for, fucking bastard??

Someone in the crowd: Who're you calling a fucking bastard, you piece of shit!

Numskull: (with a brief howl he rushes off after the voice)

Lousehead sits on the ground amidst the brawl, sheltering his head under a blanket, and feeling paradoxically at just the right time and place . . .

(*Translated by James Naughton.*)

Michal Ajvaz

The Beetle

At last I have found the information I have been seeking for years; it reveals the location of a secret passage leading to the malachite palace on the bank of an underground river, the palace where I was invited to a fête twenty years ago. In my search I have in vain read through forty-six volumes of the *Oxford Encyclopedia* which now burden my head, shifting painfully inside my skull whenever I turn in bed at night—and now, all of a sudden, I find detailed directions in a footnote on the page of a handbook about rabbit-breeding published on poor quality paper by the Association of Small Animal Breeders in a certain regional town. This was to be expected, of course! Nobody ever reads footnotes, everyone is always in a hurry to get to the end of the book as if he were paid for reading by the metre, people even learn to read faster by using special methods, and if it were at all possible, they would probably prefer to have the contents of the book injected into their brain in the form of a concentrate so that they would not have to waste their time reading. Nobody wants to interrupt his journey to descend into the dark basement of the page and come back again. Such readers are partly excused by the fact that in most cases footnotes contain only references to other books, which—if they exist at all—are inaccessible anyway because they are hidden in deep, rocky lairs. Besides, the space for the footnote is often used as a dump for junk of all sorts that gets swept there from the book, along with various poisonous words that can cause painful infections in the brain. But our dear readers would still be too lazy to make a detour even if they knew that the footnote contained a recipe for the philosopher's stone to be whipped up with ingredients from their own kitchen. I don't quite understand where they're off to in such a stubborn hurry; it seems they don't realize that what they are so breathlessly chasing through the book cannot be caught because they keep running ahead of it. A book's true message can be found only by the reader who strolls through the lines at his leisure as if he were taking a walk along the sea shore, listening to the quiet sound of the waves of language. And so the slow walker overtakes the fastest runner. What would those book sprinters think of my friend, an archaeologist who was exploring the capital of a long-lost Asian empire, half sunken in the waters of a mountain lake. To read the constitution of the empire carved in hieroglyphics on the stone façade of a high temple, he had to move laboriously along the wall, getting a foothold in the shallow recesses and clinging on to small slippery protrusions with his hands. His main difficulty was that almost every sentence referred to a footnote located under the surface; yet my friend did not hesitate to climb down the wall and plunge into the icy waters of the lake each time he came to an asterisk floating over the end of a word. As he cleared the wall of algae and molluscs to be able to read the hieroglyphic text, he could hear a strange noise like the clatter of castanets: they were the countless voracious fish of the lake gnashing their teeth as they closed in on him in smaller and smaller circles. He would then climb up the steep wall again to resume reading where he had left off, mauled by the fish, soaking wet and garlanded with algae fluttering in the freezing mountain wind, only to descend under the surface again after a short while. However, this footnote tells me that the door of the corridor leading to the underground malachite palace can be found in the back wall of an overstuffed wardrobe located in an apartment in the Prague district of Smíchov; it even gives the house number and the number of the apartment, but I cannot read the name of the street because of a beetle with shiny metallic wings who is sitting precisely in that spot, baring his enormous mandibles at me. I try to push him aside with my pencil but he bites into it, yanks it out of my hand

and throws it on the floor. I spend the evening struggling with the beetle, who in turn destroys my pencil, pen, comb and toothbrush; in the end, I tackle him with my bare hands but he bites into them with great gusto and all that time he would not budge an inch to reveal so much as a single letter of the street name. All this is taking place in the reading room of the university library, and I know that I'm never going to get my hands on the handbook about rabbit-breeding again because all the borrowed books are burnt the same day for reasons of public hygiene. (It has been calculated that the current stocks will last two hundred and fifty-eight years; after that the university library will be turned into a market hall.) Just my luck, as usual! I often get within an inch of success but at the last minute some trifling obstacle fatefully stands in my way. Once I almost won the Jubilee Marathon through the cafés of Prague but I was disqualified because I had inadvertently eaten Dr Winter's brioche. Another time I was invited to participate in the Eleusinian mysteries held in the local gymnasium in the village of Kunratice, but I couldn't see a thing because the lady sitting in front of me was wearing a tall mauve hat, and I was too shy to ask her to take it off. All those who did see the mysteries have been initiated; they claim they have achieved the point from which, according to André Breton, 'life and death, the real and the unreal, the past and the future, the communicable and the incommunicable, the lofty and the base cease to be perceived as opposites'. Not only have they achieved this point, but it seems that they have made themselves comfortable in it as in a cosy living room. They have established a brotherhood of the initiated and the members hold regular meetings in the Horymír Restaurant. Now, I am, of course, also a member and go to the Horymír every Friday because I was too embarrassed to admit that I had seen nothing and have achieved no point (while I would be quite happy to start with achieving a point where I could somehow resolve the contradiction between wanting to live a quiet, solitary life, unnoticed by anyone, and seeking attention by committing eccentric acts of provocation which often exceed the limits of good taste). And so I attend the meetings of the initiated and listen to their prattle without having the faintest idea what they are talking about, while I keep myself busy contemplating the mysterious mosaic of the brawn on my plate which resembles medieval incrustations, or the puddles of beer spilt on the brown formica table where they form mythological scenes with dragons, fairies and winged horses. I have to keep coming up with clever new tricks to conceal the fact that I haven't got a clue what the initiates are saying; as a result I live in constant dreadful tension, terrified that I am going to be found out and that the initiates are going to attack me, turn me out of the Horymír and chase me indignantly through the night streets of Prague. My visit to the underground palace could, among other things, radically change this unbearable situation—if it weren't for the mean, stubborn beetle. When I think of all the possible places he could choose to sit: he could sit on beautiful, intoxicatingly fragrant blossoms or on the breast of a sleeping maiden, he could find himself a colourful illuminated Gothic manuscript or rare bibliophilia, and if he must insist that, of all places, he has to be sitting on a book about rabbits (which is as illiterate as if it had also been written by a rabbit), he could at least move up two lines from where he is. But he has to make himself comfortable in the only spot in the world from which he can destroy my luck. What can I do? I'll have to go about it in a different way: I'll befriend people who live in Smíchov and when they invite me to their house, I'll wait for them to leave the room, then quickly step into their wardrobe and, fumbling around in the darkness, look behind their coats for the handle of the door leading into the secret passage. The problem is that such doors exist in nearly every wardrobe, except that they lead not to underground palaces but at best to some forgotten warehouse full of discarded poetry robots or to a buried steamship. (So far, seventeen steamships have been discovered buried under Prague; this phenomenon has yet to be explained but it may have something to do with the experimental addition of shredded studies in phenomenology into cattle feed.) Also, pushing one's way through the hanging clothes and coats to the back wall of the wardrobe is no mean feat: their heavy intoxicating aromas may cause unpleasant hallucinations. I myself had a graphic vision once, brought on by inhaling those dangerous vapours: in it, I was walking across Charles Bridge and in place of St Vitus's Cathedral I saw a huge tiger looking around the city with narrowed eyes. Proust describes how the taste of a madeleine dipped in limeflower tea conjured up the lost world of his childhood in Combray; when I recently caught a whiff from the half-open door of somebody's wardrobe, I immediately remembered the year of my life I spent with a certain girl in a small cottage in the middle of a deep wood made of coat stands hung with overcoats, jackets and heavy fur coats. We lived on whatever snacks we could find in the pockets; every morning we would set out with a basket, making notches on the coat stands to be able to find our way back through the immense woods. The hardest time came in winter when the pockets were covered with snow and there was nothing to eat. We would make our way through snow drifts among the snow-covered coats, and when a storm came, the heavy, icy sleeves tossed about in the wind, beat us across our frozen faces, woollen scarves flew through the air like spectres, fur caps rolled in the snow chased by foxes and wolves who took them for little animals on the run. It's a long time since I last saw the girl I lived with in the coat forest. This year I heard in the espresso bar at the Museum of Decorative Arts that she's made a career and is now a deputy minister. Does she ever remember the time we spent wandering among the snow-covered coats? Pockets, of course, are always mysterious and disquieting, and the latest fashion is to be commended for its superfluous, unfunctional number of pockets. It is true that Hegel says in his *Aesthetics* that, in comparison with the loose, uninterrupted lines of the antique dress, modern clothing, full of seams, buttons and pockets, is characterized by 'unfree forms, folds and surfaces', that its puffed-out pockets 'conceal what is sensuously beautiful in the organic formation of the limbs, namely their swelling and curving, and substitutes for them the visible appearance of a material mechanically fashioned', but we know that numerous pockets, the exact number of which is often not known even to the owner of the outfit, are poetic in the extreme as they turn a jacket or a pair of trousers into a thing as mysterious, uncanny and inscrutable as a commode with secret drawers or the grim, labyrinthine Elsinore. Pockets are spaces which resist giving themselves up, in them the outfit retains its dark *Für-sich-sein*, they are the reservoirs of miraculous encounters and revelations, bringing our clothes into strange connections with the Pyramid of the Niches in El Tajín, they are the secret recesses of our space where stranded objects acquire disturbing and demonic meanings. Usually, we reach quite mechanically into no more than a few pockets while the remaining ones are left to rest like the thirteenth chamber. When, for some reason, we put an object in one of the unused pockets and forget about it, there is little hope that we are ever going to be reunited with it again. An object hidden in the darkness at the bottom of a pocket is transformed: licked by pocket-dwelling animals whose saliva, mixed with pocket poisons, slowly erodes the protective skin of its common, non-problematic meaning, it reveals a mesmerizing aspect, a shape impossible to classify, an unknown substance which is probably the Aristotelian prime matter. Sometimes, when we are looking for something, we embark on a thorough search through all our pockets: our hands wander through them like helpless, blind animals through unfamiliar burrows, our fingertips uncertainly and fearfully feel the ambiguous forms they encounter in the enclosed dark spaces and bring them up to the light. Bewildered, we look at the suspicious items, not knowing what they are, where they come from and how they got into our pockets in the first place. The pockets of our clothes are the most remarkable archaeological sites; we may yet need to establish a new academic discipline dealing with pockets, a scholarly sinusology, a field of knowledge where speleology would meet philosophical transcendentalism. We shall have to work out the elements of the chemistry, biology, palaeontology and metaphysics of pockets. The other day, I rifled through my pockets in search of a tram ticket; the most interesting find was a folded piece of paper with frayed, blackened edges. When I unfolded it, I could see it was an envelope with my name and address on it; the envelope had been opened and inside was a letter saying, 'Dear friend, both I and my wife were utterly delighted by your wise and kind letter. I spent the whole night thinking about your excellent metaphor of the pump—I believe you have touched on the essence of all metaphysics with the utmost clarity, addressing the problem which drove my uncle from the illuminated balconies into the chill of the desert. Just as you predicted, the lobsters he so loved to eat quietly set out to follow him on their wobbly legs, forming a sad procession as they waddled along the narrow path winding through the shrubs in the garden, until they disappeared from sight at the crumbling wall overgrown with ivy. What can be done? We shall patiently continue putting cold tins to our ears, we shall go on silently and laboriously ingesting the long, somewhat slimy spaghetti, pale and phosphorescent in the moonlight, without knowing their end. After all, it happened seventy years ago in Bad Ischl. Your tale of the ghostly TV set is partly comical and partly very frightening; the only thing not quite clear to me is who is 'Frankie'—is he that pale, logical neopositivist whose mediumistic sister once materialized a compressor in a bistro? I remember she taught us a wonderful game which drove some to madness and others to illness and death. Many of those things we experienced in the time of lemon slices and transcendental beaches have meanwhile ripened in the darkness under the stairs and are now slowly surging at us down Vinohradská Avenue, past the philately shop where in a closed album rests a so far unnoticed blue stamp from the islands with an engraved image of our greyhounds who in the end denied us and savaged us. That happened, I believe, on the famous airship named Laetitia. In case you have come to the conclusion that this tiny stamp betrays more than we would like to admit, I can't say whether or not I agree, or whether I approve of the carefully constructed plan which is possibly hatching in your mind at this very moment; however, there is every indication that I am going to show a great deal of understanding for certain necessary measures that, taken out of the strict context known only to two people in this city, may appear to the uninitiated observer in a somewhat macabre light. Kindest regards from me and my wife, we shall impatiently await your next letter.' And underneath all that, an illegible signature. I peruse the letter again and again, and for the life of me I can't remember who it's from, nor do I understand what it's about. Yet I must have read it before, because there is a note jotted on the margin in my handwriting: 'kidney pie!!!' (A symbol or a secret password?) It is possible that the letter refers to the period in my life when a group of friends and I performed allegorical pantomime sketches depicting Kant's twelve categories on the concrete stages of beer gardens around Braník, Zbraslav and Chuchle. That merry time brings to mind a series of images which could be very enlightening, but it is necessary to bring this text to a conclusion because the tip of my pen is inexorably approaching the bottom of the page where, like a shore drawing closer and closer on murky seas, emerges the dirty green top of the desk in the university library reading room where I am writing these lines. On it, I see the faded inscription 'Remember!' next to a dried blood stain, the last trace of the strange and as yet unexplained events that took place here twelve years ago and about which I could write an eight-hundred-page ghost novel. (You may have heard about the 'case of the crawling book'.) The available space grows narrower, I have to make my letters smaller and smaller and compress each word like an accordion. What a pity, I still wanted to tell you much more about my journey to the malachite palace, about my descent down the marble staircase bordered with white statues of deer, the end of which plunged into a warm, viscous, sweet-smelling purple mush, about an unexpected encounter in the wardrobe, about my duel with five masked ninjas on the roof of the National Theatre, about a lachrymose monster in the compartment of a train riding through a snow-covered landscape; I still wanted to tell you who was the beetle sitting on the book about rabbits, what the book was and who the rabbits were, but nothing more fits into the narrowing gap. I could perhaps resolve the problem by continuing past the lower edge of the page and writing the end of the story on the top of the desk, and then I could tell you which desk it is so you could come here and finish reading, but I realize that somebody could use the opportunity and become interested in the various coded messages written in ball-point pen on the desk tops, which could lead to the divulging of certain closely guarded extragalactic connections, and anyway, the position of the desks changes daily because they are removed every night when the reading room is used as an ice-rink. And so I ponder the images pouring from my pen and try to figure out which one of them could be used to conclude this terrifying tale, but none seems to fit, probably because our notions of what an end should look like are quite false, we cut up action into finished narratives to be able to stack them up neatly in our mind like chopped wood in a shed; yet no event is intrinsically an end, any more than it is a beginning or a middle. As Empedocles says, 'there is no growth of any of all mortal things nor any end in destructive death, but only mixture and interchange of what is mixed'; if it were possible, I would paste up these written pages into a Möbius strip so that my story would have no beginning and no end, and it would be fitting to do this just now, as I have reached the same point from which I had started, that is, the reading room of the university library. Why not? After all, a little while ago you were willing to come here just to be able to read the end of the story on the desk top, and so you should not find it difficult to paste up the text as required. You have surely heard about the mythical serpent Oroborus who bites his own tail. And so: at last I have found the information I have been seeking for years; it reveals the location of a secret passage leading to the malachite palace on the bank of an underground river, the palace where I was invited to a fête twenty years ago . . .

(*Translated by Alexandra Büchler.*)

Ludvík Vaculík

extracts from the novel
How to Make a Boy

May 1987   It is the end of May. In April, Josef wrote nothing and he doesn't want to do any more writing. It makes no sense at the present time; everything has been decided: Pavla is in her third month. Which brings an end to introspection and to the luxury of depressions. He is in good health. The rest is a matter of strength.

She went to see the doctor one morning while he was sitting at his desk in the bedroom, printing out copies of his Easter column which began with the sentence, 'I'm making a cat-o'-nine-tails and thinking of the government.' For years now he has been writing something other than what he wants and needs to write. When he heard the key in the lock, he went into the hall. Pavla was standing in the doorway, holding a bouquet of flowers, an elated expression on her pale face framed with dark hair. 'I'm pregnant and I bought you flowers,' she said in her loveliest voice, joyful and humble. He took the flowers from her, helped her out of her coat, and with mixed feelings of shock and relief he kept repeating the sentence, 'I bought you flowers.' It reassured him. He put the flowers on the kitchen table and Pavla set about cooking lunch, without changing; she didn't want to take off her pretty dress. He sat at the table, watching her. She worked carefully, keeping her elbows from her sides, her belly from the work top. She would immediately wipe off every splash of water. She told him how differently the nurse and the doctor treated her now that she was registering for childbirth rather than for abortion. And vitamins, advice, recommendations. Josef watched her, thinking: this is the right thing to do, but how am I going to tell them at home? From time to time she stopped in mid-motion and turned to him, astonished. 'I'm going to have a baby,' she would say. Then, 'So you've knocked me up!' and she burst out laughing. And, after a while: 'Do you want to . . . fuck . . . right now?'

Fierce, cruel desire, immediate. Running, she tore off her clothes and was there before him. As soon as he embedded himself in her, he was startled to feel his disobedient juice gather and surge into the tip, even before he started 'fucking'. 'I'm sorry,' he said. 'It's all right,' she said. 'It's for you. From now on I'll do it just for you. I don't want to excite him.' She was lying there fulfilled, looking at his face, tenderly ruffling his hair. He reckoned that it must have been perhaps the fourth time she had done this: focused exclusively outside herself, on him. Leaving, he glanced at her belly: it was indeed slightly different. There was a third being.

After Easter Josef received a telephone invitation to a 'conversation' with the secret police: they were to meet in the Expo Restaurant. Awaiting him were the same men who had interrogated him recently. They told him to order something. He asked for coffee and for his own bill. They immediately broached his old question: to be or not to be? 'We know that you'd like to travel. A man of your reputation and talent'— Josef made a face—'should travel. It might even help you achieve a better view of our society. We've been authorized to offer you a passport if you sign a statement promising to abide by Czechoslovak law while abroad. You can formulate the text yourself.' He did not hesitate a moment: nothing and never! Then he replied: 'Of course I'm not going to break the law. Do you ask other people to sign such statements? I'm no different from anybody else.' They stirred their coffee, thinking. 'You're wrong. In your case we're responsible for your behaviour.' Hmm, that was certainly true. He realized how many people he himself was responsible to: what would he tell his friends, what confusions would he cause? They went on, 'Times are changing and so are we. We don't want to be unfair. Or is it perhaps that our suggestion isn't convenient at this particular time?' Here it comes!

They finished their coffee, talking about nothing in particular, and asked for the bill. Josef paid his own. They had a receipt made out, then shook his hand. Unwittingly, he held the hand of the man who was a ridiculous figure in Pavla's novel a little longer. The man gave him a surprised look. On his way down to the city centre he imagined what the man was going to do when he read this. Dear Pavla, he repeated to himself, dear Pavla! How am I to protect you all? I'll have to, somehow.

It was a little arrogant of him but he headed for the book-binder's to collect the bound typewritten copies of Havel's *Redevelopment*. He had a good look around Valentinská Street before entering the building; he looked again when leaving. So here it is again: to be or not to be. Had he decided to be then, many years ago, when they first put the question to him, he would no longer be today. What would have become of me? he asked himself.

What would I be today, he asked, had I then firmly turned down Pavla's invitation to our first date? How does one reject a woman who excites him and wants him? Which of you knows how to do that? He remembered the day when he was lying in Pavla's bed and nobody, nobody, not even the secret police knew where he was: he was meant to get up and return to his former life, leave the house and the room where they were simply a man and a woman, walk out into the street and so officially reclaim his fate. The thought made him ill and he said to the very young woman, 'Now I wish that this wall would open'—it was a wall facing away from Prague—'and behind it would appear an entirely unknown landscape. I would leave here and walk. I would recognize nothing, nothing would remind me of anything I know.' It didn't happen. He went out into the familiar street. But he would return to the woman. Was it because in her apartment she had a wall facing an unknown and innocent landscape? Yet the wall never opened up for him like the woman to whom it belonged.

When she became pregnant he was astonished at how

many unknown things it was possible to encounter on old ground, and when he tried to find the right time to tell his wife, he failed: almost every day she would buy and bring home little things for her first grandchild. In the end, she had to find out from strangers.

15 December 1988   I am not exaggerating: the boy falls and hurts his head at least twenty times a day. Then he cries a lot. The only remedy is to pick him up and hold him. I don't know whether I have changed in the few years since we had our daughter, Lucie, or whether now we have been given something completely different from what she was: she never evoked such strong feelings of compassion and fear in me. She was gentle, fragile and lovely, the way she was expected to be. She behaved appropriately to her gender and age: I'm a good little girl and I'm trying to lift the tiny printed beetle from the pillow with my tiny little finger, I've been trying for ten minutes and nothing! While the boy is eager to rise above what he is for the time being: above his strength and ability. When we were at Josef's mill during the holidays, Jiří Ruml paid us a visit and witnessed what happened: the boy was following us, gurgling and making his usual noises, when suddenly, out of the chaos of sound, came the sentence, 'I shall act.' Ruml froze and stared down at him. 'Did I hear right?' he said.

30 January 1989   Until today the boy called me 'Ma-a-a': when I appeared in the door, when he wanted to be picked up or sit on my shoulders and look at the river through the window. Today, he started calling me 'Pa-a-a'. The previous word was a spontaneous sound of need, more of an interjection; this one is a new form of address. He has a precisely shaped, beautiful, firm head with soft hair, brown with reddish glints. I look at his older photographs—he has been remarkably faithful to his own image. Lucie was the one who changed during her first year.

It occurred to me that he is so forceful and strong because

he burst into life with an accumulated charge, having been kept from being born for such a long time: since when? Since Lucie's birth or since my first meeting with Pavla? He had wanted to be in the world, he had been waiting, and it is a terrible thought that he might not have been born, that nobody might have granted him that gift. I worry that my feelings for him may be unmanly. I realized it today, when we were visiting somewhere and I was holding him on my lap, kissing his head: a silly, sentimental old man? And I remembered instantly how much my own father loved me. He treated me with passionate tenderness, even when I was already ten, fifteen years old. How he would hug me to him when he returned from work after a long shift. When I was leaving home to go out into the world, he would kiss me on the lips. He treated my younger brothers with the same tenderness. Isn't a father's love for his son really a form of self-love? A peculiar phenomenon, the identification of son and father. I think of the boy all the time, underneath all my other thoughts. When he's not around, I fear for his safety. When I find him safe and well, I consider it almost a lucky escape. This is surely pathological: but is it really? Pavla is ironing, the phone rings, she goes to answer it: at that moment the boy could pull the iron down on top of himself. It doesn't happen because he follows her to the phone. 'Careful!' I say and point to the iron and the boy. 'So what?' she protests. 'He followed me, didn't he?' But one day he may not follow her. Then she adds, 'You're here too, aren't you?' I say that if I weren't here it would have been the same, and she says, 'Well, you ought to be here!' 'Some fathers can't be home because they work as locomotive drivers, for example.' 'But you don't work as a locomotive driver, do you?'

30 March 1989   The boy throws tantrums. If he wants a shoe and I don't give it to him, he stands in one spot, bawling and bawling. But he is also building up his patience. He tidies up and puts things back in their place. He works all the time. Children like him do not as yet need their own corner, their desk, their place. He is always trying to push his way among

us, where he belongs. Yesterday, when I took him in my arms, washed, fed and ready for bed, he suddenly looked at me, scrutinizing me for a long time, calmly, thoughtfully. As if he became aware of me in a way different from other times: as a separate being, not just a feature of the world that is there for him.

It is hard for me to think that everything I have done with him so far is forgotten. If I died, he wouldn't remember me. He presses his cheek tenderly against mine. I hum a tune in his ear, he stays still for a while, then turns his other ear. I do my carpentry: he collects the cut-offs and plays with them. I feel as if I were in the workshop of my godfather, the joiner: I am the joiner and it is me who is playing with bits of wood on the floor.

11 April 1989   Pavla asked me to reread her novel, which she claims is now finished, the one about stupid Josef to whom she *had to* be unfaithful because he let her have an abortion; that's the long and the short of the story. I read it again with a sense of being wronged, and I can't say anything any more: I no longer know how she perceives me, in what ways she reduces my being. All these years, she has lived not with me but with the offence I have caused her. Her novel confirms that these days literature likes to draw on evil. Good is not appealing or interesting, it creates no drama. There is no reason, for example, why Pavla should write about what I do with the children, what I manage to overcome within myself and within society, how I serve—her, the children and others. She doesn't understand that my attempt to bring together my small children with my grandchildren, my grown-up sons with this new family, is a feat much greater than some book!

5 May 1989   Everything is in blossom at the same time— apple trees and lilacs, snowdrops and tulips.

'Pick those things up and put them in the basket,' I tell the boy, who collects the clothes he had previously taken out of the basket and puts them back. 'Hold this for me,' I say. He grabs the strip of wood I am sawing off. 'With both hands,' I say, and he clasps the wood with both little hands.

I still don't know how to write this. There is a whole universe in the head of a small child and I fear for that head. The sitting room, as Pavla calls it—I call it a hovel—has been turned into a workshop. I'm building a bed here. It will be high, with steps to climb up, like one of those huge brickwork stoves they used to have in village houses, on top of which they slept in winter: a refuge in the corner, a warm stove for everything. It will be for playing and horsing around, for lying in when you're ill and for reading, for crawling into and for lounging, for thinking. It's going to have a railing and drawers. Pavla has called it the ark: when the Vltava rises to our windows, we'll simply set sail. The boy climbs through the timber structure and I can feel his strength, his movements, his joy and perceptions. The planks form a ceiling above his head and walls all around him; he finds his way through the internal cross-pieces. From his perspective, the bed is like a barn. We won't be able to take it with us if we ever move house; hm, I should have thought of that. The room smells like the house of my godfather, the joiner. I have to lend the boy every tool I take into my hands. The building of the bed, the sounds, the hammering, the singing are as important as the bed itself. I feel like the master of a large country estate. I do it for the children: for their eyes and ears now and for their memories later. The whole bed will be joined with pegs; there will be no nails. But for the moment I have to use a provisional nail here and there; the boy immediately wants a hammer and nails. I give him a piece of wood, a nail and a hammer: he grasps the end of the handle and his hand sinks under the weight. But who has told him to hold the hammer closer to the head to be able to lift it? Is it an inherited instinct or the knowledge of physical laws acquired by a seventeen-month-old man?

2 February 1990   We've been swamped with vigorous life—political, literary, social. There's always someone sitting

around the house. Pavla has the habit of talking endlessly. The phone rings every ten minutes and somebody wants to speak to me or to her. At the time of the 'revolution', I sometimes gave five interviews a day to foreign journalists. Then I began throwing people out. They come here and it doesn't occur to them that there are children to be bathed, dinner to be cooked ...

The other day we were walking along the embankment past Mánes. There was a crowd watching a video in the gallery window. These days, Lucie wears a tricolour on her blouse, a little heart with Havel's name; nearly all the children in her class have one. Suddenly, she noticed my bare lapel, looked at her mother and said: 'Why is neither of you wearing a tricolour?' Indeed, everyone around us had one. 'I've got one,' I said: I was carrying the boy dressed in a jacket with blue, white and red stripes.

13 August 1990   A question occurred to me: what is the boy's purpose in my life? Is it simply that I am to compare myself with the father of my previous sons and search for old mistakes? Vulgar opinion has it that we achieve this kind of self-knowledge with our grandchildren. It is not true: the consequences are not the same. All the responsibility and effort lies with the young parents; the grandfather with his belated wisdom only makes a nuisance of himself without mending his own ways.

The boy is a figure of happiness: he circles round the apartment on a tricycle, calmly and carefully avoiding things in his way, he makes sounds, he entices us to play, to take part in his enterprise. He borrows from my drawer whatever he fancies and he puts it back again. He tugs at my hand, wanting me to link up with him to play locomotive and carriage. I am busy and he says, 'I don't like you, go 'way.' When I forbid him to do something, I explain the reason why. If he accepts it, he says, 'I'm twuly sowwy.'

May–December 1991   Josef often imagined how Pavla

would get rid of him. There was always the possibility—which he considered unlikely—that they would continue living together at an ever-slowing tempo, with ever-diminishing strength, that she would also slowly cool down and their relationship would develop into a collaboration, a family affair full of practicalities. They shared two fields of interest: the children and literature. Yet it seemed more likely that he would suddenly die and she would mourn him. But he also thought that one day she might forge a sensual bond somewhere and fall in love, because that was what she used to say: 'Every one of my men was meant as love.' Josef also remembered her view that, if you can't get enough at home, you have the right to satisfy your hunger elsewhere. But how could they live with that? He would watch her escapes and returns, and the decision about how to go on would be up to him.

It happened differently. She simply sent him away when she no longer needed him, just as she had discarded her previous men; only with him it happened after a much longer time because his task took longer to perform: two children and a nice apartment. She was also counting on earning money because the bans had been lifted and she knew how to work hard. It happened in May when Josef expressed his view on women, marriage and family in an interview for a women's magazine. He could have put it more cautiously, not admitting that he considered it a mistake for people to leave their marriages; a mistake he had been humbly working off ever since. He thought that he had said—for that was what he had in mind—that he cared for Pavla; but when he looked for the words in the text, they weren't there! Pavla, who was aware of his view and had suffered for it, could not bear the idea that he had made it public. It was a reason for something to happen between a man and an offended woman; Josef could see that he would have to do 'penance' for his cleansing 'confession' but he thought that the sanctuary dedicated to what they both valued would endure. He was wrong.

What happened next belongs in a different volume; this one wants to stick to its main character. At the moment when Pavla gave Josef his marching orders—in the street!—the boy said, 'Y'know what happened?' And he showed him his tiny finger: it was slightly grazed and there was a little scab on it. Josef bought himself two large cardboard suitcases. He waited for the time when nobody would be at home and he went there to fill them up. But it was a desperate task: what to do first, what to take with him and what to leave? The box with the boy's old shoes? First of all he took his heart pills and a pile of mail that had to be dealt with. Superstitiously, he felt he had to decide on the one thing he would leave behind: otherwise the breakup would be sealed for ever. He walked through the rooms that were unexpectedly, unbelievably tidy and he understood the taunting message: I don't need anyone to educate me! Dragging the suitcases down the stairs, he corrected himself: This is to show you that I'm starting a new life! He had to return several times to confirm the changes in the apartment. Like the disappearance of all the photographs of him and Pavla together.

The bed! He would bequeath that to the boy. Looking at it, he realized the beastliness of her honest decision: she assumed the right to put an end to his sleeping next to the boy. She robbed the boy of the beauty of holding his mother with one hand and his father with the other. She robbed Lucie of their singing. Just like that. She . . . it's unbelievable! She values herself so highly that she just orders three people: You won't live together! She prescribes to the father: You will borrow your children as if in a soap opera. If she's not a cow, I don't know who is! He filled his suitcases, fearing the sound of the key in the lock, fearing the sight of that creature in the doorway. When he imagined her, it seemed to him he would have to embrace her and abolish the whole stupid nonsense. But he trembled with the fear of rejection. He looked out of the window at the river where he saw two boats setting out and one mooring. You knew that she would not allow you to grow old next to her. How could you have thought that one day, together with the boy, you would build a workshop here, a study, a work-room?

He decided to go abroad for as long as possible, but it could be for only three months; no benefactor was willing to finance a longer stay. When he told his wife, Marie, she considered it sensible. Saying goodbye to her was the most difficult part of this step: they both knew they were losing precious time together. Everything that had happened since a certain time had been a mistake. Yet, had he not made those mistakes . . .

He returned before Christmas. He decided that Advent would be the latest time by which he could expect a sign from Pavla. But she held out: Christmas, a tree, Christmas Eve, carols. What a strong character! He was glad he'd escaped. Then it was he who could not hold out: after Christmas he borrowed the children and took them to the mountains. Am I a widower and you orphans? Long live the Socialist family! There was a lot of snow; they went sledging. It was freezing. Everything was all right, even the food he prepared for them, yet he felt they were an invalid group. Towing the sledge along, he thought about the kind of solution he would be prepared to accept if he had to admit that Pavla didn't want him. But there was a gap in his reasoning: the point was not that she wouldn't want him, but that she simply wanted her man to love her. That brought back his old idea that she didn't love the men she chose, though she demanded that they love her. He was beginning to realize that he loved Marie; if it wasn't too strong a word. Every day he went to bed exhausted. The boy slept between him and Lucie. Sometimes he would cry and call for his mummy before falling asleep. 'Mummy's not here,' Josef would repeat to him. 'But why?' repeated the boy. 'She has to write,' he would say instead of: She doesn't want to be here.

On New Year's Day, Pavla appeared on the doorstep and said, 'Will you turn me away?' Turn her away? Goodness! Several thoughts crossed his mind: how good it was for the children; how difficult it must have been for her to go back on her resolve; how she would never forgive him for that; how she threw his neat, male sadness into disarray. 'I've come to the conclusion that I made a mistake, and that we should try again for the sake of the children. I have forgiven you.' The last sentence was accurate: she felt no guilt and he should be grateful. For the life of me I'm not dragging those suitcases back, he thought, and said, 'I'm not going back into service, Pavla. I believed that this time you were serious. I had to travel some way away from you. But, for the children, let's be together as much as we can.' She said, 'I understand you. I know about your journey away from me, but we can still be friends, and then we'll see.' That was sensible, that's what he had been hoping for!

At night she wanted to make love. She had grown hungry during those seven months. His friends had been wrong; he trusted her, he knew her sense of honour. Yet he felt as if he were being unfaithful.

29 March 1992   These beautiful children. I am afraid that this is the end. The drawing on the other side of this sheet of paper is the boy's map of a hidden treasure. I am powerless even before my own writing. Never again—I promise myself.

The cause of yesterday's argument does have its place here, after all: but it would be unfair. Pavla is truly, helplessly unhappy. After her 'return' at New Year, she expected me to step back into the same position from which she had thrown me out. I wrote her a letter then, saying, 'I think you've returned out of sheer necessity. Had you found someone else in the meantime, you wouldn't have come back. It was not the outcome of some deeper understanding, you simply couldn't carry your revolt any further. Why don't you renew your resistance?' She replied that she loved me. Then I had a stroke. She visited me in hospital and I felt sorry for her: it would have been kind of me to resolve your dilemma.

21 April 1992   In the car, Lucie tells us about a girl in her class whose mother is a Jehovah's Witness; that means she knows when the end of the world will come, and the girl has

brought the news into the classroom. The boy says that he knows what the end of the world will be like: 'One morning it stays dark an' den you start to lose your memowies.'

I ask: who is it who has spoken through the boy? Most likely myself.

9 August 1992   Pinned down by wires and tubes, I am going through hell: all those unfinished matters I had been putting off, unsorted papers I wanted to destroy. The bad relationship with that last Pavla which I should have tried to overcome and mend. Not having said goodbye to Marie. All the half-finished ideas.

I'm writing in pencil, lying down, and my handwriting is illegible because I am no longer used to it. Most of all I miss the boy. He is now probably in my car, on his way to his mother. My grown-up middle son came to collect him.

They threaten to keep me here for some time, although my pulse and blood pressure appear to be all right. We are now waiting for the blood tests. I love the boy because he is me and I pass myself on to him. I love Marie because she was my first woman and because she is good. We went on a wonderful trip with the boy—Blansko, Macocha and Punkva. But I also suffered because it brought back memories of her in our youth. In those days, we used to walk everywhere, distances that today are so easily crossed by car. It is a shame. She was a beautiful woman.

Josef woke up into darkness. Was he really awake? He blinked and the darkness didn't disappear and he didn't know whether he could see. It should have been morning but it was not. He remembered nothing. He knew nothing, except that he might still exist. He didn't understand what had happened. It was morning and the darkness had not ceased, and he had no memories: you start to lose your memories! Yes, that was a memory! The boy! He tried to move: he felt a deep, overwhelming pain. He realized he'd had an operation.

When morning comes, he will draw a picture of good news for the boy.

(*Translated by Alexandra Büchler.*)

Jáchym Topol

extracts from the story
A Trip to the
Railway Station

The city was changing. Above it, as dependable as in the tenth century or any other time, the moon hung in the night's dark gateway, sometimes full and puffy like the face of a drunk, at other times floating in the clouds, almost invisible, a glassy bauble that didn't burn but still drove the city mongrels mad. Here in this glow, whenever the moon climbed to its cool intensity, lovers would drink off the last of their bottle and hurl themselves at one another, nibbling corners off love supreme, the killer would sneer as he twisted his knife in the wound, and here in this light, dear Mommy would suddenly do something atrocious to her little papoose, and the golden force flowed down over the tracks of trams and trains and they glistened brilliantly in the flood of light . . . The Lord of the Earth caught hold of the dark at its centre and turned the night inside out like freshly peeled skin. Then the sun would blaze in the sky, beating down on walls and pavements, and only then was filth filth and decay decay and now you could see them. This searing sun caused blood to move slowly and lazily, turning sweet, or just the opposite, it made the pumps work so frantically the blood seemed ready to burst right out of its confines. That's how it always seemed to me, nothing pretty about it.

The city was changing. Iron grilles and shutters left pulled down for years and gone to rust were given fresh coats of paint and often a sign with somebody's name on it. Dusty cellars and dirty beer joints in what used to be the Jewish quarter were cleverly converted into luxury stores. You could find steamer trunks from the last century, a book dictated by

Madonna herself, with a piece of her chain included, pineapples and fine tobacco, diaries of dead actresses and trendy wheels from old farmers' wagons, whips and dolls and travel grails with adventurers' blood in them, coins and likenesses of Kafka, shooting galleries with all the proletarian presidents as targets, rags and bones and skins, anything you could think of. In the back of one showcase were two statuettes, half dog, half man, stooping under heavily laden wicker baskets, their glassy eyes watching you over their shoulders, and maybe they even knew your name. They were the statuettes of the devil, and they stood there for a long time before anyone bought them. I was relieved when they finally disappeared, but the very next day in their place stood a catwoman figurine with green eyes, inlaid with precious stones, and raven-black hair. The hair was human. Pozener was the name of the company that owned the shop, they were from Vienna and their logo had the horns of a bull in it.

The city was changing. Old broken walls were torn down, ads were pasted up over cracked, mysterious maps in the roughcast plaster, pavements were newly laid, barriers of sheet metal and wood that had stood for years vanished overnight. New owners took charge of dilapidated buildings and tried to convert them into hotels, pubs, wholesale glass and crystal shops, travel agencies. Trousers, coats, wooden toys, frankfurters, newspapers, gingerbread and gold were sold on the street out of ground-floor apartments, and the idea of declaring income was a joke. Nothin' sleazy 'bout money, the sleazeballs said, and they parcelled up the streets and squares to fit the size of their stands. On the periphery of the city and in the outlying districts, new centres sprang up around discos, mini department stores, new bars and restaurants.

But it wasn't enough to quench my thirst for life. I searched for a way to wear out my vigorous mind in business activities, working my way up to literary mercenary, a dealer in words, a street-smart hack. Most of the people in the neighbourhood were more successful. Dunar the crook, blackmailer and wino became lord of Nightland, a disco that reeked with the stench of burnt flesh from the hot rocks tossed from one mafioso client to the next. Come again sometime, Dunar told the emissary from one of those nasty foreign outfits that came to Prague in the rush for the rain of gold. Come again, he told the smart-ass who so confidently demanded a premium for protection, and I'll kill you. They shot the guy the next week, he probably came just to have some fun, and they didn't even give him a chance to trot out his offer a second time. Show this to Mommy, Dunar told the guy's date as he expertly snapped her collar-bone in two. Then his heavies worked her over a little bit more, just enough so she'd barely survive, and tossed her on to a rubbish tip outside town, all rolled up in the crime-flecked carpet together with the dead protection expert.

Stumbling by Nightland back to my dump at about 6 a.m. I saw Dunar perched on the bonnet of his BMW, having breakfast. Three or four half-drunk flunkies were prancing around him with a bravura worthy of a changing of the guard, serving him up roast chicken and salads, gold-plated toothpicks, baskets and dishes, drams and bottles, the air pulsed with the sounds of ABBA. Dunar let out a belch and flung a bottle of wine at me. Scram scribbler, he roared, and I made myself scarce. Some time back he had asked me to write him a few pieces in praise of his 'entertainment paradise', and even though I was paid a king's ransom I still hadn't turned them in. Apparently he hadn't lost faith in my genius, because the bottle smashed against the wall about five yards wide of me and none of his Dobermans came snorting for my throat.

The factory workers were walking to work with last night's hangover splitting their heads. Hey Franta, Dunar greeted them, hey Luboš, hey Ládín, how's tricks? Nothing mean about the way he said it, and his BMW sat sparkling like a great big black beetle, the bonnet supporting its load of deli fare without damage, Dunar was obviously having himself a ball with his flunkies and bodyguards. The working stiffs smiled, their innards invisible, but they knew that he knew that they knew. They were of one blood. Plain and simple, the Master had come to town to pull the chair out from under your rear, the soup from under your spoon, shove it right in your eye. The Master's going to make slaves of your sons, and what's more, he's going to take his followers, your daughters and wives, and sell 'em on the street, flesh by the pound. Hey Miloš, hey Jožín, you sonofagun, ciao guys, ciao, ciao. One-time classmates and buddies and cagemates and workmates from the factory, one-time brothers from school, church, the Party, the army. Was a time they lived together, side by side, so to speak, fist with fist, idle gossip with ratting to the cops. Nowadays they just swallow hard on their spit, on their envy and hate. One day one of them is going to break his head open. Maybe soon, maybe not, when the time is right.

The city peeled off its stern and gloomy face of the past, the mask of rotting Bolshevism, and replaced it with a thousand others. Some were the smiley make-up faces of clowns, and who'd give a damn if those wacky old circus-ring alcoholics smelling of sawdust and animal dung covered up a few little pox-marks here and there, or a two-bit scar from a two-bit stab wound? Brightly coloured buffoon kissers painted on for rowdy youngsters, for female sightseers from around the globe, for the first shy kisses and fleeting touches, for the first marijuana cigarette in the mysterious twilight of foreign lands wrapped in a web of legends, for wanna-be artists in a haze of romance, rust under their nails from the Iron Curtain, behind which—at long last!—no more tank parades now, just Punch and Judy shows for sons and daughters from well-to-do families with fabulous passports who came to Eastern Europe to go wild. Expecting a menagerie they found a jungle, expecting a jungle, they found a warehouse of scrapped stage scenery, searching for the Spirit and the mirror-faced Bogeyman got them . . . for dour intellectual females who had cast off Morrison and Kerouac at the age of seven, then existentialism and phenomenology between eleven and sixteen . . . and all that junk and then drugs and then, once cleansed, they loved Jesus so they could start up with some other male, the harpies, and then they were men-haters with well-rounded views on what was nonconformist and environmental and witchy and lesbian, and wore out their resigned and scornful Czech landladies with all their opinions, delivered in words, words, words . . . Sooner or later every lunatic with a couple of crowns, a world view and a vision set down in this city and founded organizations or movements or newspapers, or checked into town with never-ending cables wrapped round their waist for the new TV, one you could look at for a change, creating CULTURE or at least some cute little sect for the local suckers or some limited liability company, it's nothin' but paper, right? . . . and when the money ran out, they vanished, the city and its speculators sucked them up like a sponge.

It just about killed me too, this city . . . evenings with the fortune-teller . . . new owners tailored other parts of town into apparel for respectable businessmen, banks and change offices, varicoloured flags fluttered over the ruins and hired guns took potshots at pigeons with air rifles so their cloacal ammunition wouldn't disturb the digestion of the suits whose shits run the circuit with utter discretion . . . and still other city districts contorted into the professional spic-and-span face of the player, the try-hard, the type who's born to lose in spite of his agile fingers and lifelong training, because he's sick, condemned by nature, a weak piece. Some streets still made you feel the best thing to do was drug yourself till you dropped. And in some corners, dark and damp with black sewer water, you could come down with schizophrenia as easily as you catch a cold. Then again, other places seemed to emerge from the magic spell of inertia to reconnect with happier days. By some miracle, or maybe it figures, these were the oldest places, like the cathedral with the Czech kings' tombs in it and outside the low-flying pigeons, the sparrows and lazy swallows who move—as I like to put it, even though it might sound unusual for birds—with sublime sensuality—or the monastery with the abbot they tortured so many times.

I was walking through South Station with a hangover, examining the colourful covers of pulp novels, detective stories and pornography, their titles resonating in the slow-motion ache of my brain, and they're points on a world map too: 'Here are lions' and here's *A Thousand Sex Slaughters* and here's *Black Mary* and here's *House of Spiders* and here's *Mutiny of the Robots*, and if you stand on tiptoe you can also catch a glimpse of *Cooked Alive*, a novella, and *The Maid's Dream* and *Reign of the Fist* and *Street of Terror*. Next to that's a vegetable stand, and the heavy aroma of Asian unknowns and dill and oregano and cinnamon and olives piquant and lemons and raisins form a unique smell-screen wafting over towards *King of the Mutants* and *Maneater*, and next to that the toilets stink. The private newsagent runs them too, and he also sells porno videos.

I'm standing there pissing into the trough, watched by the paper eyes of a painted slut, her legs spread wide on the cover of *Teenage Prostitute*. You like to jerk off? says the guy standing next to me. My hungover brain fails to issue the command for a lightning punch in the face, so I go on standing there and, Huh? I ask, starting to play stupid. It's the *pissoir* owner himself who's addressed me, an entrepreneur. Could he too be setting up some sort of movement or centre? How To Change Your Life in Harmony With Yourself How to Get Rich German in One Hour Lose Weight in Three Days of Gorging, etc.? Yeah, I see you round here, he goes on. I work next door, I explain so he won't think I'm a Snooper, but he probably does anyway. You like to jerk off? Jerk what? I reply, giving him my best baffled-innocent look. He tosses a glance towards the door to make sure no one's coming and: Just between us, if you like to jerk off, we could make a deal on a peep show. Huh? Yeah, all you do is jerk off in one of the stalls and they watch. Who? Come off it, perverts, for Chrissake. So it's to be strictly a business deal between two grown-up men. Nothing happens to you, they just look. How many times can you jerk off all the way? Listen, you got long hair, I stick a helmet with horns on that mop of yours and it's instant Viking. Uh-uh, I groan. Don't make too much where you work, do you? he says with a disapproving look at my shabby suit, but he's from the sticks, what does he know, this cotton here's brand-name. Sorry, I tell him, doesn't grab me, and I leave him standing there, no coin tossed into his little plastic dish.

I watch the swarm of nomads inside the railway station. No wonder the bushes in the front are such fierce competition for the public toilets if he goes around hassling every Viking like that. Cash. How much would he have given me anyway? With a filthy mug like his, I'll bet he does the really kinky stuff himself. Helmet with horns? Yeah right, just the thing to make it easier for the rent-a-cops to nab me! Cash, cash, cash. And there sure isn't any point in money-making without a pinch of excitement thrown in, can't argue with that.

I had a real soft spot for South Station. It was a throwback to the times when railway stations got the same kind of respect that airports get nowadays. Art nouveau metal holding up the vaulted ceiling, holding together the glass. Pink and green flowers so high up in the corners that the miniature drawings engraved on them were impossible to make out. Back then maybe artisans still believed that God could see their creations. At least some of them were careful, that's for sure. No freethinker could've come up with spirals like those, look at how they all coil around each other. Then again, I thought, maybe it's some kind of Freemason symbolism, and I stood there, following it up into infinity till it gave me the chills. Then suddenly, out of the darkness and mist of the cosmic tunnel I was so happily tumbling into, emerged the image of Jules Verne. On one of my better days, I had traded some idiot a carton of Gauloises for a Jules Verne daguerreotype by Rondé. Afterwards the guy's elder brother just about killed him for being so stupid and they came to plead for it back, but I didn't budge an inch: a deal's a deal, even in bestial times. The wooden doors on the cloakrooms were art nouveau too: the hinges with nymphs, the hasps and mountings, as big as about six of those slabs of particleboard that pass for doors. As if they'd been built for men of gigantic stature. In fact it was as if the entire railway station had been built for some race now long extinct. If any of those Titans actually turned up here, the local riffraff would no doubt turn tail and head for the hills, and I wouldn't be far behind. But the consummate carpenters from the other end of the century left behind no holes in their work.

I still wanted to go to the waiting room and admire the enormous tiled stove for a while. Back in the old days, the Red monsters had adorned the place with a Proletarian Corner and a Militiaman Guard of Honour, and I often spent time there, the only visitor, in quiet meditation. I fortified myself with a cup of coffee from the stand in front of the station, and just as the timepiece in my brain returned to ticking tolerably I spotted a familiar face on a bench: Hey Mičinec!

Mičinec had enough years on me to have taken me in more than once: I'd swapped him my father's watch for some pieces of broken bottle, he'd slashed me with his skates over the Maškalířová girl, snapped my Little Bison bow in two, burnt me with his lighter, ratted on me, accused me, laid the blame on me for everything that ever got broken or stolen in the building where we lived with our families. But now our fathers had crumbled to dust and the remnants of our families were scattered throughout institutions, studio apartments and boneyards. That watch would look pretty old-fashioned these days, and odds are that fetching red-haired creature had turned into a fiery old hag by now, so let bygones be bygones: How goes it, Mičinec? Sitting twisted up on the bench, he was grumbling something to himself, left hand pressed to his side. He turned my way, his eyes pure panic, then threw his head skyward, tensed up, fell silent. His hand slid from the bench, his side was covered with blood.

The day I found Mičinec and saw the man who survived Auschwitz continued in the bookshop and the hallway beneath it. On top of that I had a few business matters to settle with Piotrowski, my favourite desk chief at the paper. He was looking for an apartment. Me, I had my daily bread on the line and butter to boot.

P: I'm going outta my skull, twenny-eight years old and I can't come up with a thing. A hundred thousand crowns I need, even for the smallest place around, and all I got is half that!

ME: I got something for you. Remember Peters & Gimblers?

P: Yeah.

ME: They want forty pieces over the next three months.

P: Ads or articles?

ME: Either one, same difference. They supply you the brochure with the specs. But they're looking for dailies. You got that, right? Two, maybe three people everywhere, right?

P: Yeah sure, but the cash is spreading thin. How about you, not interested?

ME: Nah.

P: 'Cause they test on animals, is that it?

ME: Yep, that company is in league with Satan, no doubt about it.

P: And who isn't? What else you got?

ME: Then there's Multicorp Nuclear. It's a biggie. You send out letters to mayors saying that people want the plants in their town. Here's a list of sleazeball engineers, mercenary types. Do interviews with 'em, buy a few expert evaluations, the works. But you only get it long enough to look it over and there's a deposit on it. What they're after is detailed pieces in all the political rags, especially outside Prague. You got things covered outside the capital too?

P: Something'll turn up, yeah.

ME: I bet.

P: They supply brochures too, facts and figures?

ME: I've got all that right here, plus photos. You giving me Thailand or not?

P: Once everything's going smooth and I start turning a profit, then I'll give you the job. But anyway, I don't get it. Why run off and screw around for a year in Thailand when you got that Holy Land deal?

ME: How do you know about that?

P: I have my sources. I know the ins and outs.

ME: Thailand's just insurance in case it ends up the old beard-strokers don't give me the nod. I just want out. I'll be a great correspondent. For your paper I'll do anything.

P: Uh-huh.

ME: Hm.

P: Hey, get this: today I was reading in *100 plus 1*, you know, that newsmagazine? Twenty-three million girls turn sixteen in China every year. Is that intense or what?

ME: Incredibly intense.

P: Damn, twenty-three million Chinese sweet sixteens! It's unbelievable! Just blows my mind.

ME: Can't even fathom it. It scrambles your brain.

P: Actually, it's like trying to picture the millions they slaughtered in those concentration camps.

ME: Yeah, maybe all those teenage girls balance it out.

P: Could be. That gives it a positive spin. You think the world is actually balanced out like that somehow?

ME: Hey, here's a lane change for you: for the first time ever, China voted against the Khmer Rouge in the UN!

P: Really? And you got it?

ME: Yep, about twelve thousand bytes.

P: You promised eighteen. Where's it from?

ME: Some *Economist*, some *Herald*, the *Globe*, you know, a few of my own amazing new insights, the usual. If it's too short throw in a map. Got any photos of those Commie bastards?

P: You're making more work for me. How about those chopped-off heads I've got over my desk? They're Malaysian actually, but no one'll know the difference. Wait a second! We've got Pol Pot with that little girl! The one where he's handing her the flag!

ME: Great, put it in. And I've got Pakistan and Kashmir with the Aziz murder, ten thousand bytes, give or take. Then there's the famine in Sudan, that's about eight thousand, no big deal. How about slavery in Moldova?

P: Nah, too boring. We need something on the home front, something with sort of a human touch. Couldn't you do some of those good little gypsies? Or maybe some youth stuff?

ME: Had so much of that it makes me puke.

P: How about children's homes?

ME: For Chrissake!

P: Take it easy, you can handle it in an evening.

ME: OK, but you pay for the trip: petrol, food, the works.

P: Come off it, you're not going anywhere and you know it.

ME: You paying or not?

P: You bring the receipts?

ME: Deal. And hey, what do you say to some poems, you know, sex and death?

P: No interest.

We parted filled with mutual understanding. I saw some children playing Heaven, Hell, Paradise* in front of the Church of St Bruno, scribbling chalk on the asphalt and hopping around as if nothing were wrong, as if the universe weren't expanding and contracting, as if the world weren't at best a dubious lump of combustible matter, ready to burst into raging coloured flames at any moment. They acted as if nothing was wrong, the kids, as if they didn't have a clue, as if they hadn't sucked it in with mother's milk. But they know all right, those shrewd little scriveners, I said to myself, they just don't give a damn.

Across from the church, an Australian had set up a self-serve grocery shop. His name was Hořica. The place used to be nothing but an ordinary hole-in-the-wall, selling brooms, lamps and pharmaceuticals and smelling fiercely of detergents and poisons to combat moths, rats, snakes, fleas, scorpions, sow bugs and other kindred vermin unleashed in massive doses from the generous hand of the Lord. And why does He do that? Just take it easy, brother, that's part of the secret. In place of its former stench, the shop now gave off a peculiar sanitary scent, almost like rubber.

Come right in and happy shopping, I was instructed by a gorgeous girl paid to say crap like that. I don't need anything, I said, but the angel-for-hire had already turned her attention elsewhere. And you know what else, I roared, this is what I call harassment! Get out of my face, you bimbo! She disappeared into the shop and I set out after her, grabbing a shopping basket on the way. She floated off past the cash register to where a tall, pale man was standing: Hořica, the Australian. I know everyone in this neighbourhood. Before I had the time to size them up, though, I was walloped by a formidable shock from the Australian, a biting chill that lashed my face. I did my best to return the shot, but I was too tired and they were too far away. Hořica walked up to me:

* The Czech version of hopscotch.

Go ayvay, pleez, he said. I could tell he was too strong for me. Defeated and humiliated, I decided it was best to make tracks. I walked down the street, a little older, a little wiser, a day just like any other, a new crop of stubble poking out of my skin.

Word was out that they had the sixth part of *Tumulus on Mars* at the bookstall on Gasworks Street. That would really hit the spot right now, I thought, and headed in that direction. I practically jumped for joy when I reached the stall and saw the men in blue overalls, heaving bag after bag of books out of the overflowing bed of their pick-up truck. Maybe they'd also have *Planet of the Beetles*, Part II.

I'd had a fabulous time with Part I. In a frenzy of industriousness I had rewritten the entire book, making the invading Earthlings into cowboys and the Beetles into Indians, crossing out space buggies and writing in mustangs. From the six-eyed beauty Moia I created the red-haired Mary Anne, while Akis, the ultra-intelligent professor, became Benny Brets, the hare-brained pistol-packer. The beetle chief, Ribis the meat-eater, I made into Crazy Moccasin, a more or less acceptable Apache degenerate. It was a nice little game, remaking the subterranean domed crystal palace into a ranch, the ray guns into bona fide six-shooters. I even came up with my own title: *Autumn on the Chequered-Q Ranch*. I sold the hodgepodge to a publisher called Copperpot and loafed around in bliss for the next three months, writing stupid poetry and snooping around for my next money-maker.

I'd have to wait till next time, though, they didn't have the goods. The men in blue loaded the books into orange crates, whatever didn't fit they threw on to a blanket. The vendor stuck a sign with a 5 drawn on it on to the crates. I was the first one over. *We Were Here Too* caught my eye. Šimková. And *8,000 Days in Siberia*, goddamnit, I know that one. *Faded Photograph* and *Kites to a Missing Person* right next to each other. Hey, you got *Gulag* marked down too? I asked. Nope, the salesman said, but you want something special, try this, and he handed me *Nightmares of Jáchymov*. That's those uranium mines, they pounded 'em good down there. I know, I said, rummaging through the books. Kratochvil, the Czech

J'accuse. Kaplan and Hejl's *Report on Organized Violence*. And there was more. Concentration camp memoirs. *Executions and Tortures of the Fifties*, a cyclostyled list of names. The trial of the Sonya resistance group. *The White Legion* right beside it. And short stories by Jan Beneš. Ginzburg with a torn cover. Marčenko and Djilas. *The Wooden Spoon*. *The Katyn Pits*. Stránský, Rambousek on the Commie-killing Mašín brothers, *Breakout* by Hejda, all of them neatly gathered together. In one big heap. How is it you got all this stuff on the same subject so cheap? I asked. Raided the warehouse of some organization, political or somethin'. They were hard up for cash, you can bet. Would've been better off recyclin', though, nobody buys stuff like this anymore, people've got other things on their minds these days, the wheeler-dealer said.

By now several potential customers had turned away from the crates in disgust. How much you want for these bum bandits here? asked a fat guy, from the looks of him a purebred yokel. Every little bit of this A-1 readin' material goes for fifteen, the salesman announced. And have you got *Twenty-First-Century Casanova*? a teenaged boy inquired, guitar in hand. Git, the salesman growled at him. These goods here, he confided to the hayseed, is strictly for the over-eighteens. I'll take the Kratochvil, I said. And that list of the guys who were tortured to death. All rightie, that'll be two fivers. Don't tell me you study that stuff? Yep. And don't look at me like I was some kind of sadist. Now just hold on, the vendor chuckled, I can throw him in too, lookie here, and suddenly a purple notebook of de Sade materialized in his hand. Fine then, I said. You want both parts? Sure, at least I won't have to worry what to get my mum for Christmas. Ho ho ho, we laughed together.

I hadn't got a shoulder bag, so I carried the books in a sack. That Kratochvil is pretty hefty, especially if you're run-down. The meeting with Piotrowski had gone well, looked as if it would bring in some profits. But *Planet of the Beetles* Part II was still stuck in my head. I wonder how much I could squeeze out of Part II of *Autumn on the Chequered-Q Ranch*? Or should I do *Winter* Part I maybe? I could have Mary Anne get pregnant. With a redskin, for example. Sure, it'd be tough for them, but then again I could teach the world a lesson in racial tolerance. What if I threw in some black slaves too? Naw, save that for some other time. If Copperpot falls for it, that is. He thinks I'm sort of shady. But so what, if things work out, I'm out of this country anyway. I can grind out the next part of the story somewhere else. Just to be sure, though, I went to take a look round the bookshop.

I spotted Věra at a tram stop standing next to some old-timer with glasses. She waved, barked something into the man's hearing aid and ran across the street to me, dodging the cars.

Hi! I shouted. The trams were making such a racket you couldn't even hear yourself think.

So what's up? When do you leave for the Holy Land? Věra shouted back. The machines rattled off.

I'll never understand how come the Free Synagogue chose you of all people, she went on.

Well, I've been studying a lot, reading books and stuff.

That's a load of bullshit, you're just lucky is all.

Well, the Lord watcheth over me.

Come off it.

You know how it goes, they just pull a name out of a hat, and I'd have got a passport sooner or later anyway. Plus there could be a war there and they're all nothing but Russkies.

You are glad you're going though, aren't you?

Yeah, sure, it's the fatherland and I haven't got any kids here, so what do I have to lose.

Bet you didn't talk like that in front of the people from the agency.

Course not, I only talk like this with you.

So will you put in a good word for me there at the Wailing Wall? Talk about a fake.

You bet. Hey, by the way, who are you with? Who's the old-timer?

A tram rattled by in its tracks and I lost sight of the old man. Věra had to shout again.

That's Špicek, you know, the one who survived Auschwitz.
What?
Špicek, don't tell me you've never heard of him?
Sure, read every one of his books. Is he alive?
You bet, never even set foot out of Prague.
He's still alive? That's really Špicek? No shit?
What, are you kidding? You want to meet him?
Yes. I mean, no. Not here. Well all right. But not right now.

We waited for the trams to pass: first the one with a sign that said 'I've gotta have it!' (it wasn't clear what), then the one with the smiley bubbles. The next tram, with the Camel ad on it, wasn't so noisy.

I thought he died in prison.

Just about. When they locked him up in seventy-seven that was almost the end for him.

Unbelievable. So he survived the uranium mines in Jáchymov, I shouted, fifteen years!

I can't hear you, Věra said.

Yeah, just saw his memoirs in a crate a few minutes ago. Oh, never mind. Wow, uranium, he survived all that. And Auschwitz too! I mean, climbing the fence to get out of there and all!

I thought you said you'd read all his books.
Well, some of them I just breezed through. He still writes?
Probably. Why don't you come over and ask him yourself?
I can't, uh-uh, maybe some other time.
Well, I have to get back to him.
Absolutely, he's an old man.
And give a call before you leave.
Yeah, you bet.

I set off again for a little trip to the railway station, it was right nearby. In the winter gardens, where the locomotive is, I heard some sounds from up above, looked up and caught sight of a shadow in the glassy heights of the art nouveau vault, as though a buzzard was up there flapping its wings with a little mouse in its claws, or maybe a goldfinch. The brutal creature had a firm grip on its prey, and I heard a squealing in my ears, so high-pitched that it hurt. I could almost feel the predator's claws sinking into the goldfinch's heart with the strength of steel, the strength of a machine. Then he must have finished off his victim with a few blows of his beak because the mouse stopped squealing, abruptly, like the chop of an axe, and I could only imagine the slow, floating movement of wings on high. Maybe it was just a hallucination. I stood there twisting my neck upwards, but there was nothing left to see, and maybe my chin was quivering a little and that was the day

I saw the man

who survived Auschwitz

and then I went back out to the street and found a bookshop where there was a good chance they might have Part II of *Planet of the Beetles*. You never know, on some shelf, maybe in a display case, trash like that could easily be lying around with all the rest like it was no big deal. But of course that's your book, of course, I'll put it away for you right here, said the saleswoman at the entrance, Jamborková read the name-tag on her jacket. I'll hold on to it for you while you have a look around. I deposited the Kratochvil in her outstretched hands. OK, thanks a lot, I said, and I headed for the shelves with the colourful books. You're coming with me, said a man in a black uniform. Behind him was another and behind him Jamborková. Look now, don't go making any trouble, you come in here and steal our books and we're going to take a walk to the office. They had me surrounded, Jamborková was holding the Kratochvil as if it was some kind of court exhibit. We've caught plenty of others with tricks like yours, she said. What's going on here, what are you talking about? I gathered my courage for a follow-up sentence, but by that time we'd already reached the office, actually a cellar beneath the pavement. Empty out your pockets, said the cop. Well, lookie here, our little boy goes for the sick stuff, said the other cop as he tore the paper bag with de Sade in it out of my hand. How much have you lifted here, you bum? Either you confess, or you're going to pay for everything that's been stolen here in the last six months, said Jamborková, that's the law! And put your stuff on the table, you creep! roared the cop. But I didn't steal anything, I'm just a reporter, I babbled. One cop gave me a rap on the head and twisted my arms behind my back while the other one started going through my pockets, and My oh my, he chortled, pulling out my knife. Seems there's more here than meets the eye, isn't that so, young man? Not quite your average smokes, Máňa, here, take a sniff, he said, handing Jamborková the two home-rolleds from my pocket. I gave up defending myself

> because that was the day
> they robbed me
> that great day
> when I saw the man
> who survived Auschwitz
> and everything had
> its own dimensions
> and some of it
> was real

and when I dragged myself home that night I didn't even bother to cover up my two black eyes, and anyway Dunar wasn't standing by his BMW. I could tell from the pain pulsing in my old wound that a storm was on the way and that I would go home and write incomplete lines, one under another. I ran across a dog dragging a fish head along the pavement and I remembered Mičinec and I read somebody's forgotten newspaper in the night tram. The dark and the fog were thick enough to slice, but I hadn't got anything to slice with. A little boy emerged from round the corner with a pack on his back and a key round his neck, sobbing slightly. He probably ran away from home to hide out on Petřín Hill *en route* to America, direction: maybe Shanghai.

> And then he'll meet
> girls one day
> get to know them and probably beer
> and self-education
> and some sort of job

and everything else too
nothing will pass him by
if he survives
and that was the day
of the Trip to the Railway Station

and then I was home and I heard the chorus.

CHORUS: so what's up little brother
how goes it kid? how's life?
come on you know P will come up with a place
before Mičinec runs into the knife
and you finish writing *Planet*
and everything has been before
and it always will be
and some things take a turn for the better
and some don't.

ME: I'm trying I'm living
and I just took a little walk
through town and I think
I'll keep my hands clean and if not
then just a little bit dirty.

CHORUS: come on you be happy
kid
and no more complaining
today you saw a man
who survived Auschwitz
do you know of any mercy more momentous
in today's eventful times?
could you value
any sign
more than that?

ME: course not thanks thanks
thanks
course I know what it's all about
I know

I felt it
and I feel it
but
I could use some sort of message
'cause I admit
I'm kind of mixed-up.

CHORUS: take this then:
look out for yourself and be good to your neighbours
and have at least minimal respect
for strangers as long as you live in this world and
wash yourself once in a while
and that's it
that's absolutely all you need.
Take care now—
and lots of luck.

The chorus faded away, and it was from me but wasn't me.
What's so wise about that? I asked my pillow. Let's try to get
some sleep, I said, see what that does, maybe something'll
come to me in a dream. Then I looked out the window. It was
getting light.

(*Translated by Alex Zucker.*)

About the Authors

Many of the titles mentioned here were first published in samizdat or exile editions, and it is difficult to date them without a degree of confusion. The dates therefore refer to the first traceable publication, whether official, samizdat or exile. The majority of these works have been re-issued in the Czech Republic since 1989. Titles of English editions appear in round brackets with the date of publication.

Michal Ajvaz (1949) was born in Prague. He is the author of poems *Vražda v hotelu Intercontinental* [Murder in the Intercontinental Hotel], 1989, short stories *Návrat starého varana* [Return of the Old Komodo Dragon], 1991, and a novel, *Druhé město* [The Other City], 1993.

Alexandra Berková (1949) writes fiction and scripts for radio and TV. She has published a collection of short stories *Knížka s červeným obalem* [The Book with a Red Cover], 1986, and two novellas, *Magorie* [Magoria or Loonyland], 1991, and *Utrpení oddaného všiváka* [The Sufferings of Devoted Lousehead], 1994. A story from her first book was included in the Picador anthology of Eastern European fiction *Description of a Struggle*, 1994.

Zuzana Brabcová (1959) was born in Prague. Her first novel, *Daleko od Stromu* [Far From the Tree], 1987, is considered to be one of the most significant literary statements of the generation which grew up in the stifling atmosphere of the 1970s.

Ota Filip (1930) was born in Ostrava and since 1974 has lived in Munich. Writer, journalist and editor, he was blacklisted in 1960 and sentenced to prison in 1969. He has been writing in German since the early 1980s, and is the author of two collections of short stories and ten novels including *Cesta ke hřbitovu* [The Road to the Cemetery], 1967, the four-part *Nanebevstoupení Lojzka Lapáčka ze Slezské Ostravy* [The

Ascension of Lojzek Lapáček from Silesian Ostrava], 1974, 1975, *Poskvrněné početí* [The Maculate Conception], 1976, *Café Slavia*, 1985, *Die Sehnsucht nach Procida* [Longing for Procida], 1988, and *Lebensleerläufe* [Curricula of Idle Lives], 1993.

Ladislav Fuks (1923–94), one of the most important modern Czech writers, was born and lived in Prague. His first novel, *Pan Theodor Mundstock*, 1963 (*Mr Theodor Mundstock*, 1968), was followed by two collections of short stories, *Mí černovlasí bratři* [My Blackhaired Brothers], 1964, and *Smrt morčete* [The Death of the Guinea Pig], 1969, and eleven novels, including *Variace pro temnou strunu* [Variations for a Dark String], 1966, the acclaimed *Spalovač mrtvol*, 1967 (*The Cremator*, 1984), filmed by Juraj Herz in 1968, *Příběh kriminálního rady* [The Story of the Police Commissioner], 1971, *Obraz Martina Blaskowitze* [The Picture of Martin Blaskowitz], 1980, and his monumental panorama of life in Vienna at the turn of the century, *Vévodkyně a kuchařka* [The Duchess and the Cook], 1983.

Jiří Gruša (1938) was born in Pardubice and used to live in Prague. Since 1980 he has lived in Germany, where he was appointed Czech Ambassador after 1989. Poet, prose writer, author of children's books, critic, translator and editor of 1960s literary magazines *Tvář* and *Sešity*, he was active in the samizdat Petlice [Padlock Editions] together with Ludvík Vaculík, and in 1978 was held in custody in connection with the publication of his acclaimed novel *Dotazník* (*The Questionnaire*, 1980). His other works include three collections of poems and the prose works *Mimner*, 1972, *Dámský gambit* [The Queen's Gambit], 1973, and *Doktor Kokeš Mistr Panny* [Doctor Cocker, Virgin Master], 1980.

Bohumil Hrabal (1914) was born in Brno-Židenice and lives in Prague. A prolific writer, he has developed an idiosyncratic and highly influential narrative style inspired by the poetics of surrealist automatic texts and the vernacular rhythms and vocabulary of ordinary conversations. His work, now being published in an annotated collected edition, includes some forty volumes of novels, short stories, poems and occasional texts, including his selected short stories *Automat Svět*, 1966 (*The Death of Mr Baltisberger*, 1973), and novels *Ostře sledované vlaky*, 1965 (*Closely Observed Trains*, 1968)—made into a highly acclaimed film by Jiří Menzel—*Obsluhoval jsem anglického krále*, 1971 (*I Served the King of England*, 1989), *Příliš hlučná samota*, 1976 (*Too Loud a Solitude*, 1990), *Postřižiny*, 1970, and *Městečko, kde se zastavil čas*, 1978 (published together under the title *The Little Town Where Time Stood Still*, 1993), *Vita nuova*, 1984–5, and recent occasional texts *Listopadový urgán* [November Hurricane], 1990, and *Aurora na mělčině* [Aurora Aground], 1992.

Ivan Klíma (1931) was born in Prague, where he still lives. One of the most popular of contemporary Czech writers, his work was banned between 1970 and 1989 while published worldwide in translation. Author of novels, short stories, theatre and radio plays, children's books and essays, including short-story collections *Má veselá jitra*, 1979 (*My Merry Mornings*, 1985), *Moje první lásky*, 1985 (*My First Loves*, 1986), *Moje zlatá řemesla*, 1989 (*My Golden Trades*, 1992), and novels *Milostné léto*, 1972 (*A Summer Affair*, 1990), *Soudce z milosti*, 1986 (*Judge on Trial*, 1991), *Láska a smetí*, 1988 (*Love and Garbage*, 1990), and, most recently, *Čekání na tmu, čekání na světlo*, 1993 (*Waiting for the Dark, Waiting for the Light*, 1994).

Jiří Kratochvil (1940) was born and lives in Brno. Author of short stories, novels, radio and theatre plays, his work was banned in 1970 when his first short-story collection *Případ s Chatnoirem* [The Chatnoir Case] was withdrawn from distribution. His trilogy of novels *Medvědí román* [The Bear Novel], 1987, *Uprostřed nocí zpěv* [Song in the Middle of the Night], 1989, and *Avion*, 1995, published to critical acclaim and the second was translated into Spanish, German and French. Collections of his short stories are *Orfeus z Kénigu* [The Orpheus of Kénig], 1994, and *Má lásko, Postmoderno* [Postmoderne, My Love], 1994.

Věra Linhartová (1938) was born in Brno and since 1968 has lived in France, where she is curator of oriental art at the Musée Guimet in Paris. Her five prose works published during the 1960s—including *Prostor k rozlišení*, [Space for Differentiation], 1964, *Meziprůazkum nejblíž uplynulého* [Intersurvey of the Nearest Past], 1964, and *Přestořeč* [Despitespeech], 1966—brilliantly question narrative conventions and the possibilities of language. Since 1970 she has been writing in French and her published work includes *Twor* and *Portraits carnivores*. She is also the author and editor of studies and theoretical works in the field of art history.

Arnošt Lustig (1926) was born in Prague and since 1968 has lived in the USA, where he lectures at the University of Washington. Novelist, journalist, editor, author of film and TV scripts and radio plays, his numerous short-story collections and novels, most of which reflect the traumatic experience of Jewish life under Nazi occupation and in concentration camps, include *Noc a naděje*, 1958 (*Night and Hope*, 1976), *Démanty noci*, 1958 (*Diamonds of the Night*, 1978), *Modlitba pro Kateřinu Horowitzovou*, 1964 (*A Prayer for Katerina Horowitzova*, 1985), *Dita Saxová*, 1962 (1979), *Z deníku sedmnáctileté Perly Sch.*, 1979 (*The Unloved*, 1985), and an English translation of some of his short stories, *Indecent Dreams*, 1988.

Ewald Murrer (1964) was born in Prague. His first collection of poems was *Mlha za zdí* [Fog Beyond the Wall], 1992, followed by poems and short texts *Vyznamenání za prohranou válku* [A Medal for the Lost War], 1992, and a short prose work, *Zápisník pana Pinkeho* [Mr Pinke's Notebook], 1993. His poems appeared in the Penguin anthology, *The Child of Europe*, 1990.

Sylvie Richterová (1945) was born in Brno and is professor of Czech literature at the University of Viterbo in Italy, where she has lived since 1970. As well as prose and poetry, she has published literary studies and translations of Czech authors, including Věra Linhartová. She is the author of collections of short texts *Návraty a jiné ztráty* [Returns and Other Losses], 1977, and *Místopis* [Topography], 1981, which were republished together with *Slabikář otcovského jazyka* [Primer of the Father Tongue] in 1991, novellas *Rozptýlené podoby* [Dispersed Images], 1979, and *Druhé loučení* [The Second Parting], 1994, and poems *Neviditelné jistoty* [Invisible Certainties], 1994. She has published her work in Italian and French under the name Sylvie Richter.

Josef Škvorecký (1924) was born in Náchod, north-east Bohemia, and lived in Prague before emigrating in 1968 to Canada, where he was professor of English at Erindale College, University of Toronto. Together with his wife, the novelist Zdena Salivarová, he established 68 Publishers, the key exile press which issued the work of banned Czech and Slovak writers. Novelist, poet, scriptwriter, editor, literary critic, translator, film and jazz aficionado, his first novel *Zbabělci*, 1958 (*The Cowards*), established him as a major figure of post-war literature. His numerous publications include several collections of short stories, novellas *Legenda Emöke*, 1963, and *Bassaxofon*, 1967 (*The Bass Saxophone*, 1978), and novels *Tankový prapor*, 1971 (*The Republic of Whores*, 1993), *Mirákl*, 1972 (*The Miracle Game*, 1990), *Prima sezóna*, 1975 (*The Swell Season*, 1982), *Příběh inženýra lidských duší*, 1977 (*The Engineer of Human Souls*, 1984), *Scherzo Capriccioso*, 1984 (*Dvořák in Love*, 1986). A versatile and prolific writer, he is also the author of several detective novels, including *Smutek poručíka Borůvky*, 1966, (*The Sad Demeanour of Lieutenant Borůvka*, 1973), and *Lvíče*, 1969 (*Miss Silver's Past*, 1974). An English translation of some of his essays, *Talkin' Moscow Blues*, was published in 1988.

Jáchym Topol (1962) was born and lives in Prague. Poet, novelist and founding editor of the leading literary and cultural journal *Revolver Revue*, his three poetry collections published in samizdat between 1985 and 1988 were re-issued under the title *Miluju tě k zbláznění* [I Love You Madly], 1991; his second collection was *V úterý bude válka* [The War

Will Be on Tuesday], 1992. His first novel *Sestra* [The Sister] was published to critical acclaim in 1994.

Ludvík Vaculík (1926) was born in Brumov, eastern Moravia, and lives in Prague. Novelist, journalist, essayist and editor of *Literární noviny* [The Literary News] in the 1960s, author of the famous 1968 'Two-Thousand-Word Manifesto', and founder of the key samizdat Petlice [Padlock Editions], which helped keep underground Czech literature alive in the 1970s and 1980s, his work was banned for twenty years but he has provided an ongoing commentary on the country's cultural and political life through his regular feuilletons. His novels *Sekyra*, 1966 (*The Axe*, 1973), and *Morčata*, 1970 (*The Guinea Pigs*, 1974), were translated into a number of languages and established him as a major novelist of his generation. They were followed by diary-novels *Český snář* [The Czech Dreambook], 1980, and *Jak se dělá chlapec* [How to Make a Boy], 1994. An English translation of his feuilletons, *A Cup of Coffee with My Interrogator*, was published in 1987.

Michal Viewegh (1962) was born and lives in Prague. His second novel, *Báječná léta pod psa* [The Blissful Years of Lousy Living], 1992, won him instant popular recognition and was translated into Dutch and German. His most recent publications are a collection of literary parodies *Nápady laskavého čtenáře* [Ideas of the Kind Reader], 1993, and the novel *Výchova dívek v Čechách* [The Education of Young Ladies in Bohemia], 1994.

Permissions

These pages constitute an extension of the copyright page.